Sugar Spinelli's Little Instruction Book

I can't believe my eyes. There's our young, conservative lawyer, Blair Townsend—bidding on a cowboy! That reckless adventurer Scott McKay sure doesn't seem her type. Especially now that she's raising that nephew of hers, who I hear is quite a rascal. Maybe she's looking for someone to give her a hand with the boy. I gotta say, Scott does look deceptively steady and respectable in that jacket and tie. I wonder if Blair knows what she's getting herself into. Because if she doesn't, there's going to be fireworks—and I sure hope I'm around to see them....

Dear Reader,

We just knew you wouldn't want to miss the news event that has all of Wyoming abuzz! There's a herd of eligible bachelors on their way to Lightning Creek—and they're all for sale!

Cowboy, park ranger, rancher, P.I.—they all grew up at Lost Springs Ranch, and every one of these mavericks has his price, so long as the money's going to help keep Lost Springs afloat.

The auction is about to begin! Young and old, every woman in the state wants in on the action, so pony up some cash and join the fun. The man of your dreams might just be up for grabs!

Marsha Zinberg
Editorial Coordinator, HEART OF THE WEST

It Takes
A Cowboy
Gina
Wilkins

HARLEQUIN®

TORONTO • NEW YORK • LONDON
AMSTERDAM • PARIS • SYDNEY • HAMBURG
STOCKHOLM • ATHENS • TOKYO • MILAN • MADRID
PRAGUE • WARSAW • BUDAPEST • AUCKLAND

Gina Wilkins is acknowledged as the author of this work.

ISBN 0-373-82589-7

IT TAKES A COWBOY

Copyright © 1999 by Harlequin Books S.A.

This edition published by arrangement with Harlequin Books S.A.

® and TM are trademarks of the publisher. Trademarks indicated with ® are registered in the United States Patent and Trademark Office, the Canadian Trade Marks Office and in other countries.

Visit us at www.romance.net

Printed in U.S.A.

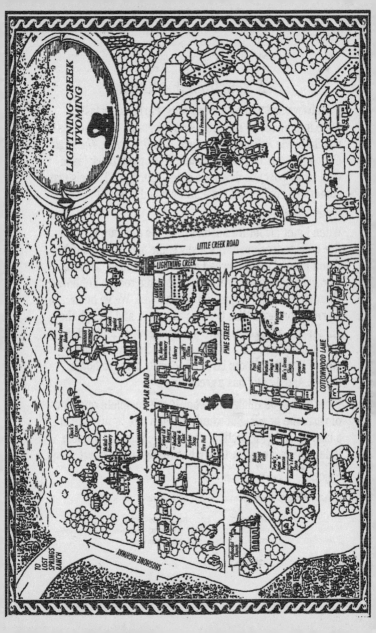

LIGHTNING CREEK
WYOMING

A Note from the Author

I've always had a thing for cowboys. Perhaps my tastes were influenced by the television programs I watched as a child—*The Rifleman, Bonanza, The Big Valley, The High Chaparral, Lancer* ("Johnny Madrid" in tight, black jeans with silver conchos down the side—oh, my!). There's just something about a man in a Stetson and a pair of slant-heeled boots....

When I met my future husband, he was a skinny, six-foot-five college freshman with a shy smile and a great laugh. When I found out he owned a palomino named "Diablo," a gray mare named "Freckles" and had a roomful of horse show ribbons and trophies, I was hooked. We've been married for more than twenty years now, and though the horses are long gone, there's a little cowboy still left in this businessman. He still has his saddle, and the same pair of Dan Post boots he used to wear in those horse shows. And he still has a great laugh.

Blair Townsend thinks a cowboy is the complete opposite of what she needs. But when she buys one by mistake at a charity bachelor auction, she soon learns that it does, indeed, take a cowboy to win her well-guarded heart.

Enjoy,

Gina Wilkins

For all those women with a weakness
for Stetsons and boots.

CHAPTER ONE

WHEN SHE'D FIRST heard about the plan, Blair Townsend had thought a bachelor auction was a desperate and probably futile scheme to save the financially strapped Lost Springs Ranch for Boys. A bachelor auction? Were they joking? What made these people think they could possibly raise a significant sum of money by parading a group of former ranch residents in front of a bunch of man-hungry women? Selling the guys off like...like prize bulls?

Blair had pessimistically predicted that there would be more men up for auction than there would be women to bid on them. And as for the media coverage they were hoping for...she'd thought they would be lucky to get a mention in the *Lightning Creek Leader*.

Now, as she gazed in awe at the TV news vans and reporters crowding the ranch grounds, she was perfectly willing to admit that she had been wrong.

She didn't know how they had done it, but somehow ranch owner Lindsay Duncan and director Rex Trowbridge had pulled off an amazing feat. They had a sizable group of gorgeous bachelors, a stadium full of enthusiastic bidders and a whole herd of reporters there to cover the festivities. The public relations benefits alone should go a long way toward helping Lindsay save her ranch—and the lost young boys who needed it.

Blair groaned at the thought of lost young boys. That

particular problem hit just a bit too close to home at the moment. A group of boys dashed past her, shouting, laughing, their destination the peeled-log forts and jungle gyms that made up the recently renovated playground. Though somewhat rowdy, they looked as though they were having a great time. It hadn't occurred to her that so many youngsters would be in attendance at a charity bachelor auction. Now she wondered why she hadn't expected it—this was, after all, a boys' ranch.

Maybe she should have brought Jeffrey. It might have been good for him to socialize with other children today. And yet...did she really want him spending time with the residents of Lost Springs? Wasn't he difficult and rebellious enough without the influence of this group of troubled boys? She'd spent a lot of time lately worrying that if things didn't improve soon, Jeffrey was going to be a prime candidate for a residential program for boys who were headed for serious problems.

She put a hand to the back of her neck, squeezing the muscle that had tightened there—something that had been happening with uncomfortable regularity since her ten-year-old nephew had moved in with her six months ago. A familiar burning sensation in her stomach made her reach into the pocket of her cream-colored cardigan for a roll of antacids. She popped a couple in her mouth and chewed grimly. The chalky taste made her grimace.

Wanting something to wash away the residue, she looked toward the crowded pavilion where food and drinks were being sold to an eager throng of customers. The tantalizing, smoky smell of barbecue wafted toward her, making her lick her lips. She had only come to observe the activities today, not to participate in them, but she could at least contribute to the cause by purchasing a soft drink and maybe a hot dog. She would love to indulge in a spicy barbecue sandwich, but she was afraid that would only intensify her heartburn.

Barely thirty, she thought ruefully, and she had to eat like a little old lady. And to think she'd moved to Lightning Creek, Wyoming, to *reduce* the stress in her life! But that had been before she'd become responsible for Jeffrey.

Several acquaintances greeted her as she approached the barbecue pavilion, people she had met during the year since she'd moved to the area from Chicago to take over her uncle's law practice. Lindsay Duncan, the ranch owner and one of Blair's clients, rushed by with a clipboard in her hand and a slightly harried look on her face. She gave Blair a distracted smile; Blair sent her a bracing thumbs-up in return, knowing Lindsay didn't have time for conversation just then.

Blair really hoped this gamble would pay off. The ranch had been in Lindsay's family for fifty years. Innumerable boys had been housed here, a significant number of them going on to lead successful, productive lives rather than the bleak, dead-end futures they'd faced prior to being assigned to the Lost Springs Ranch. Some had been orphans, some children whose parents had been unable or unwilling to provide for them, others had been deemed incorrigible and had been sent here as a last resort before reform school or jail, but all had been given the finest of care and the best of opportunities. Many had taken advantage of the education and counseling they'd received to turn their lives around. Blair knew that the owners and staff of the ranch grieved over every boy who could not or would not be helped.

That thought made the back of her neck tighten again. She was determined that her brother's son would not become one of the sad statistics.

Deciding to forgo the hot dog, she ordered a diet soda from one of the volunteers running the concession booth, a woman whose fairly amiable divorce had been one of Blair's first cases in Lightning Creek. "There you go, hon," fifty-something Arnette Gibbs said as she exchanged a cup of soda for Blair's dollar bill. "Enjoy."

"Thank you, Arnette. Looks like business is booming."

The woman's plump face beamed. "They're keeping us hopping, that's for sure. My goodness, would you look at that crowd gathered around Shane Daniels! If he don't stop signing autographs, he'll never get to the arena in time for the auction."

Following the direction of the older woman's gaze, Blair frowned. "Who is he? A singer? An actor?"

Arnette blinked in surprise that Blair hadn't recognized the name. "Honey, he's a rodeo champion. One of the best bull riders the circuit has ever seen."

"Oh." Blair's frown deepened as she studied the outright idolatry on the faces of the boys crowding around the handsome cowboy. A bull rider? Hardly the type of role model she would choose for her nephew.

"The auction's about to get started," Arnette announced, pointing toward the rapidly filling arena. "You better get over there before all the good ones are gone."

Blair's eyebrows rose. "I didn't come to buy a man. I'm only here to support the fund-raiser."

"Wouldn't hurt you to bid on one of those fine young hunks," Arnette advised cheerfully. "Just because I decided I didn't want to spend the rest of my life catering to Jesse Gibbs's every cantankerous whim don't mean I can't appreciate a pair of broad shoulders and a nice, tight butt. Sure makes for a pleasant diversion on a lazy weekend."

GINA WILKINS   13

Laughing and shaking her head, Blair moved away from the folding table that had been set up as a sales counter, giving the people in line behind her a chance to be served. She sipped her slightly watery soda as she strolled toward the arena to watch the auction. She couldn't help but be curious. It was certainly a beautiful day for the event, unusually warm for mid-June, the sky that intensely clear blue she'd come to identify with Wyoming. Rolling, wildflower-dotted pastures spread into the distance, crisscrossed by fencing, and on the horizon loomed the purply Wind River Range.

A colorful handmade quilt flapping from a branch of an enormous oak tree caught her eye. Blair loved pieced quilts, appreciating the effort and history that went into each one. A raffle box on a folding table had been set up in front of the quilt, along with a banner that read Converse County Hospital—35 Years of Sharing and Caring. A smaller sign proclaimed that proceeds from the quilt raffle would be donated to the Lost Springs Ranch for Boys. So many local organizations had pitched in to help today.

Impulsively, Blair stopped at the table, reaching into her pocket again as she greeted the striking redhead manning the raffle table. "Hello, Twyla. That's a beautiful quilt. I'd like to buy some raffle tickets."

Her cheeks unusually flushed, her manner a bit flustered, the hairstylist who had been cutting Blair's dark blond chin-length hair for the past year reached for the roll of raffle tickets. "Hi, Blair. How many tickets do you want? They're a dollar each."

Blair glanced at the bill she'd pulled from her pocket. "I'll take ten."

Twyla took the bill and handed Blair ten numbered

tickets. "The emcee will announce the winning number over the PA system after the auction. Good luck."

"Thanks." Blair glanced wistfully at the quilt's lovely log cabin design. "I'd love to win that."

Someone else approached to buy raffle tickets, and Blair drifted toward the practice arena that had been built for the use of the boys on the ranch. The risers surrounding the arena were filling rapidly, mostly with women. Women of all shapes, descriptions and ages, she thought in amusement, glancing from a group of giggling teenagers to a couple of silver-haired women in spangled jogging suits. As she took an empty space near the front, she noticed that most of the people around her clutched glossy brochures filled with pictures of the men to be auctioned.

"Isn't that a fine-looking group of studs?" the young woman beside Blair asked with a sigh, eyeing the men beginning to take their places in the folding chairs behind the auctioneer's podium. "Lordy, what I wouldn't give for a weekend with any one of them."

Blair smiled at the brunette, who appeared to be in her early twenties. "Are you going to bid?"

The young woman laughed and shook her head. "I'm sure they'll all go for more than I can afford. Some of these guys are famous, all of them are prominent in their fields, and there are some seriously rich women here to bid on them. Women from other states, even. I just came to make a donation to the fund-raiser and watch the fun. And maybe to fantasize a little about doing something wild and crazy with a good-looking stranger."

Wild and crazy. Sounded like a description of Blair's family. The Townsend reckless streak was notorious for spurring on impulsive and imprudent behavior. It was a part of her own nature that Blair had been suppressing for years, ever since it had become clear that someone in her family had to be responsible. That task had fallen to her at a very early age.

She looked again at the men assembling behind the podium, talking among themselves, some posturing good-naturedly for the women who hooted and whistled and flirted outrageously from the audience. If ever there was an opportunity for a woman to do something daring, this auction was it. They *were* an exceptionally intriguing-looking group of males. Not all of them could be called classically handsome, but it was obvious they were all comfortable with who they had become since leaving the ranch. They'd progressed a long way from the lost boys they'd once been. It must have been a sense of gratitude and obligation to the ranch that had brought them back for this rather odd occasion.

Blair looked from one self-consciously smiling male face to another. Each of them had at one time been in trouble, poised on the brink of potential disaster. Yet they had all chosen to turn themselves around. To make something of themselves. To…

Her eyes suddenly widened. Why hadn't she thought of this before? She didn't want Jeffrey spending time with the boys currently at the ranch, but would he benefit from talking to one of these *former* residents? A man who had been faced with a troubled future but who had chosen the path to success and responsibility instead? Jeffrey had never had a responsible, dependable male role model. Any one of these men would understand what rejection felt like. What it was like to be angry, confused, rebellious, defiant. Maybe they could share the secret of putting those negative emotions behind them so they could get on with their lives.

What if she bought one of these men to spend a weekend with Jeffrey, be a role model for him? It was a crazy idea...but she was desperate enough to give it serious consideration as the emcee took the podium and tried to calm the excited crowd so the auction could get under way.

Her thoughtful gaze moved from one bachelor to another. She wished she had one of those brochures so she could read their bios, pick the ones who seemed most responsible. She tried to make some guesses strictly on appearance. The famous rodeo champion was rejected immediately. A footloose, daredevil cowboy was not at all what she had in mind. Jeffrey's father was both a wanderer and a thrill-seeker, and he had certainly not been a good influence on his son.

No, she most definitely did not want a cowboy.

A couple of the other bachelors looked a bit too non-conformist for her taste, she mused as her gaze skimmed across a guy with an earring and a ponytail. What she needed was a man who looked as though he understood the importance of conforming to the rules and expectations of society.

The auctioneer finally had everyone's attention. "So, ladies, put your hands together for our first bachelor, Dr. Robert Carter."

Doctor? Blair straightened with interest as an absolutely gorgeous man stood and stepped toward the podium. A ripple of appreciation went through the audience, followed by wistful sighs when the man whimsically kissed Lindsay Duncan's hand. Blair noted his fabulous looks—what woman wouldn't?—but she was more interested in other details of his appearance. The expensive, conservative haircut. His elegantly casual clothing—a navy golf shirt and crisply pressed khakis. The auctioneer introduced him as a successful pathologist, following that up with an amazing list of professional and personal accomplishments. A weekend with this man, Blair thought, tapping her chin, could be exactly what Jeffrey needed. And she would be making a donation to the ranch, a charity that had become close to her heart during the past year.

The bidding for Dr. Robert Carter started at five hundred dollars. To the apparent delight of the woman sitting next to her, Blair bid six hundred. Within minutes, the amount had risen sharply, as had the level of noise from the giddy, keyed-up crowd. Blair dropped out of the bidding at five thousand dollars. The guy looked nice, she thought, but there was a limit to how much she was willing to pay for a weekend that might not accomplish anything, anyway.

"See?" the brunette next to Blair said with rueful amusement. "I told you there are some high rollers in the crowd today."

"You were right," Blair said as the bids topped eight thousand and kept climbing.

The handsome doctor sold for a staggering amount. Blair gasped in surprise—as did a number of others in the audience—when the auctioneer called the name of the winning bidder. Sugar Spinelli was seventy-five years old and had been married for half a century! What did *she* want with a young stud of a doctor?

Blair was still shaking her head in amazement when the next bachelor was called to the stand. Again, bidding was brisk, though Blair sat this one out. When rodeo star Shane Daniels took the stage, there was a near frenzy of bidding. She didn't participate in that one, either.

It really had been a dumb idea, she told herself as the auction proceeded. She hadn't expected the bidders to be so serious about this. It seemed that every winning bidder had a serious agenda motivating her, spurring on high dollars and fierce, though generally good-natured, competition. Blair's reason for participating was a valid one, but maybe she'd been foolish to even hope she could solve Jeffrey's problems by buying him a weekend mentor.

By the time a half-dozen bachelors had been auctioned off, Blair was losing interest, her attention caught again by the tantalizing smells drifting over from the barbecue grills. One of those smoked turkey legs sure sounded good. Maybe, now that her stomach had settled a little, she could handle one. Maybe she should buy another batch of raffle tickets for that beautiful quilt. Since it didn't appear that she was going to be buying a bachelor, she might as well donate to the cause in another way. And she really would love to have that quilt....

"Now, ladies, our next bachelor is Mr. Scott McKay. Scott owns a—"

The latest bachelor's credentials were drowned out by an outburst from somewhere behind her. Blair turned automatically to see what was going on. It seemed that one of the women had gotten so excited she'd fallen completely off her seat at the end of a row, landing flat on her well-cushioned bottom on the dusty ground below. She wasn't hurt, Blair noted in relief; in fact, she and her friends were laughing almost hysterically, drawing a lot of shushes from others in the audience who were straining to hear the auctioneer. Blair watched the woman stand with the assistance of a solicitous ranch employee, dust off her too-tight jeans and climb onto her seat, where she and her big-haired friends dissolved into giggles again. Only then did Blair turn, thinking again of that turkey leg. Maybe if she...

Her wandering gaze landed on the bachelor currently on the auction block, and she felt her jaw drop. She closed it quickly, trying to clear her suddenly clouded mind. Must be lack of food, she told herself. Maybe an overload of sound and activity. It couldn't possibly be that she had just been struck dumb by the sight of an attractive man in a beautifully tailored suit.

The bidding had already climbed to fifteen hundred dollars by the time she could think clearly. She looked at the guy again, trying to be objective. He wasn't as movie-star gorgeous as the first bachelor, the doctor she had tried to buy earlier. But he was…intriguing. His hair was a rich, glossy brown that glinted in the sun. It was brushed neatly back from a tanned, angular face creased by sexy dimples. From where she sat, his eyes looked very blue, his teeth very white. He held his chin tucked down a bit, so that he seemed to be looking up from beneath his lashes. His brow was creased in an endearingly bemused expression, as if the rowdy attention he was getting from the audience was something he hadn't expected when he'd signed up for this.

His dark suit fit him to perfection, displaying impressive shoulders, a solid chest and narrow hips. He wore a snowy white shirt and a boldly colored geometric tie. His western boots made her frown a bit, since they didn't quite fit the image, but then she smiled, deciding he'd probably worn the boots as a tribute to the ranch. Regarded in that respect, it was actually a very sweet gesture.

Someone bid twenty-five hundred dollars.

He certainly looked like a conservative, respectable businessman, Blair mused. And that somewhat befuddled smile could indicate a slight shyness that Jeffrey would identify with. Whatever problems Scott McKay had faced as a boy, he'd apparently put them well behind him. Would he know what to say to a child whose hurt and anger were propelling him down the wrong path?

"Do I hear three thousand dollars?" the auctioneer sang out.

Blair drew a deep breath and lifted her hand, calling once again on the Townsend boldness she so rarely indulged.

"All right. You're back in the bidding," the young woman at her left said with a laugh.

Someone else bid thirty-five hundred, followed by a bid for four thousand.

Once again, Blair's hand shot into the air, raising the stakes to forty-five hundred.

"He *is* pretty," the brunette mused. "And he sure sounds like a fun date."

A fun date? Was there something Blair had missed that she should know? The bidding rose to five thousand dollars, more than she'd intended to spend. She gulped and upped it to fifty-five hundred.

"Wow. You must really like that sexy smile," the woman next to her murmured.

Blair almost answered that the man's sexy smile had nothing to do with this. She was buying him for her nephew, not for herself. Although, if she *was* buying a man for herself, this was definitely one who...

She shook her head, telling herself to concentrate on what she was doing—and why. She waved her hand again when the bidding rose to sixty-five hundred. Scott McKay looked in her direction and grinned.

"Oh, lordy," the brunette said with a sigh.

Oh, lordy, Blair echoed silently, her nerve endings all aquiver from the smile he'd sent her way.

"Sold for sixty-five hundred dollars," the auctioneer

called. "The residents of Lost Springs Ranch greatly appreciate your generosity, ma'am. Now, let's hear a warm welcome for our next bachelor...."

"Way to go!" The woman beside Blair cheered, clapping Blair on the back. "You bought yourself a hunk for a weekend."

"Oh, but I..." Blair's words dissolved into a groan as the full impact of what she had done sank in. What on earth was she going to do with a hunk for a weekend?

HAVING ALWAYS BEEN the type to want things settled very quickly, Blair wrote out her check to the auction officials, then immediately went looking for Scott McKay. She wanted to let him know exactly why she had purchased his services—just in case he'd gotten the wrong idea.

She didn't find him among the other bachelors milling in the arena, surrounded by their buyers and other admirers. She finally located an auction volunteer, a young man who nodded in response to her question and led her to one of the cozy one-room, one-bath cottages where overnight guests and visiting directors were occasionally housed. "He's in here," he said, and knocked on the door. "Mr. McKay? Your buyer wants to meet you."

Blair's cheeks flamed. She didn't particularly like being referred to as his buyer. It sounded so ridiculous.

The cottage door opened. And Blair discovered that Scott McKay was even more attractive close up than he had been from the risers. So polished and dignified, she thought in approval. Obviously an important businessman. He looked her over as the volunteer hurried away, leaving them alone. "Hi. So you're the one who bought me?"

"Well, um, yes. I'm Blair Townsend."

"And I," he said, giving her a smile that could have melted concrete, "am delighted."

Oh, heavens. Blair cleared her throat. "Mr. Mc-Kay..."

"Scott. Please, come in."

"Well, I—"

He reached out, took her arm and hauled her into the neatly furnished little cottage, talking the whole time. "I gotta tell you, Blair," he said, closing the door. "I was a little worried about who would buy me. Did you see the women out there? Some of them looked like they wanted to eat us alive. And that little granny who bought Rob? What do you suppose *she* wanted, a grandson for a weekend?"

"I'm not—"

He reached for his tie, yanking it loose and over his head, still knotted. The movement mussed his hair from the neatly brushed-back style of before, causing a heavy lock to fall forward on his forehead. "I'll tell you, I wouldn't have done this for anyone but Lindsay. I'd rather bungee jump off the Empire State Building or wrestle the meanest bull ever born than stand up on that auction block again."

Bungee jump? Wrestle bulls? That didn't sound like something a conservative businessman would say. "Scott, I..."

He tossed his suit jacket over the back of one of the chairs and reached for the top button of his shirt. "Anyway, I hope they made enough money today to keep them afloat—maybe enough positive PR to keep the donations coming in. Too many kids out there would be in a spit-load of trouble without this place."

"Yes, I know it's—"

"Thanks to people like you, Lindsay's got a real

chance to make it. Sixty-five hundred dollars…well, that was incredibly generous. I'll have to make sure,'' he added with a grin, ''that you get your money's worth.''

He stripped off his shirt and tossed it toward the same chair that held his jacket. His bare chest was broad, tanned…and made Blair's heart almost stop. Her fingers curled at her sides—she assured herself it wasn't an effort for her to keep from reaching out to touch all that lovely expanse of male skin. She lied, of course.

''Mr. McKay!'' she sputtered. ''What are you *doing*?''

''I'm changing clothes,'' he said with a smile that was suspiciously bland. ''I hate wearing suits, but I thought we were supposed to dress up for this thing. Come to think about it, Lindsay was the one who suggested the tie. I'll have to figure out a way to repay her for that.''

He snatched a duffel bag off the couch and moved toward the bathroom. ''I'll finish changing in here. Help yourself to something to drink, if you like. There are sodas and juice in that little fridge. I'll be out in a minute.''

The bathroom door closed in her face. Blair stared at it in dismay. What had just happened here? The dignified, conservative businessman she'd spent a large chunk of her savings on had transformed right in front of her eyes into a bare-chested, fast-talking crazy man.

Oh, how she wished she had read one of those auction brochures before she had made such an uncharacteristically impulsive and imprudent gesture!

She should probably leave now, admit defeat and consider her monetary loss a donation to a very worthwhile cause. She wasn't at all sure Scott McKay would be the right person to get through to Jeffrey. Pushing a picture

of his gorgeous bare chest out of her mind, she took a
step toward the exit.

"Hey, Blair!" Scott called through the bathroom
door. "Would you mind pouring something cold for me,
too? After sitting out there in that arena all afternoon,
I'm damned near dried out."

Blair sighed. His words reminded her of what a generous and unselfish gesture he had made on behalf of
the ranch. She would have absolutely hated being pa-
raded in front of a hooting, cheering crowd. Maybe Scott
was still just a little nervous and hyper after that experience. That would be understandable, she thought, remembering the slightly bemused expression he'd worn
during the auction.

Maybe she should give him a second chance.

"Soda or juice?" she called out.

"Whatever you're having, darlin'."

Darlin'. She swallowed a groan, tried again to forget
how good he had looked a moment ago and poured orange juice into a glass she found in a cabinet beside the
mini-refrigerator. She didn't want anything for herself.
She sincerely hoped Scott would reappear with his hair
neatly brushed again, maybe wearing a polo shirt and
khakis—something suitably conformist and respectable.
Something that would convince her he was the right man
for the job she had in mind.

The bathroom door opened and she turned, holding
out the glass of juice she had poured for him. And then
she nearly dropped it on the floor when he stepped out
and she got a good look at him.

"Oh, damn," she said in consternation. "You're a
cowboy."

CHAPTER TWO

FOR SOME REASON, Scott was getting the idea that Blair Townsend wasn't overly enthusiastic about the purchase she had made. In response to her comment, he glanced automatically at the clothes he'd just pulled on—a blue-and-white-striped denim shirt, a pair of jeans cinched with a worn leather belt and the boots he'd had on earlier.

Regular-type clothes, he thought with a frown. Why was she looking at him as if he'd just switched heads instead of shirts? "I've been called a cowboy a few times," he acknowledged. *Among other things.*

She seemed to brace herself. "Rodeo?"

Reaching for the juice glass, he studied her face, reading disapproval in her expression. When he'd first met Blair Townsend, he'd been relieved that his buyer was young and very attractive—he still shuddered when he wondered what that older woman had wanted from a weekend with poor Rob Carter. He thought Blair looked rather prim and uptight in her conservative clothes—a cream-colored short-sleeve sweater set, pearl necklace and tailored slacks. It was a more professional-looking and less casual outfit than most of the ranch guests had been wearing that afternoon, but other than that, his first impression of her had been quite positive. Now he was beginning to wonder if the old lady might have been more fun. "I rodeo sometimes—when I feel like it."

"What do you do when you don't feel like it?"

He shrugged. "I've raced cars, motorcycles and speedboats, and I have a few other hobbies that keep me entertained. What do *you* do?"

She sighed, her expression changing from consternation to resignation. Pulling a roll of antacids out of the pocket of her cardigan, she popped one into her mouth. "I eat a lot of these," she murmured.

He couldn't help smiling at her rueful tone. He wondered if she was some sort of high-powered executive. She sure had the look. Her honey-blond hair was cut for practicality in a chin-length bob she kept tucked behind her ears. No wispy bangs to soften the look. Understated makeup—not that her fair, clear complexion needed artificial enhancement, he mused, studying her dark blue eyes, naturally rosy, rounded cheeks and soft, full lips. She was of medium height and slender. Pretty, he thought, but practical.

He hazarded a guess. "Accountant?"

"Lawyer."

He nodded. *Close enough.*

"So, Counselor, you looking for some relaxation? Trust me, you've bought the right guy. By the time our weekend is over, you're going to throw the rest of those antacids in the trash. We're going to have a great time."

She shook her head. He might have liked her to look a bit more intrigued by his promises. "That wasn't the reason I bid on you, Mr. McKay. Actually, I think I've made a mistake. Maybe it would be best if I just consider my check a donation to the ranch and we'll both forget about arranging a weekend. I'm sure you're very busy. I know Lindsay and Rex and the others greatly appreciate the time you gave them today. It was extremely generous of you."

"Now, just hold on a minute," he said, holding up a hand. "You spent more than six thousand dollars for a weekend in my company. You must have had some reason for doing so."

"Well, yes, but—"

"So, what did you have in mind? And what have I done to cause you concern?"

She cleared her throat and started to speak. He interrupted her, motioning toward the tweedy couch pushed against one wall. "Why don't we sit down and get comfortable, and then you can tell me all about it."

"That won't be necessary. This won't take long."

Scott wasn't the easily riled type, but Blair Townsend was starting to irk him a bit. What the hell had she bought him for if she didn't want anything to do with him? Had she been so offended by the sight of his bare chest? Or—his pride stung a bit—so disillusioned?

"I'd like to sit for a few minutes," he said, keeping his tone mild.

She looked momentarily abashed. "Of course. Please, feel free to take a seat."

Staying where he was, he motioned toward the couch again, indicating that he would be seated when she was. Given little choice, Blair moved to the couch and perched on the edge, her back very straight, her chin high. Scott sank into the chair opposite the one that held his jacket and shirt. He slouched comfortably, stretched his legs in front of him and crossed his booted feet. He set his empty juice glass on the floor beside him, then laced his hands over his stomach. "Okay, what was your plan? And why'd you change your mind?"

"It was an impulse, really," she answered, suddenly looking flustered. "I don't act impulsively very often, and I really shouldn't have.... Anyway, I only came to watch the events today, not to participate. Buying a bachelor was the last thing on my mind when I left home this morning.''

He nodded, growing increasingly curious. ''So, what made you decide to bid on me? Was it my big blue eyes? My irresistible smile? My charming personality?''

''It was the tie, I think,'' she murmured, sticking a pin directly into his ego.

''The *tie?*''

She nodded rather glumly. ''I had this sudden, crazy idea that I could buy a role model for my nephew, Jeffrey. He's living with me, and he's going through a difficult time. He's angry and rebellious, he doesn't care about his grades, he isn't making friends. He seems to have no interest in planning for his future. So, I thought maybe one of you men who have been through rough times and still managed to turn out successfully would have some influence on him. You know, maybe have a good talk with him and convince him of how important it is to follow the rules and focus on the future.''

He felt his eyebrows rising as he digested her unexpected explanation. She had bought him for her nephew? Remembering all the wolf-whistling women who had cheered him from the stands, he wondered how he'd ended up with this one. Not that he was complaining, exactly, he thought, studying her flushed face. ''So you want me to have a bracing man-to-man talk with your nephew.''

She cleared her throat. ''That was my original idea. But now I think maybe...''

She'd changed her mind, he realized. Somewhere between him taking off that tie and coming out of the bathroom in his regular clothes, she had decided he wasn't the right one to talk to her nephew, after all. It was a good thing, he thought with a wince, that he had developed a pretty good self-image during the past few years. If he was the sensitive type, Blair Townsend just might have hurt his feelings.

What he should probably do was shrug his shoulders, agree that this had all been a mistake and let her go on her way, both of them having made their contribution to an extremely worthwhile cause. He was no one's mentor, no kid's role model. The very idea should have made him laugh. But something about the way she looked at his scuffed boots got his dander up. Her nephew could do worse than to take advice from him. And Blair just might find herself enjoying some time with him, as well.

"So what weekend is good for you?" he asked matter-of-factly.

She blinked. "What do you mean?"

"You bought me to spend a weekend with your nephew. Let's go for it. Tell me when you want to do it, and I'll set everything up."

Blair shook her head. "No, really. I think—"

"You said he's angry and rebellious and headed for trouble, right? You want him to talk to someone who's been there, someone who had to choose between freedom and jail, right? Well, lady, I'm your man."

Blair looked at him thoughtfully. "You really think you can get through to him?"

"I'm no psychologist," he admitted. "And I'm sure no expert on kids. But I came to this ranch as mean and angry and rebellious as any kid they'd taken in before. There were some who predicted I'd be in prison before I turned twenty-one. Instead, I own a successful ranch and serve on the board of directors of several civic organizations. I pay taxes and vote in every election. You might say I'm a respectable citizen—though I guess there's a few who'd define me in other ways."

"You own a ranch?"

"Yeah. Didn't you read the brochure?"

"I told you, I didn't intend to buy anyone. It was just an impulse when the idea occurred to me about Jeffrey."

"So now that you know I'm an upstanding guy, you want to give it a shot?"

"Well…" She rubbed the back of her neck, as if it had suddenly tightened. "I guess it wouldn't hurt for you to talk to him."

"Might even help," he murmured.

"I suppose that's possible."

He wasn't flattered by the lack of confidence in her voice. It only made him more determined to prove he could do this.

Scott McKay had never been one to back down from a challenge.

"This will work out just fine," he said, rubbing his hands together. "When d'you want to do it?"

"You're sure you don't mind?"

"Hey, for your generous donation to the ranch, talking to a kid is a small favor for me to do in return."

She dug into the leather purse she'd worn over her shoulder and pulled out a thin calendar. "Jeffrey and I are free next weekend. Beginning Friday, he has a three-day break from school."

"School? Isn't he out for the summer yet?"

"No, he still has a couple more weeks."

"So you want to get together next weekend."

"If that's convenient for you. Are you available then, or do you need more time to—?"

"Sure, that'll work."

She looked surprised at his quick acceptance. "Don't you need to check your schedule?"

"I don't keep a schedule. If you want to go next weekend, that's when we'll go."

"How can you run a business if you don't keep a schedule?"

"I improvise a lot." He uncrossed his ankles, then crossed them again in the opposite direction. "Okay, so beginning next Friday, you and Jeremy and I will—"

"Jeffrey."

"Sorry. You and Jeffrey and I will spend some time together, get to know each other, have a good time. Do you have any specific plans?"

"What I would like for you to do is talk to Jeffrey about how crucial it is for him to focus on his future. He needs to know that the grades he makes in school are important, that he has to cultivate the right friends and make the right choices."

She made it sound as if she was trying to get the kid into Harvard. "How old is he?" he asked, thinking that if the boy was just fifteen or so, she could cut him a little slack. He'd have some time left to have fun before he had to seriously buckle down. Now, if he was, say, a senior in high school, he'd better…

Blair started to answer, but a knock on the door interrupted her.

"Excuse me a minute." Scott stood and opened the door. Joseph, the ranch teen who'd been assigned as Scott's host for the day, smiled shyly at him. "They're wantin' to take some pictures, Mr. McKay. Out by the arena. Miss Lindsay wants to know if you can come."

"Well, I…"

"Go ahead, Scott. I have to leave, anyway. My nephew's expecting me." Blair stood, slung her purse over her shoulder and handed him a business card. "My numbers are on there. Give me a call after you've checked your calendar and we'll decide where to meet—unless you change your mind, of course, which I would completely understand."

"I'll call you."

She nodded, hesitated, then stuck out her hand. "It was very nice to meet you."

Because her rather stiff, proper manner amused him, he couldn't resist taking her hand, then tugging on it to pull her closer so he could brush a kiss against her cheek. "It was very nice being purchased by you. I'll be in touch."

Her face was flushed again when she pulled away. She murmured something incoherent and fled, though she made an obvious attempt to be dignified about it.

Joseph grinned as he looked at Blair's rapidly retreating back. "I think you flustered her, Mr. McKay."

Scott returned his grin. "I think you're right. "

And you ain't seen nothing yet, pretty Blair Townsend.

BLAIR WISHED just once Jeffrey would look happy to see her after they'd spent a day apart. But when she stopped by her aunt's house to collect him after the auction, he greeted her with the same unenthusiastic mumble she heard from him every afternoon when she picked him up after work. Her retired aunt, Wanda, lived next door to Blair, so Jeffrey stayed with her after school until Blair got home—a convenient arrangement for all of them.

"Did you like the videos we rented for you to watch this afternoon?" Blair asked Jeffrey.

He tossed his shaggy hair out of his face—he refused to wear a neater, more conservative cut, and Blair hadn't insisted on that yet since there had been so many other problems to tackle. "They were kind of lame," he grumbled about the films she had so carefully selected. "I wanted to see the new slasher movie. All the guys have seen it but me."

"I don't think *all* the fourth graders at your school have seen that movie. I'm sure there are plenty of parents who agree with me that it isn't suitable for children your age."

Jeffrey shrugged one shoulder. "Whatever."

"Get your things and we'll go have dinner."

He ambled off without looking back.

Blair turned to Wanda Townsend, who hovered nearby. "Was he much trouble?"

Wanda shook her gray head, her eyes dark with concern. "He just sat in front of the TV all afternoon, watching those films. I asked if he wanted to go outside and play, but he wasn't interested."

It had been Wanda's late husband, Edgar, who had started the law office Blair managed. She and her uncle had been discussing Blair leaving her stressful, incredibly demanding position with a firm in Chicago and becoming a partner in Edgar's practice. Just as she had decided to agree to his offer, Edgar had died of an unexpected heart attack, leaving his practice to Blair. It still distressed her that they'd never had the opportunity to work together. Instead, she'd had to scramble to catch up with his cases ... keep his office afloat. She'd lived here only six months and was just beginning to feel comfortably settled in Lightning Creek when her brother, Kirk, had arrived with his motherless son in tow. Three days later, Kirk was off on another of his crazy get-rich-quick schemes, and Blair had been left with her sullen, resentful nephew. Six months had passed since that day, and there had been only a couple of telephone calls and a postcard from Kirk since.

Wanda had tried to help with the boy, but never having children of her own, she'd often been at a loss in the face of Jeffrey's moodiness. Blair had no experience with children, either, but she'd made a valiant effort to give the boy a good home. She'd bought and read dozens of parenting books, spent several hours in consultation with the counselor at Lander Elementary School and had tried to help Jeffrey find friends and interests here. Her efforts had been met with little reward. Every time she thought she was getting through to him a little, he pulled back again.

He seemed to make a determined effort to hold other children at a distance. His grades were not good, though Blair knew he was much brighter than he let on. He refused to participate in sports, Scouts or any of the other diversions Blair suggested to him. And he was growing increasingly belligerent toward authority. She was becoming more and more worried that Jeffrey was a prime candidate for the Lost Springs Ranch for Boys—either that or reform school.

Was it any wonder she'd gotten desperate enough to buy him a role model for a weekend?

Jeffrey trudged into the room, dragging his backpack behind him. "I'm ready."

"Tell Aunt Wanda thank-you for letting you spend the afternoon with her."

Jeffrey gave Blair an annoyed look, but muttered, "Thanks."

"You're welcome, dear. I'll see you Monday after school."

"Yeah. See ya." Jeffrey headed for the door.

Blair and her aunt exchanged worried glances. "I really think you should consider getting him some professional counseling," Wanda murmured. "Maybe there's a medication that could help him."

Blair cleared her throat. "Actually, I'm taking Jeffrey to see someone next week. Someone who has a great deal of experience with troubled boys." She saw no need to add that her expert was a cowboy, not a counselor, especially since her aunt seemed so encouraged by the news.

They were both getting desperate, it seemed.

BY WEDNESDAY AFTERNOON, Blair was beginning to wonder if Scott McKay had forgotten all about her. If they were supposed to get together on Friday, they needed to make plans. Coordinate their schedules. Perhaps make a list of the things she wanted Scott to talk about with Jeffrey.

She would feel a lot better about all of this if she could just make a few lists.

Maybe she should call him, she thought, sitting in her office Wednesday afternoon, too distracted to concentrate on the stacks of paperwork piled on the desk in front of her. Scott hadn't given her his number, but she imagined it would be easy enough to get it from Lindsay Duncan. She could call him and simply ask if something else had come up. Or if he'd perhaps changed his mind.

But he was the one who had talked her into agreeing with this outing, even after she had decided it wasn't such a good idea, she reminded herself. Why should *she* call *him?* It was his responsibility to follow up on his offer.

Still, she had paid sixty-five hundred dollars for a weekend of his time....

Her phone rang just as she was telling herself she

should probably write off the donation and forget the whole thing. She picked up the receiver. "Blair Townsend."

"Ms. Townsend, this is Carolyn Roberts. I work for Scott McKay."

"Yes?"

"Mr. McKay asked me to call you to inquire if ten o'clock Friday morning is a convenient time for you and your nephew to meet him."

Blair wondered why Scott hadn't called her himself. She glanced at the calendar, though she knew nothing was written on it for Friday. She'd been keeping that day open for this. "Ten o'clock will be fine. Where does he want me to meet him?"

"At the Lightning Creek airstrip. Do you have a fax machine?"

Blinking in surprise at the unexpected question, Blair replied, "Yes, I do. Why—"

"If you'll give me your fax number, I'll send you the list of items Mr. McKay recommends that you bring with you."

A list? While Blair approved of lists in general, she wondered why Scott was sending her a list of supplies. Just what was he planning, anyway? "May I speak to Mr. McKay?" she requested, thinking this would be much easier without the middleman—or rather, middle person.

"Mr. McKay is in Japan. He won't be back in this country until Thursday evening."

"He's in Japan?" Blair parroted blankly.

"Yes. He left all the information he thought you might require. He said if you have any questions, you should feel free to call me and I'll relay them to him."

It sounded like more trouble than it was worth; much

easier to simply go along with Scott's plans. Had that been his intention?

Carolyn Roberts recited her telephone number, which Blair quickly jotted down. "Call me anytime tomorrow if there's anything you need. I'll fax Mr. McKay's list to you within the half hour."

Blair felt a bit dazed when she hung up the phone. What was Scott doing in Japan and why had he had his—secretary? assistant? housekeeper? mistress?—whatever she was, call Blair? And what was this list being faxed to her?

She prowled the office for ten minutes before the fax machine rang. She practically pounced on the pages it spat out. One look at the list had her sinking bonelessly into her chair again.

Clothes for three days—jeans, T-shirts, lightweight jackets. Hiking boots. Sunscreen. Toiletries. Favorite pillows and teddy bears.

"Cute," she m..tered, reading the last. "Where on earth are you planning to take us, Scott McKay?"

She should probably call Carolyn back immediately and tell her the weekend was off unless Scott called personally to discuss his plans—even if he had to call from Japan. Blair didn't care for surprises, and she was not an outdoorsy type. This list hinted strongly at both possibilities.

But then she pictured Jeffrey hiking along a nice trail, enjoying the fresh air and wonders of nature, responding—despite himself—to Scott's easy, cheerful banter. Apparently, Scott had arranged for them to stay in a rustic lodge or cabin. Perhaps he could take Jeffrey fishing or something, which would give them a chance to talk while male bonding. Blair wouldn't mind sitting on a porch swing with a good book while Scott tried to communicate with her nephew. She hadn't had a vacation in the entire year since she'd moved to Lightning Creek—nor the year before that, actually—and she could use a break.

Maybe she'd even do a little hiking herself, she mused, imagining a leisurely amble along a well-marked path with frequent stops to sniff a wildflower or read a park information sign.

She'd lived in Wyoming for a year and hadn't even seen Yellowstone Park yet. Was that where Scott was taking them? She supposed that wouldn't be so bad. And most important, perhaps Jeffrey would enjoy it.

She would go through with this, she thought. But only for Jeffrey.

What other reason could there be?

"WHO IS THIS GUY we're going to meet?" Jeffrey asked, not for the first time, as Blair drove toward the airport Friday morning.

"His name—as I've told you before—is Scott McKay. He's a rancher and a businessman. A former resident of Lost Springs."

"Oh, great," Jeffrey grumbled. "A geek."

"He's not a geek," Blair corrected. Not even close, she thought with an unwelcome mental image of his strong, bare chest. She ordered herself immediately to stop doing that.

Jeffrey tossed his brown hair out of his face. "So where are we going? Why'd we pack all that stuff?"

"I'm not sure where we're going, exactly. Scott's going to surprise us. It should be fun," she added, trying to convince herself as well as her nephew.

Jeffrey's grunt was not encouraging. "I guess it beats being in school," he muttered.

"Just let yourself have a good time, okay, Jeffrey? It's okay to have fun. And listen to Mr. McKay. There are probably a lot of things you can learn from him."

Jeffrey rolled his eyes and slumped in his seat, looking as if he were on his way to a root canal. Blair had to try one more time to put him in the proper frame of mind for this experiment. "Come on, Jeffrey. Surely you like being outdoors. Having adventures. Seeing new things."

"I like having adventures with my dad. Not with strangers."

The boy's sullen response made Blair's heart ache. She was trying so hard to repair the damage her careless, irresponsible brother had caused this child. But she was beginning to believe it was something she couldn't accomplish alone.

"Just give Scott a chance," she repeated quietly. "Maybe you'll like him."

The boy shrugged. "What does it matter if I like him or not? He won't be around long. Nobody is."

"*I* will be," Blair told him firmly. "Don't you doubt that."

Her nephew merely looked out the window beside him, his expression unreadable, much too contained for his years. Either he didn't believe her reassurances that she wouldn't abandon him, as everyone else in his life had, or he was afraid to believe her for fear of being disappointed yet again. But she knew she still had a long way to go before she reached him—if ever.

CHAPTER THREE

SIPPING STRONG airport coffee, Scott lounged in the metal building that comprised the office of the one-strip airport that served the private pilots of the Lightning Creek area. There weren't many people around this morning—a couple of other pilots preparing for takeoff, a mechanic who'd been hired to work on someone's two-seater, the airport owner, and his wife, who served as his partner and assistant. Scott enjoyed airports like this one and had visited dozens of them across the country, finding a bond with other flying enthusiasts who owned small aircraft.

He kept his eyes on the gravel road that approached the airport from town, watching for Blair's car. Surely she would have sent word if she wasn't going to show. He imagined she was a little annoyed with him for not calling her himself, but he'd been very busy since the auction. He'd had to leave most of the arrangements for this weekend to Carolyn, his invaluable, long-suffering assistant. And besides, he thought sheepishly, he hadn't wanted to give Blair a chance to refuse. His ego had taken enough shots from her after the auction.

It was going to take an even bigger blow if she stood him up today. Had she decided he wasn't qualified to talk to her nephew, after all?

But then he spotted a neat little white sedan bumping down the road toward the airport and he relaxed, somehow knowing it was Blair. It looked exactly like the kind of car she would drive, he mused with a smile, thinking of his own customized four-by-four. He glanced toward the green-and-white Cessna 172 waiting by the runway, already prepped for flight. He hoped neither Blair nor her nephew was a nervous flyer. Teenage boys usually liked flying, wouldn't admit their fears even if they had them.

He was generally comfortable with teenagers—even the surly ones. He made it a point to hire several for afternoon and summer work at the ranch, believing that honest work was a boost to any kid's self-confidence. He hoped he would get along well with Blair's nephew, maybe even have a positive influence on the kid. It was too bad that he and Blair had been interrupted before they could talk more about Jeffrey. It would help if he knew more about their circumstances—how Blair had ended up with the kid, why the boy was so angry and rebellious, what she had done so far to get through to him.

He tossed his foam coffee cup in an overflowing trash can and headed outside to greet them as the car turned into the graveled parking lot. Maybe he'd give the boy a flying lesson, he thought, remembering when a kindly old pilot had given him his first lesson. Teenagers usually loved to be behind the wheel of anything that moved.

He stopped in his tracks when Blair and her nephew—her very short nephew—climbed out of the car. Her nephew was most definitely *not* a teenager, Scott realized immediately. He couldn't be more than ten years old.

This was the boy Blair wanted to have buckle down and plan the course of his life? The one she worried wasn't taking his studies and his future seriously enough? The kid didn't look old enough to *spell* future, much less to blueprint it!

Rapidly revising several of the plans he'd made for the upcoming weekend, he turned his attention to Blair. She looked great, he noticed. She was dressed more casually than the last time he had seen her, in snug jeans and a forest-green camp shirt unbuttoned over a white T-shirt. Her feet were laced into a pair of hiking boots that looked small enough to fit her young nephew.

He was hit again with the attraction he'd felt for her when he'd met her after the auction. Whether dressed in her professional lawyer clothes or this outdoorsy outfit, she looked spectacular. But it was more than just her appearance that appealed to him; he was drawn to the intelligence in her eyes, the challenge in the tilt of her chin, the confident yet undeniably sexy way she walked. "Hi, Blair."

"Good morning, Scott." Her manner was briskly polite, as if she were greeting one of her legal clients rather than a weekend companion. "This is my nephew, Jeffrey. Jeffrey, this is Scott McKay."

Jeffrey tossed his longish, center-parted hair out of his face and subjected Scott to an intense scrutiny. Scott had the sensation that the boy didn't miss one detail of his appearance, from his breeze-tossed hair to his denim shirt, faded jeans and scuffed western boots. And he got the distinct feeling the kid wasn't particularly impressed with what he saw.

"Hi, Jeff. How's it going?" Scott said casually, careful not to be overly friendly.

The boy shrugged and mumbled something.

He looked so damned young, Scott thought again. So small in his oversize jersey and baggy jeans. So vulnerable behind the defiance in his snub-nosed face. Looking at this boy, Scott recognized emotions he had thought long since behind him.

He cleared his throat, determined to show the kid a good time this weekend—for Jeffrey's sake, and not just because he wanted to impress the boy's aunt. "Did you bring the stuff I suggested?" he asked Blair.

She nodded. "It's in the car."

"Great. Want to help me load the plane, Jeff?"

"The plane?" Blair repeated as the boy shrugged again. "We're going in a plane?"

He raised an eyebrow. "We're at an airport. Did you think we were going by submarine?"

Jeffrey chuckled, then looked rather surprised that he had done so. Blair glanced at him quickly, her expression softening. And then she turned toward Scott again. "I thought you flew in this morning and wanted to meet here for convenience."

"No, we're flying. You like flying, Jeff?"

"I've never been in a little plane," the boy answered, glancing at the two-, four- and six-seaters parked nearby.

"I bet you'll like it," Scott predicted, then moved toward the back of Blair's car. "The stuff's in the trunk?"

In response, she opened the trunk, still looking a bit worried. "Have you chartered a plane? Who's our pilot?"

"It's my plane, and I'm the pilot."

"You're a, um, good pilot, I hope?"

Grinning at her, he quipped, "You bet. I've had my license for a whole week tomorrow. Bought it out of the back of a magazine. You know, one of those ads that begin, 'You, too, can soar like an eagle....'"

"That's not funny."

"Jeff thought it was. He's smiling."

The boy immediately changed his expression to a scowl. "Am not."

Scott knew better than to push it. "Whatever. Got all your stuff?"

Jeffrey pulled a grubby backpack out of the car and slung it over his shoulder. "Okay."

Blair locked the car, slipped her purse beneath her arm and turned toward Scott with the general air of a turkey at Thanksgiving. "We're ready."

Scott grinned and slung an arm around her shoulders for a quick, bracing squeeze. "Trust me," he said. "it's going to be a *very* interesting weekend."

BLAIR INSISTED that Jeffrey should take the copilot's spot in the little four-seater Scott led them to. She explained that she would be much more comfortable in the back, though she was really hoping Jeffrey would find the ride more exciting in the front. She wanted so badly for him to take pleasure from the weekend, to show some excitement about *anything*. Maybe if he enjoyed being with Scott, he would be more likely to listen when Scott talked to him.

Buckled very tightly into the snug back seat, she watched as Scott matter-of-factly showed Jeffrey all the instruments and gave him a quick explanation of their purpose. After he started the noisy engine, she wasn't able to hear much of what they were saying, but she noticed that Jeffrey seemed to be listening closely as Scott continued to talk.

She remembered the look of surprise on Scott's face when she and Jeffrey had climbed out of her car. What was it about Jeffrey's appearance that had startled Scott? Whatever it was, he had recovered quickly. He'd been quite pleasant to the boy since, using a man-to-man tone that Jeffrey seemed to respond well to. Blair was aware of how much her nephew hated being talked to like a cute little boy.

The plane began to move, the engine noise increasing. Blair swallowed and tightened her seat belt. She wasn't afraid of flying commercially, but small planes made her a bit nervous. This was the smallest she'd ever been in. And how did she know Scott was a good pilot? Was she crazy to put her life and her nephew's in the hands of a man she hardly knew?

She kept her eyes on Scott as he taxied the plane to the end of the runway. He'd slid a pair of aviator sunglasses onto his nose, and that, combined with his headphones, made him look the part of a competent pilot. She began to relax a bit, reassured, perhaps, by the image he projected. There was just something about this guy that inspired confidence—which probably explained why she was here with him now.

The engines revved and the plane began to roll down the runway, picking up speed until it lifted, then climbing rapidly until the ground was far beneath them. Blair yawned to clear her ears, looking from the vista beneath them to her nephew's face. It was the first time in weeks that Jeffrey had looked genuinely enthused. She began to take heart that she had done the right thing this weekend, after all.

Forcing herself to relax, she leaned back against the seat. The droning engine noise cocooned her, isolating her from Scott and Jeffrey in the front. She could see their mouths moving and hear an occasional word, but she made no real effort to follow their conversation. She looked out the window for a while, then pulled a book out of her tote bag. It was a recent nonfiction bestseller, a densely written dissection of the political overview for the U.S. in the new millennium. She'd intended to read it for some time but had been too busy to tackle it. She planned to get well into it this weekend while Scott worked with Jeffrey.

A couple of days of reading and relaxation while someone else took care of her nephew, she thought with a sigh. This weekend might just prove to be well worth the money she'd spent for it.

She read the first page of the book, then glanced toward the front of the plane again. Scott was half turned in his seat to look at Jeffrey, leaning slightly toward the boy as he pointed to one of the cockpit gauges. The midmorning sun filtered in through the tinted glass, highlighting his glossy brown hair. His aviator glasses covered the upper half of his face, and his deep, intriguing dimples flashed beneath them. Had she been standing, her knees would have gone weak. As it was, she sank back into her seat, suddenly unable to look away from him. The wave of sheer physical attraction caught her unprepared, held her motionless for several long moments.

She didn't have time for this, she reminded herself. The circumstances were all wrong, considering that Jeffrey was sitting right there in front of her. And Scott McKay was hardly her type, anyway. She had never allowed herself to get involved with anyone strictly on the basis of physical attraction. And she couldn't see how she and Scott could have anything in common—even if he felt a modicum of answering attraction for her.

As if sensing her gaze on him, he looked over his shoulder. "You doing okay back there?" he asked, raising his voice over the engine noise.

"Yes, I'm fine, thank you." She forced her attention

to her book, not that she was able to concentrate on it. Her gaze kept drifting toward the front seats, and even she didn't believe her feeble mental excuse that she was only checking on her nephew.

She was so involved in what was going on inside the plane that she hardly noticed the landscape passing beneath them until they started to descend. She noted then that they were headed toward a grass landing strip carved out of a stand of trees surrounded by mountains. She saw no lodge or resort nearby. Surely Scott had a place for them to stay. He didn't expect them to sleep on the ground, did he?

Her stomach tensed as the plane seemed to dive straight toward the trees. The runway hardly looked long enough as they approached it. The trees and mountains loomed on either side, crowding closer the lower they dropped. At the last minute, she squeezed her eyes shut, keeping them that way until the landing was over. She opened them only when the plane came to a complete stop—still apparently in one piece.

Scott was looking at her when she opened her eyes. He wasn't smiling, exactly, but he looked amused. "Sorry," he said. "Grass strips are a bit bumpier than paved runways."

Annoyed with her momentary cowardice, she cleared her throat. "It didn't bother me at all," she lied. "You weren't frightened, were you, Jeffrey?"

The boy looked insulted. "No. I thought it was sort of cool."

Sort of cool. High praise from this particular boy, Blair mused. She supposed the landing hadn't been so bad, after all, if it had been fun for her nephew. She looked out the window, noting that the surrounding landscape was beautiful but untamed. The only building in sight was a metal hangar at one side of the airstrip. A heavy padlock dangled from the wide sliding doors. Scott revved the engine just enough to taxi toward the building.

He pulled up almost to the doors, then parked and killed the engine. The sudden silence was startling. Blair's ears were still buzzing; she shook her head slightly to clear them. Her voice sounded too loud when she asked, "Where are we?" She didn't even know if they were still in Wyoming.

"The outback," Scott replied with a grin.

She frowned. "Where?"

"Out back of nowhere." He opened his door and hopped lightly out of the plane, leaving Blair staring after him in confusion. While Scott unlocked the padlock of the hangar, Blair and Jeffrey climbed out of the plane, Blair a bit stiffly. Scott disappeared into the building and reappeared moments later driving a sturdy-looking Jeep. He parked nearby, jumped out and, with Jeffrey's help, began to transfer their belongings from the plane to the Jeep. Blair wondered again where he was taking them, but she was afraid to ask, considering the last answer he'd given her.

When the Jeep was loaded, Scott asked Blair and Jeffrey to help him push the plane into the hangar. He blocked the wheels, closed the doors and secured the massive padlock again. Then he turned to them, rubbing his hands and looking satisfied. "Let's go."

"Where are we going?" Blair asked, following him to the Jeep.

"Farther out back," he quipped, opening the passenger door for her. "You sure ask a lot of questions, Counselor."

"I like to know what's going on," she answered a bit primly, watching Jeffrey scramble into the back seat.

Scott held out a hand to assist her into the high vehicle. "Don't you like to be surprised? Just go with the flow?"

"Not particularly," she admitted. "I'm a planner. A list maker."

He chuckled. "Not this weekend, you're not."

He closed her door and loped around the front of the vehicle to his own seat behind the wheel. "Everybody buckle up," he said, starting the engine. "The ride gets bumpy."

Where was he *taking* them? Blair was beginning to wonder again what on earth had gotten into her at that bachelor auction.

"THIS IS IT? This is where we're staying for the weekend?" Blair stared in disbelief at the cabin tucked into the side of a wooded mountain. They'd spent forty-five minutes negotiating heart-stoppingly steep and winding roads to get here. The cabin hardly looked big enough for one person, much less three. And where were the other cabins? The lodge? The restaurant?

"This is it. What do you think, Jeff?" Scott asked casually.

Apparently deciding he'd been much too agreeable so far that day, Jeffrey scowled. "Looks like a dump to me."

That was unfair, Blair thought immediately. The cabin was small, but tidy and obviously in good repair. "It is not a dump," she said firmly. "It's a nice little cabin."

Jeffrey shrugged.

Apparently unperturbed by the boy's mood change,

Scott opened the back of the Jeep. "Let's get our stuff inside and unpack so we can start having fun."

Blair was afraid to ask what Scott's idea of fun might be.

To her relief, the cabin was larger than it had appeared from the outside. They entered a good-size main room. Blair noted immediately that, despite the rustic appearance of the place, the furnishings were of good quality, heavy wood with a hand-rubbed finish, the couch sporting duck-print tapestry cushions. Hunting prints hung on the wood-paneled walls. A rock fireplace dominated one wall, and another was made up of bookcases, crowded with paperback and hardcover novels. A spiral staircase in one corner led to a loft, which obviously served as a sleeping area, and two closed doors probably indicated more bedrooms downstairs. An eat-in kitchen opened off the back of the main room. The cabin was isolated but certainly beat sleeping on the ground, she decided.

"Hardly a dump," she murmured to her nephew, who only shrugged in response.

"Anybody hungry?" Scott asked, carrying the last load in from the Jeep. "Why don't we stash our stuff and then have lunch? Jeff, your bedroom is the far door there. It's just big enough to turn around in, but it's got a bed. I'll take the other small bedroom. Blair, the sleeping loft is yours."

She suspected he was giving her his usual room. "I don't mind taking one of the small rooms."

He shook his head. "These two share a bath. The loft has its own bathroom. It will be more comfortable for you, I think. Jeff, help your aunt carry her things up while I stash some of this other stuff."

Jeffrey had already settled onto the couch. "She can carry her own stuff. It's not that heavy."

Scott crossed his arms over his chest, dipped his chin and looked at the boy from beneath lowered brows. "I'm sure she's quite capable of carrying her own things, but the polite thing to do is to help her." His lazy drawl made him sound like an old-time movie cowboy, Blair couldn't help thinking, even as she bit her lip to keep from interfering before Jeffrey broke into one of his rare, but formidable, tantrums.

Jeffrey glared at Scott with the defiant scowl Blair had come to know all too well. "I don't want to. I'm hungry. I want to eat."

Scott's voice was still very mild when he replied, "We'll eat when the bags are stowed away. You take this one upstairs," he said, nudging an overnight case with his boot.

"What if I say no?" Jeffrey challenged.

Scott's smile was quick and easy. "Then you don't eat. Around here, everyone pulls his weight. Unless you're afraid this bag is too heavy for you to handle? I guess you can take her pillow up, if that's the case. It only weighs a few ounces."

The boy's scowl deepened. "I can carry the bag. I just don't want to."

"I don't know." Scott nudged it again. "It is kind of heavy. And you're sort of scrawny. Blair, why don't you hand Jeff the pillow and you carry this bag while I bring the heavier suitcase up?"

The boy let out a gusty sigh, snatched the bag in question and hauled it toward the staircase, his head high, his back straight. If he had any trouble carrying the moderately heavy bag up the stairs, his young male pride didn't allow it to show.

Scott sent Blair a grin. "Did I mention I've done some calf wrangling?"

"Well, this little calf is probably the most stubborn one you've ever taken on," she warned dryly. She noted that Scott didn't look particularly concerned.

She waited until her nephew had stomped back down the narrow staircase before she carried her own bag up. She was immediately charmed by the loft bedroom. The big iron bed was covered with a hand-pieced quilt in a colorful lone star design; it reminded her of the beautiful log-cabin quilt she'd tried to win at the bachelor auction. Someone else had won that one, and she'd ended up here.

Shaking her head at life's oddities, she continued her inspection of the room. The mirrored dresser was obviously an antique, as were the nightstand and small stained-glass lamp it held. A little round window cut into the back wall gave a breathtaking view of the mountainside. A skylight in the roof above the bed showed blue sky dotted with fluffy white clouds; at night, she would be able to see the stars.

"Scott, this is lovely," she said, turning to him as he set her suitcase at the foot of the bed. "Is this your cabin or are you renting it for the weekend?"

"It's mine. Sometimes I need a place to rest and recharge. This is it."

"It's wonderful. Are you *sure* you want to give this room up to sleep downstairs?"

"Don't mind a bit," he assured her. "Being downstairs with Jeff will give me a chance to get to know him better. He seems like a good kid beneath the bravado."

Blair bit her lip. She wanted so badly to believe there was a good kid beneath her nephew's troubled behavior. She had tried so hard to get through to him, to make up for the neglect he'd received during his first nine and a half years of life. She refused to believe it was too late to reach him.

Remembering the excitement on Jeffrey's face during the plane ride, she hoped again that Scott would be the one to help him. She was encouraged by the way Scott had bested the boy in their brief battle of wills without setting off a tantrum. "I hope you're right," she said. "Jeffrey can be…difficult."

"He's dealing with the champ when it comes to that," Scott answered with another of his quick smiles. "I want to talk to you about him after lunch. I have a few questions for you, if you don't mind."

She nodded, aware that Scott couldn't help her if he didn't know what he was dealing with.

He turned to look around the bedroom again. "I think you'll be comfortable here. The bed," he added, his eyes meeting hers as he patted the quilt with one hand, "sleeps great. I've spent many cozy nights in it."

She swallowed, knowing it was inevitable that she would think of him when she crawled beneath the covers tonight. Had that been his intention? She couldn't help wondering how many women had shared those cozy nights with him.

"We'd better get back to Jeffrey," she said, reminding him—and maybe herself—that there would be no shenanigans this weekend.

She thought she heard Scott chuckle as she turned to hurry down the stairs. He seemed to find it amusing when he flustered her. Unless she wanted to spend the weekend being laughed at by him, she was going to have to start doing a better job of hiding her reactions to him.

Downstairs, Scott produced the picnic basket he'd brought with him and set it on the round oak pedestal table at the back of the main room. "Did you say you're hungry, Jeff? We've got plenty of food here."

Jeffrey looked torn between hunger and sulking. Hunger won. He sauntered to the table, obviously trying not to look too eager. "What've you got?"

Scott unloaded fried chicken, coleslaw, fruit and brownies from the basket, along with paper plates and napkins. It was all nicely prepared and packaged and looked quite appetizing. There wasn't much conversation during the meal; everyone was too busy eating. By the time they'd finished, not a scrap of food remained. Blair didn't know what they would eat the rest of the weekend, but she assumed Scott had made plans.

Blair asked Jeffrey to help with the cleanup afterward. He did so without enthusiasm, but also without argument, probably because he knew he would lose again.

"Okay, what does everyone want to do now?" Scott asked.

Jeffrey looked around the room. "Got a TV?"

"Nope," Scott replied cheerfully. "Don't need one up here. There are too many other things to do."

"Like what?"

"Fishing. Hiking. Climbing. Watching birds and wildlife. Reading. Thinking."

Jeffrey rolled his eyes. "I'd rather play video games."

"You won't find any of those up here, either. Looks like you're going to have to find something else to do to entertain yourself."

"Why don't we go for a walk?" Blair suggested.

Scott smiled. "Good idea. I think you'll approve of the scenery I've provided. Are you up to a hike, Jeff?"

"Maybe I'll just hang out in here," the boy answered, dropping onto the couch with his ever-present backpack beside him.

"Oh, I don't think so," Scott drawled in that steely cowboy voice he'd used earlier. "Let's all go for a walk."

With a deep, long-suffering sigh, Jeffrey rose to his feet. "This is really lame," he grumbled.

Scott only laughed and casually ruffled the boy's hair. "Try to contain your enthusiasm, will you, pal? All this hyperactivity is wearing me out."

Blair would have sworn she saw a quick flash of answering amusement in her nephew's eyes, but he quenched it almost immediately. Scott definitely had his work cut out for him if he thought he could tame this little calf, she mused.

CHAPTER FOUR

IT WAS NO leisurely stroll down a neatly marked nature trail that Scott led them on, but a brisk hike through the woods. Over rocks and fallen limbs, around tree trunks and half-buried boulders, up steep inclines and down rocky hills. He pushed them like a cheerful drill sergeant, cracking jokes and keeping up a running commentary, but rarely letting them stop. Though she quickly grew hot and winded, Blair couldn't help but enjoy the walk. It was such a beautiful day, and the scenery was breathtaking. It wasn't long before Jeffrey stopped lagging sullenly behind and began to wander ahead, chasing squirrels, hopping from rock to rock, swinging on low branches.

"There really is a regular kid inside there," Scott murmured, moving close to Blair so she could hear his softly spoken comment. "Bright, too. He asked several excellent questions about the operation of my plane."

"He's very bright. His standardized test scores are well above average for his age. But his grades aren't very good, I'm afraid. Although I make sure he does his homework, I can't force him to do the work he's assigned during school hours. He doesn't like his teacher and he simply won't cooperate with her. I would hire a tutor for him, but he really doesn't need that. He knows the material, he just won't use it correctly."

Scott watched as Jeffrey charged down a hill ahead

of them, slipping and sliding down a grassy slope, his arms flailing for balance. "Where are his parents?"

"His mother died when he was four. His maternal grandmother took him in then. She's a cool, rather distant woman. I only met her a couple of times, but I didn't care for her. Still, my brother, Kirk—Jeffrey's father— chose to leave Jeffrey with her until six months ago, when her health became so poor that she was unable to care for him any longer. That's when Kirk brought him to Lightning Creek to 'visit' me. Three days later, he was off on another of his schemes and Jeffrey was left with me. We haven't seen Kirk since."

Scott frowned. "You mean your brother just dumped his kid on you without any warning?"

Blair checked quickly to make sure Jeffrey wasn't within hearing distance. She didn't want him to think of himself as dumped on her. "That about sums it up," she murmured. "I had no idea Kirk intended to leave his son with me until the morning he left. He asked if I would mind if Jeffrey stayed with me for a week or two, and then he took off. I knew right then that I'd be raising Jeffrey until he's grown."

"I hate to criticize your brother—"

"Trust me," Blair cut in, "you couldn't say anything about Kirk that I haven't already thought. He's irresponsible, unreliable, immature and selfish. He's a reckless dreamer, unwilling—or unable—to settle down and build a respectable life for himself. He's very much like our father, actually. My dad was always pursuing some crazy scheme, though he never actually abandoned his family—not until he was killed. He had decided to become a demolition expert, you see. Unfortunately, he wasn't very good at it. He blew up a condemned building—and himself along with it."

Scott turned and leaned against a tree trunk, studying her with an intensity that made her self-conscious. She'd been trying to ignore the inconvenient attraction she felt for this man, but it wasn't easy when he stood so close, his gleaming eyes focused on her face. "How old were you when your father died?" he asked.

"Nineteen, a sophomore in college. Kirk was twenty-one and living in Alaska at the time. Prospecting for gold, if I remember correctly."

"Is your mother still living?"

"Yes. After Dad died, she moved in with her widowed sister in Arizona. Since then, she's been living on investments from Dad's insurance money. Her life has been much more peaceful since my father died, but she has never stopped missing him. For all his flaws, she loved him. As I did," Blair admitted. "Unfortunately, my brother inherited all my father's worst traits and very few of his better qualities."

Scott glanced over at Jeffrey, who was investigating a small hole in the side of a hill. "How does the boy feel about his father?"

Blair sighed. "He idolizes him. To Jeffrey, Kirk has always been the exciting stranger who shows up unexpectedly bearing exotic gifts and telling adventurous stories and making extravagant promises. Jeffrey's only seen Kirk a handful of times, but he has always dreamed of the day he would take off on an adventure with his father."

"And you doubt that will ever happen?"

Staring bleakly at her young nephew, her heart aching for him, Blair moistened her lips. "Kirk didn't even tell Jeffrey goodbye when he left this time. He took off before Jeffrey woke up, leaving a note that said, 'See you soon.' I begged Kirk to let me wake Jeffrey, but he said he wasn't into goodbyes. He didn't want to see the tears."

"So he left you to deal with them instead."

Remembering Jeffrey's heartbroken sobs, Blair swallowed and nodded. "The best I could," she whispered. "I don't know how much comfort he found with me...after all, I was practically a stranger to him then. Every time I tried to put my arms around him, he stiffened and pulled away from me."

Scott nodded, as if he understood Jeffrey's behavior very well. Remembering his stay at the Lost Springs Ranch, Blair thought that perhaps Scott *did* understand—at least a bit better than she did. It was that possibility that gave her hope something positive would happen between Jeffrey and Scott this weekend.

"Do you mind if I ask one more personal question?"

She shook her head, thinking that Scott couldn't really help if he didn't know what he was dealing with. "What is it?"

"How do *you* feel about Jeffrey?"

Caught off guard, she blinked. It was something she hadn't given a great deal of thought to, she realized uncomfortably. She'd been so overwhelmed by responsibility and worry that she hadn't had time to analyze her feelings. "I...want him to be happy," she said haltingly. "I want him to make friends and get good grades and have a successful future—unlike his father and grandfather."

Scott shook his head. "You're telling me what you want for the kid, but you aren't telling me how you feel about him."

Looking toward the young boy who peered so curiously into the dark hole, Blair bit her lip. She thought of the nights she'd stood over Jeffrey's bed, aware of how small and vulnerable he was beneath his tough-guy act, wanting so badly to give him a better life than he'd had so far. The times she had ached to hug him and let him know someone cared about him, but hadn't because she wasn't sure he would accept her hug. "I'm...very fond of him."

"Hmm. I see I have my work cut out for me," Scott murmured.

Blair watched as Jeffrey grew tired of the hole and wandered off with his head down and his shoulders hunched. "Yes. He's very angry about everything that has happened to him."

Scott pushed away from the tree and gave her what appeared to be an oddly pitying smile. "I wasn't talking about the boy just then."

Before Blair could ask what he meant, he moved briskly away. "Hey, Jeff. Let's walk down to the stream and see if we spot any fish to catch later."

Blair stared after him for a moment in confusion, then had to hurry to catch up when the guys headed down the hill without looking back at her.

DURING HIS TIME at Lost Springs and in the years since, Scott had met some kids who were serious trouble. Seething, volatile—dangerous, some of them. Jeffrey was angry and sullen, which was perfectly understandable for a boy who'd been abandoned by nearly everyone he'd counted on. But he was far from a hopeless case. He was still very young and obviously bright, and it was apparent that he'd been given fundamental training in manners, though he didn't go out of his way to display them. He expressed his unhappiness in small ways—sulking, grumbling, moodiness—but hadn't yet taken it to extremes. Scott thought he was basically a decent kid, just one who was hurting and needed a way to work out his feelings.

He found it all too easy to identify with young Jeffrey Townsend. After all, he had been just like him, only worse. Who knew where he would be today, how far his rage would have taken him, if it hadn't been for the guidance he'd received at Lost Springs?

Jeffrey wasn't nearly as far gone as Scott had been. And Scott hadn't had the benefit of a committed, concerned Aunt Blair.

Leaning one shoulder against the rough bark of a pine tree, he watched Blair and Jeffrey as they stood side by side, looking into the stream for fish. They weren't touching, but they leaned slightly toward each other— as if they wanted to touch, but didn't quite know how. Jeffrey wasn't the only Townsend who had issues with family, he mused. He'd heard a lot of bitterness in Blair's voice when she'd talked about her father and brother and some distance when she'd spoken of her mother.

Scott had never claimed to be an expert on family relationships, considering how long it had been since he'd had any personal experience with such things, but it looked to him as though Blair and Jeffrey needed each other. Maybe there was something he could do to bring them closer together this weekend.

And, speaking of getting closer…

He looked at Blair again, aware of a renewed tug of attraction. He remembered the moment when their gazes had met across the bed in the loft room. He'd found himself wondering then what it would be like to share that bed with her. Would she make love as primly and methodically as she seemed to do everything else? Would it be as difficult for her to express her feelings there as it had been for her to say how she felt about her young nephew? Or would the latent spark of impulsiveness that had made her bid on him at the bachelor auction reassert itself in the bedroom?

He was surprisingly eager to discover what it would be like between them. And when she turned, noticed him watching her and sent him a quick, slightly shy smile, he knew it was inevitable that he would try to find out. Yet he doubted that Blair would be quite as cooperative about that as she'd been about the other plans he'd made for them thus far.

He definitely had his work cut out for him.

BLAIR WAS quite surprised when Scott somehow enticed Jeffrey into racing him back to the cabin. They scrambled over rocks and limbs, skidded perilously on slick spots, stumbled in occasional holes, shouted challenges at each other. And while she wanted to warn Jeffrey to be careful, Blair bit her tongue to remain silent for fear of ruining the moment. Just then, Jeffrey seemed like an average little boy, loud, boisterous, reckless, carefree. He had forgotten to be sullen and angry. And it was all because of Scott, she thought, watching as he dashed down the hill with much the same abandon as the boy. Scott was a bit eccentric and definitely unpredictable, but twice today he'd been able to connect with Jeffrey, giving Blair hope for significant progress during the remainder of the weekend.

Scott didn't hold back to allow Jeffrey to win their impromptu competition. Though the boy gave him a good race, Scott's longer legs were an advantage. He reached the cabin several seconds before Jeffrey.

"No fair," Jeffrey protested loudly, his breath ragged.

"You're bigger than me. I should have gotten a head start."

Blair's smile turned to a grimace. Jeffrey was not known for being a gracious loser. Maybe Scott should have...

"Who ever told you life was fair?" Scott drawled, leaning against a porch post without even looking winded from the race. "And what made you think you'd be getting head starts whenever you wanted them? In a race, it's every man for himself, kid. The trick is to give it your best shot—and to take advantage of your natural strengths. My legs are longer than yours—I took advantage of it. And I won. Don't expect an apology, but I will congratulate you on running a good race. You gave me quite a challenge."

Blair half expected another bout of sulking. Instead, Jeffrey only stuffed his hands into his pockets and shrugged. "Whatever," he said, but without the belligerence she had come to expect from him when he was thwarted. "What are we going to do now?"

"You and I are going to do some maintenance work," Scott replied cheerily. "Your aunt Blair is going to relax with a good book for a while. Something tells me she hasn't spent enough time relaxing lately."

"All she ever does is work."

"Very admirable." Scott was obviously speaking tongue-in-cheek. "But everyone needs to take some time off once in a while."

"I *am* still here, you two," Blair reminded them dryly.

"Of course you are." Scott patted her head, very much as if she were a favorite pet. "And very pretty you look, too, with your cheeks all rosy from your walk."

Her cheeks immediately flamed hotter.

"What kind of maintenance are we going to do?" Jeffrey asked warily, unconcerned with his aunt's plans.

Scott looked up. "I noticed some loose shingles on the roof. We need to get up there and nail them down so it doesn't leak during the next heavy rain. You aren't afraid of heights, are you, Jeff? Or hammers?"

"I'm not afraid," Jeffrey answered immediately.

As hard as she had been trying not to interfere, Blair couldn't help asking Scott rather nervously, "You aren't going to let him get on the roof, are you? Please remember that he's only ten years old."

"Ten? Heck, I was building houses from the ground up when I wasn't but five," Scott drawled, wicked dimples flashing.

"No, seriously, Scott..."

He patted her head again. "Don't worry, Aunt Blair. I'll take care of the kid." He added in an aside to Jeffrey, "Women get a little crazy sometimes when they're protecting their precious little boys."

Blair started to retort, but realized that Jeffrey was looking at her with sudden speculation, as if it hadn't occurred to him before that she might feel protective toward him—or that he might be precious to her. "I'll be careful, Aunt Blair," he promised, and again, his tone was new to her. Reassuring. Even rather sweet.

Too bad it wouldn't last, she thought pessimistically. He just wanted to get on that roof.

She leveled a look at Scott. "I'm trusting you to keep him safe."

"No sweat. He'll be fine. Now go put your feet up and relax awhile. There are cocoa and cider mixes in the kitchen, if you want. Make yourself at home." Smiling, he stepped closer to her, lifting his hand.

"If you pat my head again," Blair warned him in a low, deceptively gentle voice, "I'll bite you."

His grin deepened. "Maybe we should save that for later," he murmured, then abruptly turned away. "C'mon, Jeff, let's get the ladder."

He left Blair shaking her head as he walked around the building with the boy.

SETTLED INTO A CHAIR with a cup of hot cider beside her, Blair had been reading—or trying to read—for nearly twenty minutes when Scott came inside. It had been a bit hard to concentrate with all the pounding going on overhead. Of course, that had nothing to do with the fact that the critically touted book was as dry as the shingles the guys were hammering, she assured herself. Still, it was with relief that she looked up from the densely printed pages to greet Scott as he came in.

"Jeff and I are thirsty," he announced. "I'm getting some sodas."

"I could have brought some out to you."

He shook his head. "Keep your seat. You look comfortable. Good book?"

"I'm having a little trouble getting into it," she admitted. "But it came very highly recommended. I've been meaning to read it for some time."

He glanced at the title and scowled. "*That's* your idea of relaxing pleasure reading?"

"I don't have much time to read purely for pleasure," she answered, going on the defensive in response to his critical tone. "When I do find time to read, I feel as though I should choose something worthwhile. Something informative that challenges the reader to think and draw conclu— What are you doing?"

Scott had plucked the book from her hands and tossed

it unceremoniously onto a table. Before he answered, he
moved to the crowded bookshelf that took up one full
wall of the room and extracted a colorful paperback.
"Here," he said, thrusting it into her hands. "Have you
read this?"

She glanced automatically at the title. "No, I—"

"Good. You're supposed to be taking a break. You
can be informed and challenged some other time. *This*
is reading for fun."

"But I—"

"I have to get back outside before the kid falls off
the roof. I'll expect a full report on that book later, by
the way."

"You didn't really leave Jeffrey alone on the roof, did
you?" she demanded, instinctively starting to rise.

Grinning, he put a hand on her shoulder to hold her
in place. "It was a joke, Blair. Lighten up. Jeffrey is
safely on the ground—or he was the last time I checked.
I gave him orders to stay there until I got back."

"Maybe you'd better go check again," she suggested
through teeth that were showing a tendency to clench.
She was much too vividly aware of his hand on her
shoulder, his fingertips straying a bit too close to the low
scooped neckline of her T-shirt.

"Good idea." He made a hasty exit, leaving her to
rub her temples with her fingertips and wish she had a
roll of antacids handy.

To keep from going outside to monitor Jeffrey and
risk interfering with whatever bond Scott was forming
with the boy, she opened the dog-eared paperback. The
analysis of modern politics she'd been trying to read had
been rather uninteresting, she admitted. Not that she expected to like this book any better. The description on

the back sounded downright bizarre—which shouldn't have surprised her, since Scott had recommended it.

Hearing renewed hammering above her, she started to read. The opening was mildly interesting—a man who seemed to be contemplating suicide was distracted when a pitiful but sweet-natured dog came out of nowhere and needed immediate attention. Blair sighed. She wasn't particularly fond of dogs, but she kept reading. It wasn't long before she was totally absorbed in the novel, swiftly turning pages as the nerve-racking tale unfolded.

She became so engrossed in the book that she completely lost track of time, paying no attention to the sounds coming from above her head. When a hand fell on her shoulder sometime later, she jumped and gave a muffled shriek.

"Scott," she scolded, holding one hand to her pounding heart. "You scared me half to death."

He grinned unrepentantly. "Who'd you think I was? The mutant monster or the sadistic paid assassin?"

Swallowing hard, she set the book aside, careful to note the page number where she had left off. She wanted to know how the story ended. "Did you guys get the roof fixed?"

Looking at her a bit curiously—probably because he hadn't seen her quite so easily startled before—Jeffrey nodded. "Scott showed me how to nail shingles without hitting my fingers with the hammer. He hit his thumb once, though. Hard. He said—"

"Never mind what I said," Scott interrupted quickly and rather sheepishly. "I told you not to repeat it."

Jeffrey flashed a creditable imitation of Scott's wicked grin. "Oh, yeah. I forgot."

"Careful, kid—there's still a woodshed out back," Scott drawled in mock warning.

Jeffrey did not look notably cowed. "I'm hungry. What's for dinner?"

"Whatever critter got caught in my trap. Have you ever skinned a coon before, Jeff?"

"We're having raccoon for dinner? Eeww!"

"You don't see a supermarket around here, do you? Out in the wilderness, we have to live off the land. Forage in the woods for anything edible. Depend on nature's generosity for—"

"There's a stew cooking in the kitchen," Blair cut in mildly. "I found the ingredients in the freezer earlier. I thawed the meat in the microwave."

Jeffrey relaxed. "I thought I smelled something cooking. I knew you were joshing me, Scott. We're not eating raccoon."

Scott lifted an eyebrow. "What kind of meat do you think your aunt found in the freezer?"

Looking nervous again, Jeffrey turned to her. "Aunt Blair..."

"Beef," she assured him. "Neatly packaged and labeled."

"You two have no culinary sense of adventure."

Glancing once again at the book she'd been reading, Blair turned resolutely toward the kitchen. "I'll get the food ready while you guys wash up."

"HEY, BLAIR—this is really good," Scott said a short while later.

She glanced up from her dinner. Their gazes met across the table and held. "You needn't sound so surprised," she said, hoping her teasing tone hid her suddenly renewed awareness of him.

He chuckled. "Sorry. I just didn't know you brainy lawyer types could cook."

Brainy lawyer types. Hardly a flattering description the way he said it. She was going to have to get her reactions to this man under control before she made a complete fool of herself. "Throwing together a quick stew hardly qualifies as gourmet cooking. But as it happens, I enjoy cooking, when I have time."

"She makes good homemade pizza," Jeffrey said offhandedly. "It's my favorite."

Blair blinked in surprise. Jeffrey always ate her pizza without comment. She hadn't known he had a particular fondness for it. She promptly decided to serve it to him more often.

Scott reached for the iced tea she'd made to accompany the stew. "Homemade pizza, hmm? Sounds great. Maybe she'll make it for me sometime."

"Perhaps," Blair murmured, though she seriously doubted she'd be cooking for Scott after this weekend ended.

Jeffrey polished off his stew. "What's for dessert?"

"There are some cookies in the pantry," Scott suggested. "They're in that sealed plastic thing."

"Cool." Jeffrey carried his bowl to the sink, rinsed it and placed it in the dishwasher—one of the amenities of this pleasantly "rustic" cabin.

Watching the boy's actions, Scott murmured to Blair, "Well, at least you're training him right."

"He lives in my house, he clears his own dishes," Blair whispered.

Scott stood and reached for her bowl, stacking it with his own. "Then I should get major bonus points for clearing away my dishes and yours."

"I'm not awarding points."

He flashed her a smile. "Maybe you should start."

Scott McKay was the strangest man, Blair thought

with a bewildered shake of her head. But—in the words of Arnette Gibbs from the bachelor auction—he certainly had one fine butt, which she couldn't help noticing as he bent to place their bowls in the dishwasher.

Scott glanced over his shoulder. "Did you say something?"

Oh, she hoped not. She swiftly raised her gaze, praying her cheeks didn't look as pink as they felt. "No."

Jeffrey finished his cookies, then looked expectantly at Scott, who was preparing a pot of coffee. "What are we going to do now?"

"Still wanting to be entertained? I suppose I could do a song and dance for you. Maybe a scene from *Pirates of Penzance.* No? How about a monologue? *Hamlet*? *Richard III*?"

"Now that sounds like something I would like to see," Blair murmured.

Jeffrey rolled his eyes. "What are we *really* going to do?"

"We could turn in for a good night's sleep."

"Oh, man. It's only seven-thirty," the boy protested. "I never have to go to bed before nine o'clock."

"Remember when a few extra hours of sleep seemed more like a trial than a luxury?" Scott asked Blair wryly, then turned to Jeffrey before she could answer. "How about a board game? I have several here to choose from."

"Okay. But pick something I have a chance to win. Not Scrabble or Trivial Pursuit where I don't know as much as you guys."

"No sweat," Scott assured him. "I don't play games that require actual thinking. Pure luck, that's what I depend on."

Jeffrey seemed to approve of that philosophy. "Okay. What've you got?"

Blair couldn't help but be surprised that Jeffrey seemed interested in the game Scott extracted from a cabinet and set out on the table. She and her aunt had tried a few times to interest the boy in playing board games with them, but he'd always declined their offers, choosing instead to play video games by himself. He was definitely responding to Scott. Was it because he'd been so hungry for a man's attention or because of Scott's appealing personality?

The game was fast-paced, the outcome determined more by chance than skill. Jeffrey held his own, playing with an intense concentration that made Blair wonder if he was actually having fun. "Your turn, Aunt Blair."

She obligingly rolled the dice and moved her bright orange playing piece the required number of spaces. She landed on the square where Jeffrey's blue piece had been sitting. "Oops. Looks like you have to go back to start, Jeffrey."

"No fair!" he exclaimed, scowling. "Why didn't you move one of your other pieces? Why'd you have to send me back?"

"That's the way the game is played, Jeff," Scott interceded. "You don't want your aunt to treat you like a baby and let you win, do you?"

Jeffrey was obviously torn between not wanting to be treated like a baby and wanting to win at any cost. He poked his lip out, trying to decide what to say or do.

Scott helped him out. "Roll the dice. Pay her back."

Choosing to keep playing rather than bring the game to an end with one of his tantrums, Jeffrey reached for the dice. Scott sent Blair a quick smile, and the game went on. And, deep inside Blair, hope continued to grow that Scott would find a way to break through Jeffrey's anger.

CHAPTER FIVE

JEFFREY WAS PUTTING the game away when he discovered a large, leather-bound scrapbook stashed in a cupboard beneath the bookshelves. "What's this, Scott?"

Scott shrugged. "Just some of my mementos."

"Can I look at it?"

"If you want."

Jeffrey carried the scrapbook to the sofa and sat by Blair to open it. She couldn't resist looking over her nephew's shoulder as he turned the pages. The scrapbook was stuffed with photographs and newspaper clippings...and they all seemed to feature Scott doing something daring and adventurous.

She studied a picture of him riding a huge, angry-looking bull. Scott's left arm was thrown high in the air for balance, his right hand locked beneath a thick rope on the bull's neck. His hat had just flown off his head, and there was a look of reckless determination on his face. Her stomach muscles tightened. Funny. She hadn't realized until now that a man could actually look sexy while straddling a bull.

Another snapshot had been taken high above the ground. Scott had been captured in a spread-eagled free fall, his parachute unopened on the back of his colorful jumpsuit. He was grinning broadly at the camera, which was obviously being operated by another jumper. There were photos of Scott racing cars, motorcycles and speed-

boats, dangling from a harness as he rappelled down a
sheer rock face, navigating a kayak through churning
white water, doing a full body flip on a snowboard, even
hanging upside down from the end of a bungee cord.

"Wow," Jeffrey breathed, looking at yet another image of a daredevil stunt. "Is there anything you *haven't*
done?"

"There are quite a few things still on my list," Scott
commented, lounging in a nearby chair and looking as
if the pages they were examining held nothing out of
the ordinary.

The awed admiration on Jeffrey's face as he gazed at
Scott made Blair uncomfortable. While she could understand his fascination with Scott's adventures—after
all, she felt the same way—this was not the sort of role
model she'd had in mind. Jeffrey's father had already
set an example of footloose, irresponsible behavior; she
didn't need Scott reinforcing the notion that life consisted of nothing more than a series of reckless adventures. Despite her own occasional longings for some of
the adventures others indulged in, she had learned as a
teenager that there had to be more to life than self-
indulgence.

She reached over to close the scrapbook. "Why don't
you put this away, Jeffrey? Scott, tell us about your
ranch. It's quite big, I imagine."

"It's a sizable spread," he agreed in a lazy drawl.

"I'm sure it takes a lot of attention and commitment
to keep it running profitably. You studied business in
college?"

"I studied girls in college. When I found out they
wouldn't give me a degree for that, I had to pick something else."

Blair looked hastily at her watch as her nephew

laughed. "Well, it's getting late, Jeffrey. I'm sure Scott has a big day planned for us tomorrow. Why don't you go brush your teeth and get ready for bed now?"

"Oh, man…"

Scott stretched. "Your aunt's right, partner. I've got a lot of big plans for tomorrow. I think I'll turn in early myself."

"That sounds like an excellent idea." Blair stood, thinking she could use a little time to herself to contemplate the day's events. She picked up the book she'd been reading earlier, thinking she would read in bed for a while until she was sleepy.

"Sure you want to read that before you go to sleep?" Scott murmured as Jeffrey plodded toward the bathroom. "Might give you nightmares."

"I never have nightmares," she replied.

Something odd crossed Scott's face. "Consider yourself fortunate," he mumbled.

Before she could decide what he meant by that, he was grinning again. "If you *should* happen to have a bad dream, just give a yell. I'm sure I can think of something to take your mind off it."

Something in his tone made her face flame. She cleared her throat and turned to speak to her nephew as he stepped out of the bathroom. "Good night, Jeffrey. Let me know if you need anything."

He nodded. "Night, Aunt Blair."

She didn't kiss him good-night. She never had, though there were times when she ached to do so. But since she'd never been quite sure how he would react, and he'd never given any indication that he wanted her to kiss him, she'd always held back.

Blair glanced at Scott on her way to the staircase. "Good night, Scott."

She couldn't quite read the expression on his face. "Sleep well, Blair."

BLAIR HAD NEVER slept well in strange surroundings. The loft bed was quite comfortable, but the night sounds were different from what she was accustomed to. She dozed on and off, spending the time she was awake staring at the stars through the skylight above the bed, alternating between wondering what she was doing there and hoping the gamble would pay off.

The sun was just rising when she abandoned all attempts at sleep. She ran a brush through her hair and pulled thick socks over her bare feet, deciding her cotton pajamas were decent enough covering for breakfast. The cabin was very quiet when she padded downstairs, and both bedroom doors were closed. Apparently, she was the only early riser this morning.

Taking care to be quiet, she made a pot of coffee and gazed out the kitchen window while it brewed. What she saw outside was so appealing that she carried her coffee to the small deck attached to the back of the cabin. Huddling against the morning chill, she settled in an Adirondack chair and sipped her hot coffee, watching nature waking up around her as the sun crept a bit higher in the pinky-purply morning sky.

She could get used to this, she thought with a contented sigh, already aware that the ever-present tension in her neck and shoulders was slowly easing.

The kitchen door opened behind her, and a sleep-gruff male voice greeted her. "Good morning. Are you always such an early bird?"

She turned her head to smile at Scott, but her smile wavered when she saw him. He was so incredibly attractive. How could he possibly look this good still rumpled from sleep, his hair tousled, his shirt wrinkled and untucked over his jeans, his feet bare? She could almost laugh at how foolish she'd been to think she was bidding on a conservative, buttoned-down businessman.

She cleared her throat and tried to keep her eyes focused on his face rather than the intriguing triangle of tanned skin revealed by his partially unbuttoned shirt. "Good morning. There's coffee in the…oh, I see you found it."

He sipped from the mug she hadn't noticed in his right hand. "It's good."

She nodded toward his bare feet as he settled into a chair beside her. "Aren't you cold?"

"No. Compared to being at the top of Mount Everest during a blizzard, this early morning air is merely pleasantly mild."

She lifted an eyebrow. "You've been through a blizzard at the top of Mount Everest?"

"Well, actually, I was only two-thirds of the way up," he admitted. "The blizzard pretty much ruined the trip."

"Your ranch must be quite successful," she remarked, thinking of the adventure trips, the airplane, this lovely cabin in the woods.

"Are you asking if I have money?"

"No, of course not. I—"

"Because I do. Tons of it."

His matter-of-fact tone made her blink. "Oh. I—"

"My father was the only offspring of well-to-do parents. My mother was the only child of a filthy-rich couple. When they died, their wisely invested money and all their business holdings came to me. And I went to the Lost Springs Ranch for difficult boys."

He wasn't looking at her, but was watching a squirrel

romping through the trees. Blair studied his unrevealing profile. "How old were you?"

"Twelve when my family died. Fourteen when my grandparents shipped me to Lost Springs."

He'd been angry, Blair thought. Bitter. Lost.

Like Jeffrey.

"How long did you live there?"

"On and off until I graduated from high school. By the time I left, I knew how to channel my anger more productively."

"By climbing mountains? Racing cars? Jumping out of airplanes? Riding bulls?"

"Don't forget snowboarding and hang gliding. I've done those a few times, too."

"And your ranch? Who takes care of things while you're risking your neck for kicks?"

"I pay people quite handsomely to take care of things there."

Blair frowned. She really didn't understand Scott McKay at all. Maybe he *could* get through to Jeffrey—but did she want him to? The last thing she wanted was for her nephew to end up as reckless and unconventional as Scott seemed to be. And yet...

"Hey. What're you guys doing out here? Jeez, it's freezing."

She turned toward the door, pushing whatever she might have said to the back of her mind. "Good morning, Jeffrey."

"I'm hungry. And I'm cold."

She rose. "Then go back inside and get dressed while I make breakfast. You shouldn't be out here barefoot."

"Scott's barefoot."

"And I'm freezing my, er, toes off," Scott commented dryly. "I was just trying to impress your aunt with how macho I am."

"Aunt Blair isn't easy to impress," Jeffrey confided.

Scott chuckled. "Then I guess I'll just have to work harder at it."

Blair swallowed. That sounded a bit too much like a challenge for her comfort.

SCOTT OFFERED to help Blair make breakfast, but she declined his assistance. She liked to cook, she reminded him. She didn't mind making her contribution in the kitchen since she had no intention of climbing onto the roof and hammering shingles.

Scott chuckled. "I wouldn't ask you to do that," he assured her. "Jeff and I finished the roofing repairs yesterday. However, if you would like to haul and split firewood…"

"I think I'd rather make pancakes," she replied with a wry expression that made him want to kiss her. Actually, everything she did made him want to kiss her, he thought with an inward grimace. It was an urge that was growing stronger with each passing minute. He no longer wondered how Blair would react *if* he kissed her; he speculated, instead, about what she would do *when* he kissed her, as he fully intended to do before the weekend was over.

The pancakes were excellent. Scott was glad Blair had volunteered to cook rather than chop wood, and he told her so, making her smile. "I prefer it this way myself," she agreed.

"So what are we doing today?" Jeffrey asked around a mouthful of food.

"Swallow before you talk," his aunt advised.

Jeffrey gulped, then asked again, "What are we doing today?"

Scott set his orange juice glass aside. "I thought we'd do some fishing."

Jeffrey cocked his head with an expression of interest. "I've never been fishing."

"Never?"

"Nope. Grandma didn't fish and neither does Aunt Blair. My dad's going to take me deep-sea fishing pretty soon."

Scott happened to be watching Blair when the boy made that announcement, and he saw the quick flicker of sympathy that crossed her face. She obviously doubted her brother would ever follow through on his promises to his son. "Well, we won't be catching any sharks or sailfish today, but with a little luck we might snag a trout or two."

"Are you going to fish with us, Aunt Blair?"

"I'm not much of a fisherman," she answered with a smile. "I believe I'll stay here and finish the book I started yesterday."

Scott smiled then. "Good book, huh?"

She glanced at him to answer, their gazes meeting across the table. "Yes, it's very suspenseful. Of course, I want to get back to my other reading as soon as I finish this book," she added quickly, if without much enthusiasm.

Scott nodded gravely. "Of course. You can't waste the whole weekend just kickin' back and relaxing, can you?"

She gave him a repressive look. "It *is* possible to relax and improve the mind at the same time."

He was beginning to find it almost impossible to resist her when she turned prissy and disapproving. It made him even more tempted to misbehave, just to watch her eyes flash and her lips purse so appealingly.

He really was going to have to kiss her soon.

AN HOUR LATER, he and Jeffrey stood side by side at the rushing stream a half hour's hike from the cabin. It took all Scott's concentration to keep the boy from snagging either of them with fishhooks. Fortunately, the kid was a quick study and was soon casting quite creditably, giving Scott a chance to relax a little.

"Having fun?" he asked, skillfully whipping his bait out to a promising-looking hole in midstream.

"This is cool. Wish I could hook one, though."

"You'll get the hang of it. Just keep trying."

By noon, they hadn't caught any keepers, but Jeffrey still seemed to be enjoying the experience. Scott set his rod on the ground. "I'm getting hungry. How about you?"

"I could eat. What have we got?"

Rummaging in the insulated carrier he'd brought with them, Scott pulled out two individual-size cans of Vienna sausages, a tube of crackers, a small plastic bottle of mustard, two bags of dried fruit and some packaged oatmeal-raisin cookies. Two cans of soda were still reasonably cool; he handed one to the boy and opened the other for himself.

Jeffrey looked doubtfully at the very plain fare. "This is lunch?"

"You were expecting caviar?"

"Well, no, but…"

"Redneck picnic. Eat up."

Jeffrey pulled the ring on his can of sausages. "I don't think Aunt Blair would consider this a healthy meal."

"Hey, we've got protein, grain and fruit. What more could she ask?"

"She thinks you gotta have something green at every meal. She's really into eating green stuff."

Scott peered thoughtfully into his can. "There's some fuzzy green stuff growing on these sausages. Does that count?"

"Eeww! Gross."

Scott laughed. "Just kidding. There are too many preservatives in these cans to allow any green stuff to grow." Just to prove the food was edible, he laid a sausage on a cracker, squirted mustard on it and popped it into his mouth.

Somewhat experimentally, Jeffrey imitated his actions. They munched in companionable silence for a while, and then Scott asked casually, "So your aunt makes you eat healthy, huh?"

"Oh, yeah. You'd think we'd drop dead if we ate burgers and fries more than once or twice a month."

"Nice to know someone cares if you're eating right, isn't it?"

Jeffrey shrugged. "It gets old sometimes. My grandma never cared if I wanted burgers or nachos or burritos all the time."

"Blair wants you to be healthy. That's her way of showing she cares about you."

Jeffrey mumbled something around a cracker.

"Do you like living with your aunt?"

The boy crumbled a piece of cracker between his fingers. "It's okay…at least until my dad comes back."

"Oh? Then what?"

"Then he's going to take me with him. He travels all over the world. Never spends much time in one place. He says nothing ties him down."

Including his son, apparently. Scott kept that thought to himself, being careful not to let anything show in his face. "That's the way you want to live? Always on the move? Never having the same people around you? What about school—your friends?"

"I hate school," Jeffrey muttered. "And I don't have many friends."

"Why not? You seem like a cool guy to me."

The boy flushed a little, looking both disconcerted and pleased by the comment. "The guys at my school are all geeks and losers."

"*All* of them? I find that hard to believe."

"Well, it seems that way to me."

"Maybe you haven't really gotten to know any of them well enough to find out for sure."

Shrugging one skinny shoulder, Jeffrey muttered, "What's the point? I'll be leaving pretty soon. When my dad comes."

Scott thought about the distance he'd sensed between Jeffrey and Blair. Was Jeffrey holding himself back from her, too, in preparation for the time he would leave? And what was Blair's excuse? He'd never even seen her hug the boy. Was it fear of rejection that kept her from reaching out to him, or was she protecting herself from getting too close in case Jeffrey's father *did* come to reclaim him?

It occurred to him that perhaps Blair didn't have deep feelings for her nephew—that she saw the boy as a burden. A responsibility. A problem. The way Scott's elderly grandparents had come to think of him...?

No. He didn't want to believe Blair could feel that way about the snub-nosed kid munching crackers in front of him. Sure, maybe Jeffrey was a pain in the neck, but who could blame him? He was too confused about his future to even make friends at school.

He wondered how to work the conversation back to Blair. As it turned out, he didn't have to.

"D'you think Aunt Blair's pretty?" Jeffrey asked out of the blue.

"I think she's very pretty. Why?"

"There's this guy—Hal somebody. He hangs around my aunt sometimes, looking at her all goofy. I think he wants her to go out with him. I don't like him."

Scott didn't like him, either. As a matter of fact, he *really* disliked the guy, and all he knew about him was that his name was Hal and he looked goofy at Blair. He cleared his throat. "Why don't you like him?"

"He treats me like a dumb kid. And he keeps telling me how lucky I am that Aunt Blair took me in and how I owe it to her to make something of myself."

Scott winced. He'd heard too many speeches along that line when he was a rebellious kid. And the only thing they had accomplished was to make him even more angry and determined to do what he wanted.

Despite what everyone had said, he hadn't considered himself fortunate to be dumped on his grandparents' doorstep. He'd wanted the family he'd lost. He'd wanted the life he'd had before the fiery car crash that had taken it all from him. And no amount of preaching or lecturing could have convinced him that he was lucky.

He pushed the unpleasant memories to the back of his mind. "So what does your aunt think about this Hal guy?"

Jeffrey shrugged. "She's always nice to him, but she doesn't really smile at him, you know? Like she has to be polite, but not too much."

After giving that summary a moment's thought, Scott

decided he liked the sound of it. Blair often smiled when she looked at *him*. He determined right then to make sure she had even more reason to smile for him.

"Maybe you should ask her out," Jeffrey suggested casually. "She likes you, and you don't act like I'm stupid."

"That's because I don't think you're stupid. And as for me asking your aunt out—I don't think this is the time to discuss anything like that."

"Whatever. But it's okay with me if you want to."

Scott shook his head at the unsubtle young matchmaker. "I'm happy to know I have your approval. Now, how about getting back to our fishing? We can't go back empty-handed or Blair's going to think we're wusses."

Jeffrey tried an experimental grin. "We don't want that to happen."

"You're darn right we don't. Grab your gear, partner."

As Scott stashed the remains of their picnic and prepared to fish again, he thought about their conversation. The extent of his disapproval upon hearing that some other guy was interested in Blair had taken him by surprise. He'd known he was attracted to her, but he hadn't realized quite how much until he'd pictured her with another man.

As Jeffrey smiled shyly at him and asked another question about fishing, Scott wondered just what he had gotten himself into by agreeing to participate in that bachelor auction.

BLAIR FINISHED the book around noon. The cabin seemed awfully quiet after the nonstop action of the story. She wondered how Scott and Jeffrey were getting along—and whether Scott was taking advantage of the opportunity to talk to Jeffrey about his future. Maybe this afternoon of male bonding would make all the difference in Jeffrey's outlook. If so, every penny she had spent at the bachelor auction would be well justified.

She rummaged in the kitchen and found a single-serving can of vegetable soup in the pantry. Since Scott had told her he and Jeffrey wouldn't be back for lunch, she dined alone on the soup and a handful of crackers. She wondered if Scott always kept the kitchen stocked or if he'd made arrangements to have food brought in for this weekend. The available fare was simple, but adequate. They didn't have to worry about going hungry even if the guys caught no fish this afternoon.

After cleaning the kitchen, she wandered into the living room. She couldn't remember the last time she'd spent such an indulgently lazy day. She really should have brought her briefcase and portable computer, but not knowing Scott's plans, she hadn't been sure she'd have the chance to get any work done. Now, thinking of all the paperwork she could have gotten out of the way this afternoon, she realized she should have brought her laptop along.

Yet she was aware that the familiar knots in her neck and shoulders were gone and that she hadn't needed an antacid in more than twenty-four hours. Maybe taking a weekend off wasn't such a bad thing, after all.

The least she could do, she thought conscientiously, was to make good use of the remainder of this leisure time. She picked up the heavy political treatise, determined to finish it. The book had received a lot of attention and generated much debate among legal and political experts. The controversial conclusions drawn had piqued Blair's interest, and her only excuse for not wading through it sooner had been lack of free time. She had the time now.

Settling in a chair, she tucked her feet beneath her and opened the cover. She found the page—not very far from the beginning—where she'd left off when Scott had plucked the book from her hands and replaced it with the well-written thriller.

Fifteen minutes later she found herself standing in front of Scott's bookcase studying the titles of the mysteries, thrillers and adventure stories crammed on the shelves. Torn between vague guilt and an unfamiliar sense of defiance, she selected another novel by the author of the thriller Scott had recommended the day before. If she was going to be lazy, she might as well do it as thoroughly as she did everything else, she thought with a wry smile, curling into the chair with the paperback and a cold diet soda.

Scott and Jeffrey found her there a couple of hours later. "Still reading that…no, I see you've started another one," Scott commented cheerfully.

Suddenly self-conscious, Blair tucked a strand of hair behind her ear. "I finished the other one this morning."

Scott nodded toward the abandoned book she'd brought with her. "Not in the mood for political gossip today?"

"It isn't gossip," she felt obliged to argue. "It's a serious discussion of the current political climate in light of recent—"

"Blair, I've read the book. It's gossip—phrased in pseudo-intellectual terms, perhaps, but gossip nonetheless. And it's all bull."

She frowned. "You've read it?"

"Every page. I was stuck in an airport in Hong Kong with nothing else to read. And it was a total waste of my time. I'd have been better served if I'd spent those two hours reading something fun and entertaining rather than some overeducated windbag's interpretation of Washington shenanigans.''

"But—"

Growing impatient with the discussion, Jeffrey bounced on his feet. "Aunt Blair, come out to the porch and see what we caught this afternoon. Scott's going to cook them for dinner."

"You caught some fish?" Distracted from the literary argument, she studied the expression on her nephew's face. It was so rare that Jeffrey looked genuinely excited. She was determined not to dampen his enthusiasm. She set the book aside and rose. "I'd love to see them."

Three fat, glistening trout lay in a cooler on the front porch. Blair examined them and nodded gravely. "Oh, yes, these are fine fish. Did you catch them, Jeffrey?"

"Only one of them," he admitted, then added proudly, "but it's the biggest one."

"Wow. That *is* a big one. I wish I'd brought a camera to take your picture with it."

"Scott already did."

Blair looked at Scott in surprise. He pulled a small, one-time-use camera from one of the many pockets of his khaki fishing vest. "I always pack a camera," he explained. "Since I release a lot more fish than I keep to eat, I take pictures of my biggest catches to prove my fishing prowess."

Whatever his reason, Blair was pleased that he'd made a production of taking Jeffrey's picture with the fish. That must have made the boy even more proud of his accomplishment.

"That's a photograph we'll definitely have to frame,"

she said lightly. "Did you enjoy fishing, Jeffrey? Was it fun?"

"Yeah, it was cool. It was hard at first because I didn't know when I had a bite and then I kept letting them get away. But then Scott gave me some advice and I caught a couple that were too little to keep and then I hooked this big sucker. I thought he was going to get away, too, but I hung on and I did what Scott told me to do and I got him close enough so Scott could catch him in the net. It was really cool," he repeated, speaking so quickly his words nearly tripped over themselves.

Amused by his enthusiasm, Blair reached out without thinking to smooth his tousled brown hair. "That must have been very exciting."

Scott put one hand on Jeffrey's shoulder and the other on Blair's, linking them companionably together. "Hope you two like grilled trout. That's what we're having for dinner."

"I've never had grilled trout," Jeffrey replied. "But it sounds good."

"Great. Now all we have to do is convince your aunt to clean the fish."

Blair's eyebrows lifted. She kept her voice purposefully cool when she asked, "I beg your pardon?"

Scott laughed. "Have I ever mentioned that I like it when you do that?"

"When I do what?"

"When you act all snooty and indignant. It's cute as all get-out. Makes me want to just kiss you silly."

While Blair fumbled for a response, Jeffrey gave a muffled laugh.

Scott grinned, apparently satisfied with their reactions. "I'll clean the fish. You can make some side dishes, if you want."

Still flustered, Blair nodded. "Of course. Jeffrey, go clean up now and change into clean clothes."

"Okay, Aunt Blair." He headed obligingly for the door.

"If only he were always that agreeable," she murmured, mostly to herself, as she watched her nephew disappear inside. And then she turned to Scott with a frown. "I really wish you wouldn't do that."

He gave her an innocent look. "Do what?"

"Flirt with me in front of Jeffrey. You'll confuse him. He's too young to understand what you're like."

Scott drew himself up a bit straighter and rested his hands on his hips, studying her with a deceptively bland smile. "And what *am* I like?"

She frowned at him, reluctant to expand on her accusation. "You know what I mean."

"No, I'm not sure I do. Surely you aren't accusing me of being a compulsive playboy? A woman chaser?"

"Well, I—"

"Because if I were that kind of man, I'd have done much more than call you cute and talk about wanting to kiss you. Being alone like this with a beautiful woman would be more temptation than I could resist."

Blair felt her cheeks heat. Beautiful? Did he really think so, or was he— She frowned again and shook her head, telling herself he was simply being difficult. Again. "I didn't say you..."

He took a step nearer, so close he had only to lift his hand to touch her warm cheek. He seemed suddenly bigger, his shoulders broader. He smelled of fish and fresh air and healthy male, and the combination was surprisingly enticing. Blair couldn't help thinking of Hal Berkley, the accountant who had been asking her out for the past couple of months. The expensive colognes he wore might appeal to some women, but she found herself suddenly, unexpectedly responding to a more basic, earthy scent.

Funny. Until this moment, she'd never suspected she had a weakness for charming cowboys. But it was a weakness she refused to indulge. Like her fondness for rich chocolate, this was a craving that had to be resisted because it wasn't at all good for her.

"If I were that kind of guy," Scott continued blandly, his fingertips rising to stroke a strand of hair from her temple, "I would have to take advantage of this opportunity to try to steal a kiss from that soft, pretty mouth…"

He leaned even closer, his breath warm against her lips, which parted in automatic reaction. His fingers slipped into her hair, exerting just enough pressure behind her head to bring her up on tiptoe. His lips barely brushed hers when he spoke again. "And if I were that type of man, I wouldn't want to stop with a kiss."

Her mouth trembled against his. With every ounce of her being, she wanted to slide her arms around his neck and find out exactly what this man's kiss could do to her. And maybe it was because she wanted it so badly that she jerked backward, pulling herself away from him. She was terribly worried that just kissing Scott McKay might not be enough for her, either.

"I, uh, I'll see what I can find to go with the fish."

"Chicken," Scott murmured, his eyes mocking her.

"We're having fish, not chicken." She held her chin high as she made the bad joke, determined to prove he hadn't rattled her. He had, of course—seriously—but she saw no need for him to know it.

She'd bought a mentor for Jeffrey, she reminded herself as she went inside. Not a man for herself. If there was one thing she did *not* need in her already stressful life, it was a gorgeous, footloose cowboy.

CHAPTER SIX

JEFFREY DIDN'T seem to notice any awkwardness between Blair and Scott during dinner. Maybe it was because he was too excited about eating the fish he had caught himself, or maybe it was because Scott talked and joked and teased as easily as he had before that odd interlude on the porch. Maybe it was only Blair who felt as though something had changed. Maybe she was only imagining undercurrents of awareness sizzling between her and Scott.

Maybe too much rest and relaxation were doing strange things to her mind, she thought wryly. Compulsive workaholics simply weren't cut out for self-indulgent sloth.

"Don't you like your trout, Aunt Blair?" Jeffrey asked, looking at her plate.

She forced a smile. "It's delicious. I'm savoring it."

He swallowed the last bite of his serving. "You cooked it good, Scott."

"Thanks. The vegetables your aunt prepared to go with it are good, too, don't you think?"

"Yeah, they're fine. How did you learn to cook fish like this, Scott?"

Blair wasn't offended. Jeffrey had been eating her cooking for the past six months. It was only natural that he would be more impressed by Scott's culinary expertise.

"Experimentation," Scott answered humorously. "You wouldn't have wanted to try some of my earlier efforts."

Jeffrey turned to his aunt. "Scott can tie a fly and make it look just like a real bug. He turned over a rock in the stream and showed me a bug and then he tied a little bit of fuzz and feathers and stuff and he made it look just like the bug he found. He's got this little vise thing in his tackle box to hold the stuff while he ties it. It was so cool. Who taught you to do that, Scott?"

"Actually, I attended a class to learn how."

Jeffrey blinked in surprise. "You went to a fishing school?"

Scott smiled. "You'd be amazed how many classes you might want to take when you no longer feel that you have to go to school. There are a lot of interesting things to learn out there."

Wrinkling his nose, Jeffrey announced, "If I ever get out of school, I'm never going to another class."

"That's what I used to say, until I went to Lost Springs and figured out how to make school work to my advantage."

Jeffrey frowned as if he'd forgotten that Scott had once resided at the boys' ranch. Blair knew Jeffrey had encountered boys from Lost Springs at school; he'd mentioned occasionally that some of them were real troublemakers. He looked curiously at Scott. "How come you lived out at the ranch? Were you one of the orphans with no place else to go?"

"I was an orphan, but I had grandparents who took me in—until I gave them so much trouble they sent me to Lost Springs to be straightened out," Scott replied easily.

"Oh. I thought only serious troublemakers went there.

Some of the guys at school say Lost Springs is just a place for the punks to go until they're old enough for jail.''

"Jeffrey…''

With a quick gesture of his hand, Scott signaled to Blair to let him handle this. Since he didn't look particularly annoyed or offended by Jeffrey's insensitive remarks, Blair fell silent.

"The boys at Lost Springs aren't all punks, Jeff. It's true that most have been in trouble and that a very few will end up in jail someday, but for the most part, they're just kids who need some guidance.''

"Were you in trouble?''

Blair had to bite her tongue to keep from telling Jeffrey to mind his own business. She didn't want to encourage him to ask intrusive questions, but she had wanted him to spend time with Scott precisely because of Scott's troubled background.

Again, Scott accepted the boy's blunt question with equanimity. "Yeah. I got into a lot of trouble. After my folks died, I was pretty mad, and I didn't get along well with my grandparents, so I did some really stupid stuff. It's like I was trying to punish everyone around me because life hadn't worked out the way I wanted it to, you know?''

Jeffrey looked at his empty plate, as if the comment struck just a bit too close to home. "You weren't a punk,'' he said loyally, his rapidly developing hero worship in evidence.

"Sure I was,'' Scott replied with a smile. "And I might have turned into worse if the staff at Lost Springs hadn't convinced me that I was only punishing myself with my behavior. They made me realize that it was up to me to make something out of myself and to decide what I wanted to do with my future.''

''And you wanted to climb mountains and race cars and stuff, right?''

Scott chuckled. ''Right. I was lucky enough to have some money—unlike most of the guys, who had to figure out how they were going to make a living when they left the ranch. But I had to learn how to take care of that money, so I went to college and majored in business. Finished in three years, because I didn't want to spend any more time in classes than necessary.''

''College?'' Jeffrey curled his lip. ''More school? Oh, man…''

''School's not so bad, once you figure out how to work the system.''

That captured Jeffrey's interest. ''Work the system? What do you mean?''

Scott responded with a question of his own. ''What do you dislike most about school?''

The boy practically shuddered. *''Everything.''*

Patiently, Scott shook his head. ''I know there are some things you must like better than others. But what do you dislike most?''

After a moment's thought, Jeffrey answered, ''The picky stuff. You know, little things that don't make any difference, but the teachers still get all worked up about them.''

''For example?''

''You got a pencil and paper?''

''In that drawer behind you.''

Blair stood and began to clear away the dishes as Jeffrey pulled a pencil and notepad from the drawer Scott had indicated. She watched out of the corner of her eye as he set the pad on the table in front of Scott. Drawing an oval with a slash through the bottom, he asked, "What letter is that?"

Scott answered cooperatively, *"Q."*

Jeffrey nodded. "Right. It's my middle initial—my mother named me Jeffrey Quentin, for some dumb reason."

"A perfectly good name," Scott assured him.

The boy shrugged. "Anyway, my teacher wants me to write a *Q* like this." He scrawled something else on the pad. "Isn't that dorky? It looks like a number two, not a letter."

Laughing softly, Scott nodded. "It is a standard cursive *Q*. I remember that's the way it was taught to me, too."

"I hate it. I won't write my initial that way. Miss Greene makes us sign all our papers with our first name, middle initial and last name, and she yells at me and deducts points every time I won't write the *Q* the way she wants me to."

Blair waited for Scott to explain to Jeffrey—as she had numerous times—that Miss Greene was simply trying to teach the traditionally accepted rules of penmanship. It was her job, and she was performing it conscientiously, if a bit rigidly.

Instead, Scott commiserated with the boy. "Man, that *is* picky. Your teacher must be a total hardnose."

Blair spun to stare at Scott. That was not what she wanted him to say! "Um..."

"I can't blame you for losing patience with her," Scott continued, still looking at Jeffrey. "Or for wanting to write your initial the way you like it, rather than the way your teacher tells you to."

"Exactly." Jeffrey shot a glittering look at his aunt

as he took encouragement from Scott's input into the familiar argument.

But Scott wasn't finished. "This is a great example of what I meant by working the system. You want a good grade, right?"

Jeffrey scowled and shrugged. "I don't really care."

"Sure you do. Good grades are your ticket to getting what you want out of life. They're for you, not for anyone else. They're your proof that you played the system—and you won."

Jeffrey looked as confused as Blair was beginning to feel. "Are you saying I should make my Qs the way Miss Greene wants me to?" he demanded.

"Yeah—but only in her class," Scott added quickly when it was obvious that Jeffrey was prepared to argue. "When you're out of class, writing just for yourself, you make your letters any way you want, as long as they're readable. After all, if no one can read what you've written, then what's the point, right?"

"Uh…"

"So, anyway, you're almost finished school this term, right?"

"Yeah. So?"

"So in the fall, you'll have a different teacher, and chances are she won't give a spit about how you make a Q, as long as it's reasonably neat. Of course, she'll have some other dumb rule, but you can play that one, too, as long as it gets you what you want—the grade. It's like a job, you see. You do what the boss says at work so you'll get the pay you want, but what you do on your own time is your business."

Blair wasn't at all sure she approved of this conversation. "Now wait a minute—"

Ignoring his aunt for the moment, Jeffrey concentrated

on Scott's unusual advice. "You're saying I should do what the teachers want because it will get me what *I* want?"

"Exactly." Scott beamed at the boy as if he was delighted to be so well understood. "You aren't giving in. You aren't surrendering. You're working the system. You get the good grades you can use later, you get your teachers off your back, you stay out of trouble—which keeps everyone *else* off your back. It's a win-win situation."

"But the teachers think *they* win."

Scott shrugged. "So it makes them happy, too. A happy teacher is a less annoying teacher."

Blair definitely did not approve of Scott trying to turn her nephew into some pint-size con artist, even if he thought it was for the boy's own good. "Scott, that isn't why students cooperate in school, just to keep the teachers happy and finagle good grades out of them."

"No?" Scott looked at her blandly. "Then why?"

"Well...because the teachers know their subjects. Because being a dedicated student is the right thing to do."

"C'mon, Blair." Scott poked the pad with one finger. "Do you really think it matters diddly whether Jeff makes his *Q* this way or the other way?"

Feeling cornered, she bit her lip. She didn't think it mattered, really, but she didn't want to encourage her nephew to flout the rules of penmanship—or any other rules, for that matter.

"You made good grades in school, right? You had to study even when you didn't want to, and you had to do some things you didn't necessarily agree with, right?"

"Well, maybe occasionally, but—"

"So why'd you do it? Because it was the right thing to do...or because you wanted the grades so you could get into law school? And you had to work your butt off in law school, I'd imagine, but you did it because you'd decided you wanted to be a lawyer and you weren't going to let anything hold you back, right?''

"Well, yes, but—''

"You did it for yourself. You didn't want to flip burgers or run a cash register or other jobs that took less work to prepare for, so you did what you had to do to get what you wanted. That's all I'm saying to Jeff here. He should do well in school to benefit himself—not to please his teachers or even to please you. For himself.''

"That sounds rather selfish.''

"Self-serving, maybe,'' Scott agreed with a shrug. "But in the long run, that's what it's all about, right? He's got to learn to take care of himself, just like I did. Just like you did.''

Jeffrey cleared his throat, reminding them that he was the topic of their conversation. "Some of the kids at school say only dorks care about making good grades. They say it's no big deal to get Ds and Fs.''

"Yeah, well, we'll see how they like spending their whole lives asking, 'Do you want fries with that?''' Scott answered carelessly. "If a guy's capable of making good grades, he should take advantage of it. Keep his options open for the future, you know?''

"For my own sake, right?''

Scott grinned. "Right.''

"That's what you mean by working the system.''

"That's exactly what I mean. Get what you want out of it—and you should want the grades, because you can use them to your advantage later—and then move on. It's no big deal to write a dorky Q for a couple more weeks if it gets you an A, right?''

"And what if some of the guys call me a nerd?''

"Just smile knowingly and tell them you're playing the game for your own reasons. Let's face it, none of the guys at school care about your future. Heck, half of them don't even care about their own futures. The only real losers are the ones who just dumbly follow the crowd, Jeff. The ones who never learn to think or act for themselves. The ones who'll destroy their own lives with booze or drugs or stupid behavior just because they worry about what everyone else might say about them. Winners keep their own goals in sight and don't let *any-one* hold them back. Like your aunt. It's pretty cool that she has her own law practice while she's so young. I'll bet a lot of her friends from school who weren't willing to work so hard are pretty jealous of her now."

Jeffrey eyed Blair's face speculatively. "She still works awful hard."

"Yeah. But only because she wants to. You like being a lawyer, don't you, Blair?"

"Well, yes, but—"

Dismissing her for the moment, Scott turned to the boy. "So what you've got to do, Jeff, is decide what *you* like and go after it. That's what my friends and I learned at Lost Springs. And the ones of us who took that advice seriously have turned out very well. Most of us are doing exactly what we wanted to do. The ones who ended up in jail were too stubborn to take advantage of a good thing while they had it."

"So being at Lost Springs was a good thing?"

"For me it was." Scott glanced at Blair. "For you, it's a good thing you have your aunt. It's obvious she cares about you. My grandparents never would have gone to the trouble of arranging a weekend like this for me."

Jeffrey blinked. "This weekend is for me?"

Blair turned to stare at her nephew. "Of course it is. I thought I'd made that clear."

"You said we were spending the weekend with a new friend. You said you thought we might have a good time."

Scott shook his head. "You think your aunt went to all this effort and expense just so she could sit around here and read or cook for us while we fish and play?"

"I thought you might enjoy spending a few days doing guy things," Blair added with a smile. "Since I don't fish or tie flies or fly small planes or any of the other cool stuff Scott has entertained you with, I hoped you'd have fun with him."

She hadn't known exactly what Scott had in mind for the weekend, of course, but she'd suspected all along that he would know better than she how to entertain a ten-year-old boy. And it seemed she'd been right. Jeffrey appeared to have had a wonderful time today. She hadn't seen him so relaxed and involved since the day his father had vanished without even a goodbye for him.

"Sounds to me like this weekend has been all for you from the start," Scott murmured to Jeffrey. "Like I said, you've got a pretty good thing with your aunt. If I'd had someone like her to take me in, maybe I wouldn't have been such a punk."

Uncomfortable with the conversation again, Blair cleared her throat. "I'd say this weekend has been very pleasant for all of us. I've enjoyed the chance to relax and read. You've been hiking and fishing and you had your first flying lesson. All in all, it's been a great success."

She hoped Jeffrey had also benefited from Scott's advice about school. Even if she still wasn't sure about his working-the-system-for-personal-gain philosophy, she approved the well-meant intentions.

"The weekend isn't over yet," Jeffrey reminded them. "What are we going to do tomorrow?"

Though Blair was reluctant to dampen his enthusiasm, she needed to prepare him for the return to reality. "We'll have to leave fairly early tomorrow. You need to spend some time tomorrow evening getting ready for school Monday morning."

Jeffrey's sudden scowl was all too familiar. He hadn't magically changed his opinion about school just because Scott had pointed out its value. She could only hope the advice would have some influence in the long run. "We don't have to leave *too* early," he argued. "I don't have any homework."

"No, but you have a spelling test to study for."

"I already know all the words. I want to go fishing again tomorrow."

With a look of commiseration, Scott shook his head. "I don't think we'll have time tomorrow, partner. Not if your aunt wants to get back early. We'll have time to take another hike in the morning, see if we can spot some wildlife. Maybe we can go fishing again some other weekend."

"I want to fish tomorrow," Jeffrey insisted. "We have time."

"Jeffrey, don't push your luck," Blair advised him firmly. "You've had such a good day. Don't spoil the rest of your evening by sulking."

"Yeah, I was hoping we could play another game this evening," Scott added quickly. "You and Blair stomped me last night. I need a chance to get revenge."

Though the boy's lower lip showed a tendency to protrude in a pout, he allowed the subject of fishing to drop.

At Blair's urging, he helped clean the kitchen and then moved with them into the living room, where they selected another board game. By the time the game was under way, he was smiling again, to Blair's relief. But there was something in his stubborn eyes that warned her he wasn't going to make things easy for her when it was time to leave the next day.

ONCE AGAIN, Blair had trouble sleeping that night. Not only was she still in a strange bed, but she really wasn't all that tired, she decided. She'd spent the whole day being lazy and now found herself wide awake and restless in the middle of the night.

She read for a while, still enjoying the author's crisp, fast-paced style. But even that failed to hold her interest after a time, so she set the book aside. She was a little thirsty. She wondered if she could make it to the kitchen for a cold drink without disturbing her sleeping cabin mates. She crept to the railing that looked down over the darkened living room, noting that both bedroom doors were closed. Maybe she could...

"Should we act out the balcony scene from *Romeo and Juliet*?" a deep, quiet voice asked from the shadows below.

Blair jumped, clutching the railing with both hands. "Scott?"

He stepped into a path of dim light coming from her loft, his face upturned to her. "No, it's Romeo."

She couldn't help smiling as she leaned against the metal rail. "What are you doing down there?"

"I got hungry. Thought I'd find a snack."

"I didn't hear you come out of your room."

His wicked grin flashed. "I'm pretty good at sneaking in and out of bedrooms."

"I'll just bet you are," Blair murmured.

"Shall I sneak up to yours?"

Because she would have dearly loved to say yes, she very quickly answered, "No. I'll come down."

"If that's what you prefer," he said, exaggerating his disappointment.

She moved quietly down the spiral staircase. Waiting at the bottom, Scott reached out to take her hand for the last few steps. "Couldn't sleep?"

"No. I'm thirsty."

"Then it appears you and I are headed the same direction." He tucked her hand into the crook of his arm. "Come into my kitchen and let me impress you."

Her fingers tingled from the contact with his bare skin. "All I want is a glass of water."

"Oh, I think I can tempt you with something more interesting than that."

Blair gulped. That was exactly what she was afraid of.

He practically pushed her into a kitchen chair. "Sit right there. I'll see what I can rustle up."

"But all I want..."

He'd already poked his head into the freezer. Blair couldn't resist letting her eyes drift downward to the tight fit of the jeans he wore with a white T-shirt.

Tempting? Oh my, yes. But she hadn't forgotten her reason for being here...or all the reasons she could not get involved with this man.

He glanced over his shoulder, caught her looking, grinned when she blushed. "I think I've got something here you'll like," he murmured.

She cleared her throat. "Actually, I've decided I'm not very thirsty, after all. Maybe I should just go back...."

He set a quart of fudge ice cream on the table, dropping two spoons beside it. "No need to dirty up a couple of bowls. We can just eat right out of the carton."

Fudge. It had to be fudge. Just how much temptation was she supposed to resist tonight, anyway?

Scott took a chair very close to hers and dipped into the ice cream. He murmured his appreciation as he swallowed a large bite. "Oh, man, that's good."

Well, heck. She was only human. She reached for a spoon. Maybe just a little...

He smiled in satisfaction.

The ice cream *was* good. So good her eyes closed in sheer, sensual appreciation at the first taste. When she opened them again, Scott was there, smiling at her.

"Good?"

She smiled at him. "Good."

"I thought you'd like it."

She took another spoonful. "I love ice cream. And chocolate. I try not to indulge very often."

"Such a very disciplined young lawyer. Just what do you do for fun, Counselor?"

"I don't climb mountains. Or race cars. Or jump out of planes. I do occasionally eat ice cream and read thrillers." She took another generous bite of the ice cream.

Scott chuckled. "Sounds very...exciting."

"I never claimed to be exciting," she answered mildly. "I have a practice to manage and a child to raise. I'm lucky to have free time to get my hair cut occasionally."

He reached up to touch her dark blond bob, running his fingertips through the soft, straight tresses. "You have very pretty hair."

She didn't even blush that time. Maybe she was getting used to his ways. "Thank you."

"Would you ever like to do something totally wild and crazy, Blair?"

Several wild—and definitely crazy—ideas were buzzing through her mind at that very moment. "I have my fantasies like everyone else, I suppose."

His smile was pure, sexy sin. "Want to tell me about any of them?"

One of them was sitting right in front of her. "I don't think so."

"C'mon. Surely there's something you've always secretly wanted to do. Someplace you've always wanted to see."

Savoring another bite of the fudge ice cream, she shook her head. "Nothing I can think of at the moment."

"I don't believe that."

She made a face at him. "Whatever."

He grinned. "Chicken."

It was the second time he'd called her that. Again, she refused to react, simply dipping into the ice-cream carton again.

"Just what does it take to get a rise out of you, Counselor?"

"A great deal." With one last, longing look at the remaining ice cream, she resolutely set her spoon aside.

"I'm afraid I'm not nearly as disciplined as you are." He scooped out another huge spoonful.

"Somehow I'm not surprised by that," she commented wryly.

With a chuckle, he held his spoon to her lips, giving her another tantalizing taste of the treat. "I have a great number of fantasies. Most of them, I've gone after."

She nodded, thinking of those fascinating photographs he kept in his scrapbook.

He slipped another spoonful of ice cream between her lips. "I've always figured that life is too short to waste it daydreaming about grand adventures. I prefer to experience them."

"And if one of those grand adventures makes your life even shorter?"

"Then I go with no regrets."

She frowned and pushed his hand away when he would have fed her more ice cream. "Don't you think that's a rather selfish way to live? What about the people who care about you? Who depend on you? What about the stress and worry your reckless behavior causes them?"

He shrugged. "That's not a problem. There's no one who depends on me particularly. The ranch runs well enough without me, as do the other businesses in which I have holdings. Unlike your brother, I have no children to pine for me. I might be selfish, but I've been very careful I'm the only one who risks getting hurt."

Blair found that hard to believe. There had to be people who cared whether Scott lived or died. He was too vibrant, too charming, too compelling. She couldn't imagine that he lived like a monk, and she didn't believe the women he romanced were all able to protect their hearts from him. This was a man who would be all too easy to love, even for someone who knew from the beginning that it was not a wise emotional investment.

So why was he saying these things to her now? Was this his way of warning her not to expect too much from his flirting? If so, she could have assured him his precaution hadn't been necessary. She made a production of stifling a yawn. "As entertaining as this has been, I really should go back to bed. I have a long day ahead tomorrow."

He capped the ice cream and rose to replace it in the freezer. "I feel a bit like Jeff. I'm not quite ready for our weekend to be over."

She crossed her arms. "I haven't thanked you yet for all you've done for Jeffrey this weekend."

He lifted an eyebrow. "I haven't done much. Just took him fishing."

"You've done more than that. He's had a very good time this weekend. He needed a man's attention, and you've given it to him. You've been very kind and patient even when he was difficult. I just want you to know I appreciate it."

Looking uncomfortable, Scott shrugged. "He's a cool kid. I've enjoyed spending time with him."

She bit her lip. It felt good to hear someone say something nice about Jeffrey for a change. To think someone had actually enjoyed being with him, whether Scott was being honest or just being nice.

"He's very fond of you, you know," Scott added conversationally. "He just doesn't know how to show you."

Her arms tightened defensively around herself. "Do you really think so? Or is he just tolerating me until his father comes back? Not that I believe that's going to happen anytime soon, if ever."

"No, I think Jeff really cares for you. But maybe he isn't sure how you feel about him."

Blair stared at him. "Of course he knows I care about him. Why else would I care whether he eats right or gets good grades or has someone to watch out for him when I'm tied up at work? Why would I work so hard trying to keep him safe and happy?"

"He's a kid, Blair. He needs things spelled out. He doesn't know how to read between the lines. As far as he knows, you do all that stuff because you think you have to.''

"Why, that's—"

"All too common," he cut in. "I know what it's like to be a kid who feels like an unwanted burden. I know how frustrating it can be to have to feel grateful for every crumb of attention or affection."

Almost before she became aware of it, the bitterness in Scott's eyes disappeared behind his usual lazy smile. "I'm only suggesting you let the kid know how you feel. Maybe give him a big hug every once in a while. He might stiffen up at first. Maybe he doesn't think he needs or deserves hugs and kisses. But trust me, he does. And eventually, he'll learn how to respond."

The voice of experience again? Had there been someone at Lost Springs who had given Scott hugs even when he hadn't realized he needed them? Or had he only wished someone would? And was Jeffrey really hungry for physical affection, even though he tended to draw back every time she reached out to him?

Scott held up both hands, palms outward. "I'm not trying to interfere between you and your nephew. It was just a suggestion, take it or leave it."

She nodded. "I appreciate your advice. That's why I asked you to spend time with him this weekend."

He smiled and dropped his hands. "You didn't exactly ask me. You paid big money for me."

"Yes, I'm aware of that," she replied dryly.

He reached out to touch her cheek. "I'd like to think you got your money's worth."

"I bought you entirely for my nephew. I'm quite satisfied with your efforts so far, thank you."

He moved a bit closer. "You remember those fantasies we talked about earlier?"

Her throat tightened, and when she replied, her voice emerged as little more than a strained whisper. "Yes."

"There's one that's been tempting me for two days now. And you know how I am about resisting temptation." He'd leaned his head toward her as he spoke, so that his lips were only an inch or so from hers.

Though her lips were tingling like crazy, she tried to speak more firmly. "Then it's a good thing I'm a pro at resisting temptation, isn't it?"

His hands were suddenly on her shoulders, drawing her toward him. "Do you *always* have to be so cautious and practical?"

"Somebody has to be. In my family, I was the one."

"Steady, sensible Blair. So…dependable."

The word didn't sound like a compliment the way he said it. She frowned, her lower lip protruding slightly in a way that felt uncomfortably like one of her nephew's famous pouts.

Scott groaned. "That does it."

Confused, she gazed at him. "What do you—?"

His mouth was on hers before she could finish the question.

CHAPTER SEVEN

MAYBE THE FUDGE ice cream had weakened her, undermined her defenses. Maybe sleep deprivation was clouding her mind, making her act in a way that wasn't at all like her. Or maybe she just couldn't wait any longer to find out what it was like to kiss sexy Scott McKay.

She rested her hands on his shoulders, clenching his T-shirt in her fists. Her lips softened beneath his, then parted, implicitly welcoming him inside. He promptly took advantage of the invitation, deepening the kiss until she was aware of nothing but that contact between them.

He slid his hands slowly down her back, fingertips tracing her curves through the practical cotton pajamas. He left behind little trails of tingles, filling her mind with images of what it might be like if there were not layers of fabric between them. Her pulse raced, and her knees went weak. Scott's hands tightened on her hips, pulling her closer. Their thighs brushed, and Blair became aware that she wasn't the only one who was reacting physically to the kiss.

He murmured his pleasure at her response, then changed the angle of the kiss to introduce her to a whole new level of sensation. And Blair melted into his arms like fudge ice cream left out in the sun.

She couldn't have said what it was that shocked her back to reality sometime later. A sound, maybe. A mental kick from her common sense. Whatever the cause, she became suddenly aware of what she was doing—and who she was doing it with. She pulled herself out of his arms, stumbling a little but quickly righting herself. And then she simply stared at him, wondering what on earth had gotten into her.

"Oh, yeah," Scott said after a moment, his voice gruff. "That was definitely one of the fantasies I've had in mind since I met you."

She drew a deep breath into lungs that had been emptied by his embrace, trying to force coherent thought into her mind, which felt much the same way. "Now that we've gotten that behind us..."

"I can't wait to do it again," he finished, reaching for her.

She skillfully evaded his hands. "No."

"No?"

"No. It was an impulse. The natural outcome of a cozy, late-night conversation over fudge ice cream. It won't happen again."

Hands on his hips, he lowered his chin and looked at her through his lashes in a pose she was beginning to recognize. "Never?"

"Never."

"Why?"

"Why?" She realized she was blankly parroting him. Swallowing, she tried to regain command of a situation that had rapidly gotten out of control. "I think it's obvious that this isn't a good idea. We're here because of Jeffrey, and that's the only reason. I'm not interested in anything else."

"You seemed very interested a few moments ago," he murmured.

"Yes, well, that was a mistake."

"Kissing me was a mistake?"

"Would you please stop repeating me? Yes, it was a mistake. It won't happen again. You aren't interested in a long-term relationship that would interfere with your adventuring, and I don't indulge in short-term flings. Even if I didn't have an impressionable child to be responsible for, that isn't my style. There's really no point in letting something like this happen again."

"So why *did* you kiss me, Blair?"

After a momentary hesitation, she gave a slight shrug. "Let's just say I have an occasional fantasy of my own." And had Jeffrey not been sleeping so close by, she might very well have indulged herself, she realized with half-guilty regret.

Scott lifted his head, and a glimmer of what might have been amusement appeared in his eyes. "You be sure and let me know if there are any other fantasies I can fulfill for you."

"I'll do that," she answered coolly.

For some reason she couldn't begin to fathom, he was suddenly in a cheerful mood again. He made an expansive gesture toward the doorway. "Allow me to escort you back to your staircase."

Eyeing him suspiciously, she moved ahead of him and resisted the impulse to run. She didn't look at him as she started up the stairs. "Good night, Scott."

"Good night, Blair. Pleasant dreams."

She'd made it almost to the top when he spoke again, his voice a deep rumble in the shadows. "Blair?"

She paused. "Yes?"

"You're deceiving yourself if you think that's not going to happen again. And next time, you won't push me away."

He'd disappeared into his bedroom before she could

think of the words to adequately express her disagreement with his outrageous prediction.

She never should have given in to her curiosity, she told herself with a muffled groan. It had been a mistake to give an inch to a man who never hesitated to take a mile.

IT WAS NO SURPRISE that Blair hardly slept a wink during the remainder of the night. She tossed and turned, dozed, then woke to replay Scott's kiss at least a dozen times in her mind. She worried that something similar would happen again—then feared she would regret it if it didn't. It was almost dawn when she fell into a restless sleep, which meant that it was a bit later than usual when she woke. Dragging a hand through her tangled hair, dreading that first moment when she would see Scott again, she stumbled into the bathroom to make herself presentable. She quickly showered and dressed, thinking it better if she didn't go down in pajamas this morning.

Scott's bedroom door opened just as Blair reached the bottom of the stairs. He stepped out, yawning, looking as though he'd managed little more sleep than she had. He paused when he spotted her. "Good morning."

"Good morning," she replied, not quite meeting his eyes.

"Sleep well?"

"Very. You?"

"Oh, yeah. Great. Looks like Jeff's sleeping in." He nodded toward the closed door of the other bedroom.

"Yes. I'll wake him when breakfast is ready."

"Need any help in the kitchen?"

"No, that isn't necessary, thank you."

He nodded. "Then I'll take advantage of the empty bathroom to shower and get dressed."

Deciding the encounter hadn't been too awkward under the circumstances, Blair went into the kitchen and rummaged for breakfast supplies. She found oatmeal and brown sugar, a combination Jeffrey often requested. She assumed Scott liked oatmeal, since he kept it stocked. While the oatmeal cooked, she made orange juice from frozen concentrate, stirring it vigorously with a long, wooden spoon.

By the time Scott ambled in, his hair still damp from his shower, three steaming bowls of oatmeal were on the table, along with toast and juice. "Looks good."

Wiping her hands on a paper towel, Blair stepped toward the door. "I'll go wake Jeffrey."

She would prefer not to remain alone in the kitchen with Scott, considering what had happened last time.

She tapped on the door of her nephew's bedroom. "Jeffrey, it's time to wake up." Receiving no response, she turned the knob and opened the door. "Jeffrey? Breakfast is…"

There was no one in Jeffrey's room. The bed had been hastily made up, and Jeffrey's pajamas were thrown over the back of a chair. She glanced toward the bathroom shared by the two downstairs bedrooms. The door was closed on this side; she tapped on it. "Jeffrey?"

When there was no answer, she rattled the knob. The door opened beneath her hand. The room was empty.

Frowning, she left the bedroom. He wasn't in the living room, and she didn't see him in the loft. Could he have slipped into the kitchen somehow while she was in his room? She stepped into the kitchen, where Scott was sitting at the table, looking hungrily at his oatmeal. "Have you seen him?"

He looked surprised by the question. "Jeff? He wasn't in his room?"

"No. Not in the bathroom, either."

"The loft?"

"I didn't go up, but the lights are off up there and he didn't answer when I called out. Did you hear him moving around this morning?"

"Not a sound. I just assumed he was sleeping." Scott stood. "Check the other rooms again. I'll look around outside."

Ten minutes later, there was still no sign of Jeffrey, and Scott looked grim when he rejoined Blair. "One of the fishing rods is gone," he announced.

"You think he slipped out to go fishing?"

"Looks that way. He must have left at least an hour ago—I'd have heard him if he'd left after that."

Blair's eyes narrowed. "Will you take me to him? He knows better than to behave this way. I intend to tell him…"

Something in Scott's expression made Blair hesitate. "What is it?" she asked sharply.

"I'll go look for him. Maybe you should wait here until I bring him back."

"Scott?" What was it he wasn't telling her? Why did he look so concerned?

After hesitating a moment, Scott admitted slowly, "I'm a little worried that Jeffrey could have gotten lost on the way to the stream. The path I led him on yesterday isn't a straight, clearly marked trail. There are quite a few winding paths he could have taken by mistake. It took me months after I bought this place to learn the surroundings, and that was with a compass and a map of the area."

"He could be lost out there?" she repeated, her voice strained, irritation changing into fear.

Scott moved toward the door. "I'll go find him."

"I'm coming with you," she said, hurrying after him.

"All right, but stay close. If he headed toward where we fished yesterday, the trail gets steep and narrow. There are some slippery places where a fall could lead to an injury."

Blair winced. Now she had to worry about Jeffrey being lost *and* hurt. She swallowed hard and stepped outside with Scott.

Twenty minutes into their hike toward the fishing spot, she was growing even more worried. There was very little path to follow, and what there was showed a disturbing tendency to branch into several directions. Scott moved confidently along the faint trail, but he'd been this way many times—unlike Jeffrey, who'd made this walk for the first time only yesterday.

Why would he have gone off so foolishly on his own this way?

As if sensing her mounting anxiety, Scott glanced over his shoulder. "You okay?"

"Yes, I'm just—" She stumbled on a loose rock but quickly steadied herself. "I'm just worried about Jeffrey."

"We'll find him."

He'd spoken with conviction. Blair hoped he wasn't just putting up a front to reassure her. She glanced to her right where another trail of sorts branched off to lead into densely wooded mountainside. She could see no differences between that path and the one they were taking; had Scott not been with her, she would have had no clue which way to turn.

It seemed like forever before they finally scrambled over a large, mossy boulder to find water, a wide, rushing stretch of the stream they had seen the first day here, though she was certain it wasn't the same spot. She didn't even think they'd come in the same direction, though again, she couldn't have sworn to it.

Scott stopped and studied the area, making a slow turn to look in all directions. "Damn."

"This is where you fished yesterday?"

He nodded, motioning to a patch of grass near the water. "That's where we ate lunch."

"He isn't here," she said unnecessarily.

"No."

She moistened her lips. "Could we have passed him on different paths? Maybe he's already been here and gone back to the cabin."

"Blair, it's more likely that he got lost trying to find this place. You saw how many turns I took. Could you find your way to the cabin alone if you went back now?"

She turned, looking at the path and the thick woods surrounding them. Could she guarantee that she wouldn't get turned around if she headed back on her own? "No," she whispered. "I'm not sure I could."

Where was Jeffrey?

"We have to find him," she said, reaching out to clutch Scott's arm. "Scott, we have to find him! He could be frightened. Hurt. He could be—"

"Blair." He covered her hand with his. "We'll find him."

She was already moving toward the path. "Jeffrey!" she called. "Jeffrey, where are you?"

Scott snagged her hand when she would have rushed away. "Stay close," he reminded her. "It won't do us any good if you get lost, too."

She forced herself to hold back and let him take the lead.

An hour later, Blair was winded, her voice raspy from calling her nephew, her legs trembling from climbing up and down inclines, over rocks and fallen limbs. Fear was building inside her until her chest ached with it. They had passed so many places where a child could be easily hurt; was Jeffrey lying even now at the bottom of a steep bluff?

She didn't realize she was crying until Scott pulled her to a stop and wiped her damp cheeks with his fingertips. "We'll find him, Blair," he said again, his voice low and gentle.

She caught her breath. "Where could he be? We've looked everywhere. What could have happened to him?"

"We haven't looked everywhere. There are still several directions he could have taken that we haven't checked yet. But I'm worried that we're circling each other. We need more searchers to spread out and cover more territory."

She moistened her painfully dry lips again, trying to stay calm. "What should we do?"

"We'll go back to the cabin and call for a search and rescue team. Then I'll head back out while you wait for word."

"You expect me to just sit alone in the cabin without knowing what's going on?"

"Blair, someone has to coordinate this search from a central location, be near my cell phone, ready to take action. I know this countryside, so it's only logical that I should be the one out looking."

What he said made sense, of course, though she didn't want to admit it. She hated the thought of being cooped up in that cabin with no idea of what was going on outside. But if that was the most helpful role she could play in the search for Jeffrey, that was what she would do.

"All right. Lead me to the cabin," she murmured, her heart sinking as she realized that she had no idea how to get there on her own.

Still calling Jeffrey's name, they made their way back. Her eyes blinded by tears, Blair stumbled more than once, but Scott steadied her. She was so worried about Jeffrey, so disgusted with herself for letting this happen. She should have been more vigilant. She should have known he would try something like this. She should have been concentrating more on her nephew and less on the man in the other bedroom. If anything had happened to Jeffrey, she would never forgive herself.

Scott's hand tightened suddenly on her arm. "Wait," he said, his tone urgent.

"What?"

His head was cocked attentively, and he was looking away from her. "Did you hear that?"

"What?"

"Call him again."

"Jeffrey!" Her voice was hoarse, but still loud enough to carry.

This time, she heard it, too—a faint, distant cry. She started impulsively in that direction, but Scott held her back, keeping her behind him as he moved quickly but carefully down a new offshoot of the path.

Jeffrey was sitting beneath a tree, his face streaked with tears and dust, a couple of ugly scrapes on his chin, his jeans ripped at the knees. His lower lip quivered when Blair and Scott came into view. "Am I in trouble?" was the first thing he said.

Blair dropped to her knees beside him, her hands trembling with relief. "Are you all right?"

"I fell down," he said with a sniffle. "I'm okay, I think, just sore and—"

She pulled him into her arms, squeezing him so tightly his words were cut off with a squeak. "Oh, my God, Jeffrey, I was so worried about you! I was so afraid...."

Jeffrey burrowed into her chest with a choked sob. "I got lost," he said in a very small voice.

"I know, sweetie. It's hard to find your way through these woods. I'd have been lost, too, if Scott hadn't been with me."

"Am I in trouble?"

Resting her cheek against his hair, Blair laughed shakily. "Oh, yes. But that can wait. Right now I'm just too happy to see you to be angry with you."

Scott crouched beside them, easing Jeffrey out of Blair's arms. "Let's take a look at you, partner, and see if you've hurt yourself."

Jeffrey mopped at his face with the back of one dirty hand. "I fell off a big rock. I thought it was the one by the stream, but there was a big hill on the other side, and I fell down it."

While Blair hovered nearby, Scott ran his hands skillfully over Jeffrey's thin limbs. "Are you in any pain? Is there any place in particular that hurts?"

"I scraped my knees. And my hands. And...and I broke your fishing rod," he added in a subdued whisper.

"We'll talk about that later, okay? Did you hit your head?"

"No."

"Can you stand?"

"Yes. I walked until I got too tired. I was resting when I heard you and Aunt Blair calling me."

Scott helped him to his feet. It was obvious from the way Jeffrey winced that his scraped knees were stiff and painful, but Blair was relieved that he didn't seem to have any broken bones. She reached out to smooth his tumbled hair, unable to stop touching him now that she had him safely with her again. "Can you walk back to the cabin?"

"Sure," Jeffrey said, trying to look tough. He took two steps, grimacing with discomfort.

Scott promptly swept the boy into his arms. "Why don't you let me give you a lift this time?"

"I can walk by myself," Jeffrey insisted, even as he wrapped his arms around Scott's neck.

"Yeah, I know. But be still, okay? I'm trying to impress your aunt with how strong I am."

"Okay." With a sigh, Jeffrey settled into Scott's solid shoulder.

Blair swallowed an enormous lump in her throat and followed as Scott began to carefully make his way to the cabin.

SOMETIME LATER, Jeffrey had bathed and his scraped hands and knees had been treated and bandaged. Dressed in clean clothing, he sat at the kitchen table behind a bowl of freshly cooked oatmeal. Rapidly recovering from his misadventures, the boy ate ravenously while the adults, who were slower to get over the morning's trauma, sipped coffee and hovered over him.

"Do you want some more orange juice, Jeffrey?" Blair asked.

"No, thank you."

"Toast?" Scott suggested.

"No, I'm fine. Aren't you guys going to eat?"

"I'm really not hungry right now," Blair answered, her stomach still queasy from fear.

"I'll eat later," Scott said, refilling his coffee cup.

Jeffrey shrugged and finished his oatmeal. And then

he pushed the bowl away, took a deep breath and said, "Okay. You can yell at me now."

Blair laced her fingers in front of her on the table, leveling a somber look at her nephew. "Is it necessary for me to point out how wrong you were to slip out without permission that way?"

Hanging his head, Jeffrey muttered, "No, ma'am."

Aware that Scott was watching them closely, Blair cleared her throat. "You frightened me out of my wits," she said. "You worried Scott, who has been so good to you all weekend. And you could have been seriously injured, if not worse, when you fell. Don't you think we have a right to be angry with you?"

Jeffrey nodded miserably.

"As it turned out, you were lost and frightened and hurt. I think you realize how wrong you were, and I hope you'll never do anything that willful and foolish again. Now, apologize to Scott for your behavior and then we'll let this go."

"I'm sorry, Scott." Jeffrey's voice was barely audible.

Scott nodded. "I'm just glad you're okay. But I hope you never do anything like this to your aunt again. You made her cry, Jeff. She didn't deserve that from you."

Jeffrey's lip was quivering again, his eyes tear-filled. "I'm really sorry, Aunt Blair."

"It's over now," she said, taking pity on him. He looked so small and vulnerable hunched in the big wooden chair. What he had done was wrong, but she couldn't bring herself to punish him further this time. Something Scott had said nagged at her. Was Jeffrey really uncertain about her feelings for him?

"I love you, Jeffrey," she said clearly and firmly. "I

would be devastated if anything happened to you. Please don't do anything like that again.''

His eyes widened, and he looked at her with surprise showing on his face. ''I only wanted to go fishing, Aunt Blair,'' he said earnestly.

She wasn't sure he'd quite gotten the point, but she nodded. ''Next time, wait until an adult agrees to go with you. Now go brush your teeth and pack your things. We'll need to be under way soon.''

Jeffrey knew when to obey without question. He nodded, stood and hurried from the room.

''You handled that well,'' Scott commented.

Blair lifted her eyebrows in response to the faint hint of surprise in his voice. ''You expected me to beat him?''

''No, of course not. I was just... Well, you didn't overdo it. You know, the preaching and lecturing.''

Was that what Scott's grandparents had done when he had misbehaved? Preached and lectured? ''It wouldn't have done any good. That's something I learned making presentations to jurors. A longer speech is more likely to bore them than sway them.''

''You must be very good at your job.''

''I've had training at being a lawyer. I don't have the foggiest idea how to raise a child,'' she said ruefully.

''You show definite potential,'' Scott assured her, and he seemed sincere behind the smile.

She made a wry face at him. ''Thanks. I suppose I'm to assume you're an expert at it.'' And then she sagged weakly against the counter as the day's events caught up with her. ''Oh, God.''

Scott rested a hand on her shoulder. ''You okay?''

''I'll let you know when I decide.''

''Harrowing morning, wasn't it?''

"I hope I never have to live through another like it."

"I'm sorry, Blair. I should have heard him slip out. I don't usually sleep so heavily—or so late."

"It wasn't your fault. I'm the one who should apologize because we've taken such advantage of your hospitality. I'll reimburse you for the broken fishing rod, of course."

"Not necessary."

She shook her head. "I insist. Jeffrey had no right to take your property. It's my responsibility to see that it's replaced."

He stroked her lower lip with his fingertip, a gleam of amusement in his eyes. "Ms. Dependability again. You're just so darned cute when you get that way."

"Scott..."

He lowered his head to brush a light kiss across the tip of her nose. "On you, responsibility is incredibly sexy. It makes me go crazy."

She forced herself to respond in the same light, teasing tone. "Oh, is *that* what does it?"

"Really cute," he murmured, then pressed his lips to hers. She knew she should pull away, but maybe she just needed the contact then. Needed a way to vent the emotions that had been building in her all morning. She rested her hands on his chest and leaned into the kiss, letting his warmth soak into her.

This kiss was different from the ones they'd shared last night. The passion was still there, simmering in the background. But there was a new tenderness this time. A new layer of meaning that Blair found even more unsettling than the physical hunger she'd been aware of before. She didn't want to get involved with this man. Didn't want to fall in love with him. And yet...

He lifted his head, ending the embrace slowly, reluctantly. "Oh, yeah," he said, his voice not quite steady. "On you, it is definitely sexy."

He pulled her closer and lowered his head again. Blair spread her fingers on his chest and held him away. "No. That's enough, Scott. I'm really not up to this right now."

He sighed faintly. "All right. But remember where we left off."

She gave him a quelling look. "Don't make any assumptions based on what just happened. You caught me at a vulnerable moment."

His grin had a wicked edge to it. "Then I'll be watching for the next one."

"Behave yourself."

"That's never been something I was very good at."

"Learn." She stepped away from him. "I'm going up to pack."

He didn't try to detain her when she walked out of the kitchen without looking back at him.

CHAPTER EIGHT

AFTER THEY'D CLEANED the cabin and packed, there was still time for a card game before lunch. The hike Scott had suggested the night before was out, of course; they'd all had enough of trekking through the woods that morning. The fast-paced card game—Scott's idea—gave them a chance to relax, laugh, put the morning's fright behind them and get comfortable with each other again. By the time it ended, things were back to normal, much to everyone's relief.

They had lunch before leaving—canned soup again. No one complained about the very plain fare, but they ate without much enthusiasm. Their departure time loomed near, and Blair suspected Jeffrey and Scott were no more excited about leaving than she was. It had been such a pleasant weekend—at least until Jeffrey had pulled his stunt that morning.

She glanced through her lashes at her nephew, who was talking with Scott. Jeffrey responded so well to Scott, who seemed to understand how the boy's mind worked. Would the lessons Jeffrey had learned during the past few days stay with him after they returned home?

Would either of them ever see Scott again?

After lunch, they cleaned the kitchen, then loaded their things into the Jeep. "I don't want to go," Jeffrey muttered. "I like it here."

"You can come back another time," Scott assured him. "We'll go fishing again—with your aunt's permission, of course."

Jeffrey's grim expression didn't alter. Blair knew her nephew had heard too many empty promises from his father to trust Scott's easy assurances. Like Jeffrey, she tended to be skeptical that they would ever be back. It was easy enough for Scott to make promises now, but real life had a way of interfering with even the most well-intentioned plans.

The plane was waiting in the small hangar where they'd left it. Scott pushed it out, transferred their belongings, then drove the Jeep into the hangar and secured the heavy padlock. Again, Blair let Jeffrey take the copilot's seat, strapping herself into the back.

"Do you need help with your seat belt, Jeffrey?" she asked, leaning slightly forward.

"No, I've got it." She heard the buckle snap into place.

Scott slid his aviator glasses onto his nose. "At least I've got someone to talk to during this flight. I usually have Cooper with me in the copilot's seat, and he's not much of a conversationalist."

"Who's Cooper?" Jeffrey wanted to know.

"My dog. Smart as a whip, but I can't teach him to carry on a decent conversation."

"What kind of dog is he?"

"Yellow lab."

"Have you had him long?"

"Since he was a pup. He's five now."

"You bring him to the cabin with you?"

"Yeah, he loves to fly. He keeps me company when I need a break from people."

"I've never had a pet," Jeffrey said with just a hint of wistfulness.

"You've never had a pet?" Scott sounded surprised. "Of any kind?"

"No. I tried to tame a stray cat once when I lived with my grandmother. I fed it every day and talked to it and stuff. He got to where he would let me pet him sometimes, but then he just disappeared. Grandma said he probably got hit by a car or something. I like cats, but Grandma said they don't make good pets."

Blair raised her eyebrows. She'd had a cat when she was growing up. It had been a wonderful pet, and a treasured friend. She hadn't thought of getting a pet for Jeffrey. Had it been suggested a few days earlier, she might have argued that her busy schedule would make it too difficult to give the animal the proper attention. But this weekend with Jeffrey and Scott had made her start to see things in a different light. She'd been so concerned with Jeffrey's physical well-being and his performance at school that she'd overlooked some of the emotional needs of a young boy. It hadn't been that she didn't care, she assured her stinging conscience; she had just been overwhelmed by the sudden responsibility of having to raise her nephew herself.

The conversation in the front seat turned to the operation of the plane, and Blair sat back, letting their words be drowned out by the roar of the engine. She made no effort to read during the flight this time. She simply watched Scott and Jeffrey, trying to analyze her complex emotions toward both of them.

"IS THAT EVERYTHING?" Scott asked when they'd transferred all the bags from the Cessna to the trunk of Blair's white sedan.

Blair closed the trunk. "Yes, that's all. Jeffrey, you have your backpack?"

He seemed almost surprised by the question, which made her realize that she'd hardly seen the battered backpack all weekend. Usually he kept it close to him, never letting it out of his sight. She'd respected his privacy about its contents, assuming he kept his most cherished possessions in the bag. As uncertain as his life had been, she didn't blame him for wanting to keep his personal belongings close by.

"I put it in the back seat," he said.

"Good. Then I guess there's nothing left for us to do except thank Scott for the weekend and get on our way."

Jeffrey's lower lip jutted in his usual pout. He didn't want to say goodbye to Scott, didn't want the weekend to end.

For once she knew exactly how he felt.

"How would you like to visit my ranch soon?" Scott asked the boy.

A glimmer of interest lit Jeffrey's face. "I've never been to a ranch."

"Then it's high time you visit one. You can't live in Wyoming and never set foot on a ranch."

"That would be cool," Jeffrey said with a hopeful look at Blair.

Knowing Jeffrey would be bitterly disappointed if Scott was making suggestions he didn't intend to follow through on, Blair looked at Scott. "You don't owe us anything more," she reminded him in a low voice. "This weekend was all you volunteered for the auction."

He gave her a quick frown. "This invitation has nothing to do with the auction. I would like you and Jeff to visit the ranch when you have time."

She had the odd sensation that she'd unintentionally offended him. She spoke quickly to assure him she appreciated the offer. "In that case, we would love to come. I'm sure Jeffrey will find it fascinating."

Scott nodded, looking appeased. "You just might find something to interest you there, as well," he murmured.

She was quite sure the most interesting feature of Scott's ranch for her would be the owner, but she had no intention of sharing that tidbit with him. She merely nodded and turned to Jeffrey. "Tell Scott thank-you," she prodded.

Jeffrey shuffled his feet and looked a bit shyly at Scott. "Thanks for taking us to your cabin and taking me fishing and everything. And, uh, I'm really sorry about getting lost and breaking your rod."

"You're forgiven," Scott assured him.

"So…we'll see you around?" Jeffrey looked torn between doubt and optimism.

Scott grinned and swept the boy into a warm, near-bruising hug. "You can count on it."

Flushed with embarrassed pleasure, Jeffrey returned the hug a bit tentatively. "Don't forget about taking me to your ranch," he begged.

"Not a chance." He set the boy on his feet, then turned to Blair, who was watching with a lump in her throat. "I'll be calling you about that visit."

She nodded. "We'll look forward to it." She held out her hand and added crisply, "Thank you for providing us with such a pleasant vacation, Scott."

He took her hand, but instead of shaking it, he held it in both of his. "You're being prissy and proper again," he said, his grin suddenly wicked. "You know what that does to me."

Her cheeks flamed as she mentally replayed the kisses

they'd shared during the past few days. She shot a quick glance at her nephew, who was watching them with interest, and gave a small tug at her hand. "Goodbye."

He didn't release her. "Hey, Jeff. Would you mind very much if I give your aunt a kiss?"

"Scott!"

Jeffrey drowned out Blair's embarrassed squeak of protest with a cheerful, "Nope. Go ahead."

"Thanks." Before Blair could pull away, Scott swooped down on her and planted a firm, warm kiss on her mouth. He didn't linger long, but she was still thoroughly rattled by the time he drew back.

"Next time," she grumbled when she could speak coherently, "ask *my* permission."

Scott laughed, dimples flashing. "At least you realize there will be a next time."

Neatly caught by her own imprudent words, Blair could only scowl at him as he stepped out of reach. "So long, you two," he said cheerfully. "I'll be seeing you soon."

Promise...or warning? Blair couldn't help wondering as she and Jeffrey climbed into her car and fastened their seat belts. She was aware that Jeffrey looked longingly through the rear window as they left the airport behind. She was all too tempted to do the same.

BLAIR HAD a few calls to make when they got home, and Jeffrey settled in front of a video game while she did so. They were back to their normal routine, she thought with a sigh. She hoped that some things, at least, had changed between them.

She made pizza for dinner, remembering that Jeffrey had told Scott it was his favorite. "It's good, Aunt

Blair," he said, which was in itself a change from his usual silence.

"I'm glad you like it. There's ice cream in the freezer, if you want dessert."

"Okay. Can I watch TV tonight?"

"For a little while. But first I want to quiz you on your spelling words to make sure you're ready for your test tomorrow."

He sighed, but nodded. "All right. But I know all the words."

"Then the quiz won't take long, will it?" she asked equably.

The quiz didn't take long at all. Jeffrey spelled every word correctly the first time.

"Very good," Blair said approvingly. "You should ace the test."

Jeffery broke into a sudden grin that was so much like one of Scott's, Blair's chest contracted. "Working the system, right?" he quipped.

"Doing well because it's the right thing to do," she corrected dryly.

"Whatever. It all comes out the same."

Blair mused again that Scott's advice had the right results but questionable rationale. "Go watch TV," she said. "But only for a little while."

"Thanks, Aunt Blair." He headed for the other room, leaving her shaking her head in bemusement.

Jeffrey had just gone to bed when Blair tapped on his door. "Jeffrey? I wanted to make sure you're okay," she said, walking toward his bed when he called to her to come in. "Your knees aren't hurting too badly?"

"They're fine, Aunt Blair. I hardly even feel them now."

She reached out to smooth his hair, pleased that he

didn't draw away this time. "Let me know if you need anything."

"I will."

On an impulse, she did something she'd been wanting to do for a long time. She bent to give her nephew a good-night kiss on the cheek. "Sleep well, Jeffrey."

"G'night." He rolled onto his side and pulled the covers to his chin. She couldn't tell if he was pleased, displeased or completely unaffected by her gesture.

She was almost to the door when Jeffrey spoke again, his voice small in the shadows. "Aunt Blair?"

"Yes?"

"Were you really worried about me this morning when you couldn't find me?"

"I was petrified. You're the only nephew I have, Jeffrey. That makes you very special to me."

He mumbled something she didn't understand.

"I'm sorry, I didn't hear you. What did you say, Jeffrey?"

"I said I love you, too," he repeated, just a little louder.

Blair's eyes were damp when she closed his bedroom door.

BLAIR HAD EXPECTED to sleep better now that she was in her own bed. And she did for a while—until a disturbing dream woke her just before dawn. A dream she blushed to remember. A dream that had prominently featured Scott McKay.

Knowing there would be no more sleep that night— or maybe fearing she *would* sleep and dream again—she climbed out of bed and took a long, cool shower.

Though Blair usually picked Jeffrey up from her aunt Wanda's house on her way home from work, they made different arrangements for Monday evening. Blair was waiting in the living room of her house when Wanda walked Jeffrey home.

Jeffrey looked curiously at his aunt when he trudged inside, dragging his backpack behind him. "How come you came home without picking me up today, Aunt Blair?"

She smiled. "I had something to take care of here."

He opened his mouth to ask another question, but paused when an unfamiliar sound caught his attention. "What was that? It sounded like a..."

He went silent when a sleek gray cat slipped into the room, pausing in the doorway to look inquiringly at the humans gathered there.

"Whose cat is that?" Jeffrey asked, standing very still.

"She's yours," Blair answered gently. "If you want her, of course."

"Mine?" the boy repeated in a whisper.

"Her name is Belle—at least, that's what her first owner called her. She's a year old and very affectionate, I'm told. She stays inside all the time where she is safe and comfortable. Her previous owner is moving to Casper, to an apartment that won't accept pets, so Belle had nowhere else to go."

"And I can keep her?"

The excitement building in Jeffrey's voice made Blair's smile deepen. "Under certain conditions."

He was already inching toward the cat, who was sitting with her tail tucked neatly around her paws, waiting for someone to pay attention to her. "What conditions?"

"She's a living creature. She has needs and feelings. She needs love and care. I will not have her mistreated or neglected."

Still moving very slowly—probably the same way he had with the wild cat he'd once tried to tame—Jeffrey knelt beside the friendly-looking Belle and extended his hand. Belle began to purr, her head arching into his palm when he stroked her tentatively. "I would never mistreat her, Aunt Blair."

"Having a pet is a lot of work. She needs fresh food and water every day, and I want the litter box changed frequently. Even when there are other things you want to do, your pet comes first."

Jeffrey was sitting cross-legged on the floor, grinning broadly as Belle climbed onto his lap, purring loudly and demanding more strokes and attention. Blair had been assured that Belle was an outgoing and child-friendly cat, but this first meeting was progressing even better than she had hoped.

"Jeffrey? Do you want her badly enough to agree to my conditions?"

He beamed at her. "I'll take good care of her, Aunt Blair. Look how much she likes me. She wants to stay with me."

"Yes, I think she does," Blair agreed gently. "She needs a home...and a friend." *Just like Jeffrey,* she thought with a surge of tenderness.

Jeffrey rose to his feet. "Come on, Belle. I'll show you my room. You can sleep with me tonight."

He moved toward the hallway, and to his obvious delight, the curious cat trotted close at his heels.

"Well," Wanda said, wiping her eyes with her fingertips, "that was certainly a successful idea. Whatever made you think of it, Blair?"

"I heard Jeffrey say yesterday that he likes cats and that he's never had a pet. I thought it would be good for him to have a pet of his own to love and care for."

"It was a wonderful idea. I don't know why we never thought of something like this before."

Blair sighed. "We've been so concerned with Jeffrey's grades and behavior that we've forgotten to address some of his other needs, I'm afraid. I've tried to make him feel safe and secure, but I'm not sure I've done a very good job of making him feel loved."

Wanda placed a hand on her niece's arm. "You've done your best for him, Blair. Considering the circumstances—the way Kirk left him with you with no warning, no preparation—I think it's more than admirable how much you've done for the boy. You've practically put your own life on hold for the past six months, and we both know it might be a long time before Kirk returns for Jeffrey, if ever."

"To be honest, I hope Kirk stays away for a while," Blair admitted in a low voice, keeping an eye on the hallway for her nephew. "Jeffrey doesn't need to be dragged from place to place in his father's wake, even if Kirk should ever decide to give active fatherhood a try. Jeffrey needs a home, a steady schedule, security. I can't see Kirk ever living that way."

"Nor can I," Wanda agreed. "Kirk really did pick up your father's worst traits. He simply doesn't seem capable of settling down and becoming a responsible parent."

"Jeffrey has a home with me for as long as he needs it," Blair said firmly.

Wanda smiled a bit ruefully. "I feel as though I should repeat your lecture to Jeffrey about owning a pet. Having a child is a big responsibility, Blair. They require a great deal of time and attention. They're demanding and expensive and very vulnerable. Even when there are other things you would rather do, the child's needs come first.''

Blair laughed softly. ''Trust me, Aunt Wanda, I've given myself that same speech already. But I love Jeffrey, and I want to keep him with me. I'm willing to do whatever it takes.''

''He's very lucky to have you.''

''I hope so,'' Blair said, thinking of all the things she'd done wrong so far.

Wanda suddenly smiled. ''Now, tell me about the man you bought at the bachelor auction. Jeffrey was almost loquacious this afternoon telling me about the weekend. Every other sentence began with 'Scott said' or 'Scott did.'''

Blair tried to keep her expression unrevealing. ''He's quite nice. He was very good to Jeffrey.''

''Jeffrey said he's invited the two of you to visit his ranch. That's not part of the auction package, is it?''

''No. He was simply being generous. Jeffrey mentioned that he has never been to a working ranch, so Scott invited us to visit his place sometime.''

''I see.'' Wanda tapped her foot. ''And?''

''And what?''

''How did *you* get along with Scott?''

''I told you, he was quite nice. Very kind to Jeffrey.''

''Hmm. I don't think he kissed *Jeffrey* goodbye at the airport.''

Her eyes going wide, Blair felt her mouth open and close, but nothing came out. After a moment, she managed to say, ''How did you—?''

''Carl Arnold. He was talking to the airport owner about flying a package to Cheyenne, and he just happened to see a certain goodbye kiss. He mentioned it to his wife, who had her regular eight o'clock Monday-morning appointment at Twyla's Tease 'n' Tweeze today. By the time I went in for my one o'clock, more than half of Lightning Creek knew that the town's pretty young lawyer spent a very interesting weekend with one of the Lost Springs bachelors."

"Oh, my God." Blair covered her face with her hands.

Wanda laughed. "Sweetheart, you've lived here long enough to know what this town is like. Kiss a man at the airport, and Sugar Spinelli and her gang have spread it all over town before he wipes the lipstick off his face."

"I cannot believe I'm the subject of lurid gossip. Aunt Wanda, I *never* do anything the gossips find interesting! I've always been so careful...."

"Too careful, maybe. You're thirty years old, Blair. It's okay to have a good time every once in a while."

"I have a child to raise," Blair argued. "A professional reputation to maintain. I don't want the people of this town to think I'm neglecting Jeffrey to carry on some fleeting fling with a cowboy."

"I'm sure no one thinks you're neglecting Jeffrey. In fact, everyone I know thinks it's wonderfully unselfish that you've taken in your brother's son. They admire you very much, and they think you and Scott McKay make a very cute couple."

Blair groaned again.

Her aunt chuckled and patted Blair's shoulder. "I have to go. Don't worry about the gossip. Just have a good time. Oh, and Blair, even though I haven't met him, I like Scott. Anyone who can make such a difference in Jeffrey's attitude in such a short time must be a good man."

Blair was still trying to come up with the words to

describe Scott when her aunt let herself out the front door.

She turned toward the hallway when she heard Jeffrey approaching, laughing. "Look what Belle's doing, Aunt Blair. She's following this shoestring just like she's on a leash or something."

Trying to put the disturbing gossip out of her mind, Blair smiled as the cat pounced victoriously on the end of the string. "I guess you've decided to keep her."

"Yeah. She's great."

"Are you going to change her name?"

Jeffrey frowned. "You don't just change someone's name, Aunt Blair. If I start calling her something else, she'll get confused. Besides, I like the name Belle. Like in the movie *Beauty and the Beast.*"

"Does that make you the beast?"

He grinned. "Real funny, Aunt Blair."

"I like the name Belle, too," Blair admitted, bending to scratch the cat's silky ears. "I think we're all going to get along very well."

"Aunt Blair?" Jeffrey said when she straightened.

"Yes?"

He hesitated, then wrapped his arms around her waist. "Thank you."

It was the first time he had ever reached out to her. Her throat tight, Blair returned the hug warmly. "You're very welcome, sweetie," she murmured in a voice gruff with emotion.

He didn't stay long, but pulled away to turn to his cat again. Still smiling, Blair went into the kitchen to prepare dinner. Maybe a little gossip wasn't so bad, after all, she thought. Especially since the weekend seemed to have been so very good for Jeffrey.

CHAPTER NINE

THEY HAD EATEN dinner and Blair had just told Jeffrey to get out his books while she cleaned the kitchen when the telephone rang. "I'll get it," Jeffrey said, and pounced on the phone before Blair could reach it. "H'lo?"

She dried her hands on a paper towel, expecting the caller to ask for her. Instead, she heard Jeffrey say enthusiastically, "Hi, Scott! Guess what...I got a cat. Her name is Belle and she's gray and she has a white spot on her nose and she likes to chase a string and Aunt Blair says I can keep her."

While her nephew spent the next five minutes chattering about his new pet, Blair mentally prepared herself for her own conversation with Scott. Though she knew just the sound of his voice would have an effect on her, she decided that she would greet him with the restrained warmth of a passing acquaintance. Not prim and proper, she thought, wincing as she remembered Scott's teasing, but not overly encouraging, either. She didn't want him to think she expected any more from him than he'd already given.

Jeffrey finally held the receiver out to her. "He wants to talk to you, Aunt Blair."

Taking the phone—and a deep breath to steady her nerves—she said, "Thank you, Jeffrey. Now go start your homework. I'll be in soon to help."

He nodded and dashed away, his cat at his heels.

Blair lifted the receiver to her ears. "Hello, Scott."

"Hello, beautiful."

Her heart tripped—*not* the way to respond to a friendly acquaintance, she chided herself.

He continued before she could reply. "The kid sure seemed happy about his cat."

"Yes, he seems quite taken with her."

"So you were listening on the plane yesterday when he said he'd never had a pet."

"I heard. To be honest, I'd never really given it any thought. Now I wish I'd thought of a pet sooner."

"You got him one the day after you learned he wanted one. I would call that a quick response."

Some of her guilt eased. "I only had to make a few phone calls to find the cat. I was told she was a very sweet-natured, affectionate pet, and so far that's proven true."

"It's a great idea. One of the first things the staff at Lost Springs does with a new resident is to give him responsibilities for the animals there. Initially it's often easier for the boys to bond with animals rather than humans. And it gives them a sense of confidence to play an important role in that animal's well-being."

"I'm sure there will be times I'll have to nag Jeffrey to clean the litter box or do some of his other pet-care chores, especially once the novelty wears off."

Scott laughed softly. "You can count on it."

"I think I've done the right thing, though," she added, still trying to convince herself.

"I'm sure you have. I know I've mentioned this before, Blair, but it bears repeating—Jeffrey's lucky to have you."

Her cheeks warmed in pleasure as he unconsciously

repeated the words her aunt had said earlier. "Thank you."

"Other than the cat, how was your day?"

"Busy. But that's typical."

"I wouldn't think there would be many legal crises in Lightning Creek."

"You might be surprised," she said, thinking of a particularly ugly child custody case she had entered into that morning.

"So you really like being a lawyer?"

She smiled at his phrasing. "Most of the time, yes."

"You said you were with a big law firm before moving to Lightning Creek?"

"Yes, an old, prominent firm in Chicago. I was a very junior partner. In maybe twenty or thirty years, I might have made a full partner."

"So what do you like better—big city wheeling and dealing or country lawyering?"

"While there are things I enjoyed about my previous position, I like being my own boss and having more control over my practice. There's more variety to my cases, so it rarely gets boring, though it does get hectic at times."

"I suspect you have workaholic tendencies."

"Maybe a few," she admitted. "But I'm making a few changes to leave me more time for Jeffrey. I'm thinking about advertising for a partner. I had planned to go into partnership with my uncle, but he died before I could join him here."

"You need time for yourself. Time to get away occasionally and just play. Have you ever been white-water rafting?"

"No."

"You live in Wyoming, Blair. You should take advantage of the state's great features."

"I'm going to a rodeo next weekend," she said, a bit defensively. "It's another charity function." One of her clients, having announced that it was past time Blair learned to live like a native, had insisted on giving her two tickets. She had decided to go for several reasons. She wanted to fit in with her neighbors in Lightning Creek, she wanted them to think of her as one of them, and she thought Jeffrey might enjoy it.

"Have you ever been to a rodeo?"

"No, this will be my first."

"You should find it very interesting." Something in Scott's voice made her think he was amused.

"I'm sure I will," she said, resigned to being the object of his good-natured mockery. Now, if only she could figure out what one should wear to a rodeo....

"Sounds like everything is going very well with you."

"It's been a good day so far." She felt as if she should cross her fingers or knock wood or something.

"I want to see you again, Blair. How would you feel about having dinner with me soon?"

"You mean you want to have dinner with Jeffrey and me?"

"I mean I want to have dinner with *you*. It's called a date. You do date, don't you?"

"Not that often," she confessed. "And especially not since Jeffrey moved in."

"Don't you think it's time you started again? You've become a guardian, not a nun."

That same thought had crossed her mind a few times—most notably since she'd met Scott. But did she really want to start down a path with so very many pit-falls?

"I don't know, Scott. What about Jeffrey?"

"He could stay with your aunt for a few hours, couldn't he? Isn't that where he goes now when you have other obligations?"

"Yes. But…"

"He gave me permission to date you, you know."

That made her blink. "I beg your pardon?"

"The subject came up somehow when I took him fishing. He said he thought I should ask you out."

"I can't believe you discussed this with Jeffrey! Scott, he's only ten years old."

"And he sees nothing wrong with us having dinner together. Neither do I. How about it?"

Blair was torn between being annoyed and amused. It embarrassed her that Scott and Jeffrey had discussed her in such a way, but it *had* been a long time since she'd had a pleasant, grown-up dinner with an attractive man. She was definitely tempted.…

"Saturday evening?" he added enticingly.

She took a deep breath, then answered rashly, "Okay. Fine. Saturday evening."

He sounded just a bit smug when he replied, "Great. I'll look forward to it. I'll call you later in the week to set up a time, okay?"

"Yes, that will be fine," she murmured, hoping she hadn't made a serious mistake. She reassured herself that she was only agreeing to dinner. A simple date. How big a mistake could that be?

"I suppose I should let you get back to your nephew."

"Yes. I promised to help him with his homework."

"Then I'll talk to you later in the week. Good night, Blair."

"Good night, Scott."

It occurred to her as she hung up the phone that she now had a date with Scott McKay on Saturday evening.

And she hadn't had to pay for this one.

THE WEEKEND with Scott had not, of course, accomplished miracles. When Blair stopped at her aunt's house to pick Jeffrey up Wednesday afternoon, she could tell immediately from Wanda's expression that something was wrong. She braced herself. "What happened?"

"Jeffrey got into a fight after school. He's been suspended for the rest of the week."

Blair was horrified. "He got into a *fight?* What happened? Who did he fight with? Is he all right?"

As if in answer, Jeffrey slipped into the room, looking braced for trouble. He sported a colorful bruise beneath his left eye, accenting the scabbed-over scrapes on his chin from his fall at Scott's cabin. The pocket of his knit shirt had been ripped at one corner. His expression was a mixture of dread and defiance.

Blair moved to his side, tilting his chin with her finger to examine his injuries. Satisfied they weren't serious, she leveled a frown at him. "All right. Let's hear it."

"I got into a fight with Jason Pritchard. One of the teachers reported us, so now we're both suspended for the rest of the week," he muttered.

"That's hardly enough information, Jeffrey. What was the fight about? Who started it?"

"He shot off his mouth."

"And who threw the first punch?"

Jeffrey's lower lip jutted outward. "He wouldn't shut up."

"So you hit him?"

He shrugged, looked at the floor and shuffled his feet, refusing to answer. But, then, he really didn't have to.

Blair sighed. " We'll talk about this at home."

Dragging his backpack, Jeffrey trudged out with only a mumbled goodbye to his great-aunt.

Wanda rested a reassuring hand on Blair's shoulder. "This is part of raising a child, too. They make bad decisions sometimes and have to be shown the consequences."

"I'm not sure how to handle this," Blair admitted wearily. "If I'm too lenient, he won't learn a lesson and he might do it again. If I'm too strict, he's likely to rebel and do something even worse."

Her aunt looked at her sympathetically. "Since I never raised a child, I'm afraid I can't be much help. All I can suggest is that you follow your instincts, Blair. They've served you well with Jeffrey so far."

"I hope you're right," Blair said, turning toward the door without much enthusiasm.

Because it was raining lightly, Blair had driven into her aunt's driveway rather than parking in her own garage and walking over to collect Jeffrey, as she usually did. Jeffrey climbed silently into her car, looking so much like the angry, sullen, withdrawn boy he'd been before that it made Blair's chest ache.

She had been so focused on her nephew that she was surprised to find an unfamiliar vehicle parked in her driveway when she pulled in. It was one of those big four-wheel-drive sport vehicles in a gleaming silver. It looked new and expensive. It looked like something Scott McKay would drive, she thought, even as the driver's door opened and Scott stepped out into the drizzle, looking lean and tough—and darned near irresistible—in denim shirt, jeans and boots.

Just what she needed to top this day off.

A flash of excitement crossed Jeffrey's face. "It's Scott!" he said, then remembered that he was in trouble and fell silent again.

Blair drove past Scott into her garage, parked her car and turned off the engine. Scott stepped forward to open her door for her. "Hi. How's it going?"

She had rather hoped that time and distance had diluted her response to this man. The moment he took her hand to help her out of the car, she knew she'd hoped in vain. A jolt of excitement sizzled all the way through her, and she reclaimed her hand the moment she was on her feet.

"This is a surprise," she said unnecessarily. "We weren't expecting to see you today."

"I know. I just happened to be in the neighborhood and I thought I'd drop by and meet the cat. Unless this is a bad time?"

"Well..."

Jeffrey walked around the front of the car to join them. "Hi, Scott."

"Hi, part—hey, what happened to your face? Were you in an accident?"

"He 'accidentally' connected with another boy's fist," Blair remarked dryly.

"Some jerk hit him?" Scott's brows drew into a scowl. "Who was it? What's being done about this?"

"Before you get too outraged, you should probably know that Jeffrey hit first," Blair informed him.

That made him pause for a moment, his gaze on Jeffrey, who huddled miserably in front of them. "I see."

"Both boys have been suspended from school for the remainder of the week."

Scott nodded. "Sounds like you've got yourselves a situation here."

"You could say that."

"Right. So why don't we talk about it over dinner. I brought barbecue."

Blair blinked. "You—"

"I figured you'd like an excuse not to cook after a long day at the office, so I stopped for take-out. You don't mind if I hang around to help your aunt yell at you, do you, Jeff?"

"Uh, no, I guess not," Jeffrey answered, looking tentatively at Blair.

This evening was definitely spinning out of her control. Scott was obviously not asking permission to stay, though he would have no choice, of course, if she asked him to leave. Knowing she would do no such thing, she pulled her purse and briefcase out of the car and closed her door with a snap. "All right, you can stay. But it's only because you brought food," she added.

He grinned. "I'll keep that in mind in the future."

They would talk later about whether this would happen again in the future, Blair decided. She had to deal with Jeffrey first.

She sent Jeffrey to put away his backpack and wash his hands while Scott carried in a box from which wafted tempting aromas. "What happened to our Saturday-night date?" she asked as she helped him set out the food on the kitchen table.

"Still on. This is simply a predate dinner."

"It might have been nice if you'd given me some warning."

"Sorry. Want me to leave?"

She could tell from his expression that he expected her to do no such thing. "Just call first next time."

"Sure thing," he said a bit too easily. "So tell me about this fight Jeff got into. What started it?"

"I don't know yet. I had planned to sit him down and get all the details as soon as we got home."

"So what are you going to do to him?"

"I suppose that depends on the circumstances."

Jeffrey entered the room carrying his cat in his arms, his expression still wary but not as sullen as it had been before Scott appeared. "This is Belle," he announced.

Scott made a production of taking the cat and looking her over carefully. "She's a fine specimen," he pronounced, cradling the cat in his arm and rubbing her head. From her blissful expression and loud purring, it was evident that she enjoyed the attention.

Jeffrey seemed pleased by Scott's approval. "She's very smart."

"Yes, I can tell. She obviously likes me."

Jeffrey grinned, then remembered to look somber again.

Blair served the dinner of sliced barbecue meat with a spicy sauce, baked beans, coleslaw and potato salad. Scott had even provided soft, yeasty rolls to accompany the meal. He kept a running, humorous commentary going as they ate, maintaining a pleasant atmosphere so they could enjoy their food.

No one mentioned the fight.

"I brought peach cobbler for dessert," Scott said when the plates had been emptied. "But maybe we should wait on dessert," he added, patting his tummy to show that he was full.

"I think so," Blair agreed, wondering if she would be able to eat another bite that evening.

Scott turned to Jeffrey then. "Ready to tell us how the fight got started?"

Jeffrey shot a quick glance at Blair, then looked at Scott. "Can't I just tell you about it? You know, guy-to-guy?"

"No," Blair said firmly. "I want to hear this, too. What happened, Jeffrey?"

He sighed heavily. "Jason made me mad."

"So you hit him."

He nodded.

"How many times have we discussed this? Violence is *never* the answer, no matter what the other boy said. Regardless of how angry you were, the correct response was to walk away. You could have discussed the incident with me this evening and we would have decided the best course of action. I can assure you it would *not* have been a fistfight."

Jeffrey swallowed and nodded.

Blair didn't look away from him to judge Scott's reaction to her words. "Do you understand, Jeffrey? Next time someone makes you angry—and it *will* happen again—I expect you to handle the situation very differently."

Jeffrey's eyes flared. "I'm just supposed to let him say whatever he wants? I'm not supposed to do *anything* about it?"

"I told you what to do about it. You come to me."

He didn't look at all satisfied with her answer. She suspected that she hadn't quite convinced him he'd been wrong to lash out. She glanced at Scott then, wondering if a man's perspective would help. Surely Scott would agree that fist fighting had been the wrong choice. "Scott? Would you like to comment?"

He seemed to have been waiting to be invited into the

conversation. He looked at Jeffrey. "Why don't you tell us what he said that made you so angry?"

Still looking furious, Jeffrey spoke in a rush. "Jason's always giving me a hard time. He makes fun of me because I'm shorter than he is and because I'm new in town and because I live with my aunt. He said he heard my dad dumped me here because he didn't want me, and he didn't believe me when I said my dad's coming back to get me. And then he said I'll probably end up at Lost Springs with the other losers, and that's why Aunt Blair was there for that auction thing, because she's planning to send me there because she doesn't really want me."

Appalled, Blair struggled for words to tell Jeffrey what utter garbage that was. Scott spoke before she could. "Do you believe him, Jeff? That your aunt doesn't want you?"

Jeffrey cleared his throat. "Well, I—"

"Because it seems to me," Scott continued, "that Blair is happy to have you here. Look at all she's done for you in the past week. She even got you a cat just because you mentioned wanting one."

"I *told* Jason he was wrong," Jeffrey assured Blair, as if he was worried that she'd been offended. "I said you weren't trying to get rid of me, but he wouldn't believe me. He just kept saying it. So I hit him to make him shut up."

"The thing is that you knew he was wrong," Scott said. "That's all that really matters, isn't it?"

"Yeah, but—"

"What he said to you was vicious and unfounded, Jeffrey," Blair chimed in. "And I don't blame you for being angry. I feel that way myself. But you were still wrong to hit him."

"Wouldn't *you* have hit him, Scott?" Jeffrey demanded, obviously hoping for masculine moral support.

Blair held her breath.

"No," Scott answered flatly, to Blair's relief and Jeffrey's obvious disappointment. "I never waste my time on jerks, and that guy is obviously a jerk. You've got better things to do than argue with morons, and you shouldn't let them get you into trouble at school or anywhere else. Remember how we talked about keeping your own best interests in mind? Letting some dipstick sucker you into a fight or taunt you into doing something you know is wrong is hardly in your best interest."

"So I should have just walked away?" Jeffrey asked, his voice subdued.

"Yeah. But with an attitude."

"What do you mean?"

"Okay, I'll show you. Blair, want to help me with some role-playing?"

She was willing to do whatever it took to help Jeffrey get the message. "What do you want me to do?"

He stood, hooked his thumbs in the belt loops of his jeans and spread his booted feet in a casual pose. "I'm standing here minding my own business and you're a jerk spoiling for a fight. Go off on me so I can show the kid what to do."

"Go off on you?" she repeated uncertainly.

"Yeah. You know. Call me ugly or something."

That was enough to make Jeffrey snort with muffled laughter and Blair smile wryly. If there was one word that did not apply to Scott McKay, it was *ugly*. But she made an effort to play her part. "Hey, you," she said, exaggerating belligerence. "You're ugly."

He gave her a raised-eyebrow glance, as if she were

a bug that had caught his attention with its buzzing. In a cool voice, he asked, "I beg your pardon?"

"I said you're ugly," she repeated, crossing her arms over her chest. "And what's that getup you're wearing? You think you're some sort of cowboy or something?"

"Whatever." He turned his back to her and glanced pointedly at his watch.

"You're ugly and your horse wears army boots," Blair said, rather enjoying herself.

The look he gave her was chilling, though there was an undercurrent of amusement in his voice when he warned, "Don't talk about my horse."

"Or what, cowboy? You going to make me shut up?"

Jeffrey was giggling now, his hands over his mouth to quiet the sound.

Looking utterly bored, Scott stifled a yawn. "Not today. I have much better things to do." And then he dismissed her with a condescending look, turned and sauntered away, his head high, almost exuding cowboy confidence.

Blair chuckled. "Okay," she said. "You win."

"You take it all back?" he asked over his shoulder.

"Oh, yes," she assured him, then added meditatively, "except what I said about your horse."

He grinned and ruffled her hair on his way back to his seat. "Cute."

"That was real funny," Jeffrey commented, his smile gone again. "But it's not that easy. What if she didn't shut up? What if she followed you and kept yelling things at you?"

"Then I'd have kept walking," Scott replied. "Without a reaction, she'd have gotten bored and gone away."

"And what if he—I mean, what if she had thrown the

first punch? Wouldn't you fight back if someone hit you?''

"I would never use my physical strength against someone who is smaller or weaker—as your aunt obviously is. So it wouldn't have mattered if she had hit first, I wouldn't have hit back.''

"Jason's not smaller than me *or* weaker," Jeffrey muttered. "What if he had hit me first?''

"Well, he didn't, of course," Blair had to point out.

"And if he had," Scott added frankly, "you might have been forced to defend yourself. A man does everything he can to avoid a fight, but sometimes he isn't given a choice.''

Blair frowned. "Fighting is never the answer.''

Scott gave her a look. "C'mon, Blair, you don't expect him to let someone beat the crap out of him, do you?''

"I would hope he would try to get away without fighting.''

"Of course. That's what we were just talking about. I said it should be the last resort. So what Jeffrey should agree to is to never again be the guy who throws the first punch, no matter what drivel someone else spouts off. Can you promise us that, Jeffrey?''

"I'll try," the boy muttered.

Scott shook his head. "Not good enough. Before I went to Lost Springs, I was in a fight nearly every day. If someone even looked at me funny, I punched him. My counselor at Lost Springs made me promise I wouldn't start any more fights and I kept that promise, even though sometimes it was very hard to do.''

"You've never been in a fight since then?''

Scott hesitated only a moment before answering,

"I've never been in one without trying everything I could to avoid it. And I haven't struck the first blow."

"Scott made a promise," Blair emphasized before Jeffrey could ask for details about the fights Scott hadn't been able to avoid. "Will you make the same promise, Jeffrey? Will you agree that you won't start any more fights, no matter what the provocation?"

"Okay," Jeffrey conceded. "I won't hit first."

She supposed that was the best she could get at the moment. "Thank you. Now, as far as the next two days go, you'll have to spend them at Aunt Wanda's house since I'll be at my office. I'm going to instruct her that you are not to watch television or play video games during school hours. You'll attend to your schoolwork and read the book you've been assigned for your book report. I want the report finished by Sunday."

"But it isn't due till Wednesday," Jeffrey protested.

"Then you'll be finished early, won't you?" she asked implacably. "You'll have plenty of time to work on it."

"Psst," Scott said behind one hand. "Better quit while you're behind, partner. She's little, but she's feisty."

Jeffrey's mouth twitched in what might have been a faint smile. He nodded. "Okay. It will be finished by Sunday. Can I still play with Belle when we're home?" he asked worriedly.

"Of course. I'm not going to punish Belle because you messed up."

He looked relieved.

"Now that we've gotten that out of the way, can we have dessert?" Scott asked with a greedy look at the aluminum pan of cobbler. "You like peach cobbler, Jeff?"

"Yeah," Jeffrey agreed eagerly, obviously relieved that the discussion of his behavior was at an end.

Scott met Blair's eyes across the table, and he smiled. As her heart fluttered in reaction, she worried about just how much both she and Jeffrey were beginning to depend on him.

CHAPTER TEN

AFTER DESSERT, Blair sent Jeffrey to take his bath. "And don't splash Belle," she called after him. "Cats hate to get wet." She'd told him that before, but thought it bore repeating since Belle was right at his heels when he left the room.

"Okay, Aunt Blair," he shouted back.

She waited until he was out of sight, then groaned and laid her head on the table.

Scott chuckled sympathetically. "This child-raising thing isn't easy, is it?"

She answered without lifting her head. "I'll never survive it."

Resting a hand on her shoulder, he gave a bracing squeeze. "Sure you will. Remember what they say about what doesn't kill you makes you stronger?"

"Just shoot me," she moaned. "Shoot me now."

He laughed. "Come on, Blair, it isn't that bad. Trust me, I've seen some rotten kids—hell, I *was* a rotten kid. Jeff's just high-spirited."

"High-spirited,'" she repeated, finally lifting her head. "Isn't that just another way of saying pain in the—"

"Neck," he supplied with a quick grin.

"Yeah, that's what I was going to say."

He urged her to her feet. "You look as though you could use a hug."

Though she was a bit skeptical of his motives, he was right about one thing—she *could* use a hug. She burrowed into his chest. "What if I handled that all wrong? What if he ends up in a tower with a rifle someday because I made him repress his anger? Or what if he knocks over a bank or…"

"Has anyone ever told you that you have a slight tendency to overreact, Counselor?"

He was teasing her, but she nodded anyway. "I know. I just worry so much about doing the right thing."

"You're doing fine."

"In the past week, he has gotten lost, scraped his hands and knees, been in a fight and got a black eye, and he's been suspended from school. If I do any better, he's likely to end up in traction or in jail."

Scott's arms tightened. "Buck up, Blair. Remember, you've got a few years yet before he enters puberty."

With a gasp, she buried her face in his shoulder again.

Laughing softly, Scott lifted her head with his fingertips. "Have I mentioned yet this evening that you look gorgeous? Very prim and professional in your neat blue lawyer suit."

Her mouth quirked into a crooked smile. "Sometimes I'm not sure if you're complimenting me or mocking me."

"Definitely complimenting you," he assured her. "I'm beginning to realize—rather to my surprise, I'll admit—that this particular prim and proper attorney appeals to me very much."

Even knowing that he was probably feeding her a line, she couldn't help but respond in a purely feminine manner. "And I have to admit—greatly to *my* surprise—that I'm rather taken with a certain charming cowboy."

He seemed quite pleased with her comment. So pleased, in fact, that he kissed her.

The teasing quickly faded from the embrace. Scott's mouth was hungry against hers, almost fierce as he claimed her lips and then urged them apart. His hands were warm through her 'neat blue lawyer suit' as they swept her body from shoulders to hips. They stood thigh-to-thigh, so that Blair couldn't help but be aware of Scott's reaction to the contact. His arousal only fueled her own.

Blair's breathing was unsteady when Scott finally lifted his head. His was ragged-edged, his face a bit flushed, his eyes glittering. "Do you know what I would *really* like for dessert this evening?"

Reluctantly, she drew herself out of his arms. "You've already had your dessert," she reminded him firmly. *And then some.*

He drew a deep breath. "I suppose it will have to do—for tonight."

He left unsaid the implication that there would be other times when neither of them would want to stop with a kiss. Though she still doubted the wisdom of this course she was taking, she was beginning to accept its inevitability. Scott didn't linger long after that interlude. He said good-night to Jeffrey, who was still damp from his bath and dressed in Star Wars pajamas, his bruised face looking sweet and innocent. And then Scott kissed Blair's cheek. "Seven o'clock Saturday evening?"

She nodded. "Pick me up here?"

"Right. I'll be counting the minutes," he murmured as he stepped away.

So would she, Blair thought in resignation.

IT WASN'T a major rodeo event Blair and Jeffrey attended Saturday morning. The competitors weren't big stars in pursuit of a heavy rodeo-champion belt buckle. This event was to benefit a local charity, and the entrants were area ranchers and teenagers, some former rodeo competitors, a few young Shane Daniels wanna-bes and others who were simply competing for fun and charity.

The audience consisted mostly of local families out for a good time on a beautiful spring morning. Dress was western casual—which meant Blair blended in well enough in her denim shirt with a red plaid yoke, comfortably loose-fitting jeans and the leather hiking boots she'd worn at Scott's cabin. In his baggy jeans, oversize jersey and black basketball shoes, Jeffrey looked more urban than western, but he seemed intrigued by the new experience.

He tossed his shaggy hair out of his face and glanced around the crowd, studying the boys who were close to his age. "Maybe I should get a cowboy hat," he muttered.

Blair rested a hand on his shoulder. "Maybe you should."

A pretty little girl with long brown hair and big brown eyes passed them with her parents. She smiled shyly. "Hi, Jeffrey."

Jeffrey straightened his shoulders. "Hey."

"Who was that?" Blair asked, noticing that Jeffrey watched the little girl walk away.

He quickly turned his gaze forward, feigning indifference. "That's Casey. She goes to my school."

"She seems nice."

"She's okay. For a girl."

"Of course. We'd better go find a seat. It looks as though the stands are filling up quickly."

The seats they found were in the center of the stands,

surrounded by a noisily enthusiastic crowd. Jeffrey ended up sitting next to another student from his school, a boy who was in the fifth grade. Blair watched as they greeted each other with nods and mutters. She wanted to nudge Jeffrey and encourage him to make conversation with the other boy, who looked quite nice—but she knew her interference would only be counterproductive. As much as she wanted Jeffrey to make friends, she knew she couldn't make them for him.

The rodeo got under way with the calf-roping event. The audience cheered and laughed as young competitors pitted their skills against fast-moving, feisty calves. Sometimes the cowboys prevailed and sometimes the calves loped away untouched, but it was all quite entertaining. Blair was concerned at first for the animals' safety, but she soon relaxed, realizing that the calves were occasionally annoyed, but unharmed.

"No, ma'am, they won't hurt them calves," the portly rancher sitting elbow-to-elbow beside her commented. "Rodeo comes from real ranch work, you know. Part of the skill is to handle the animals without damaging them."

From that point on, he seemed to think it was his duty to educate Blair on some of the finer points of each event. He kept up an amusing running commentary, including dry comments about the competitors, giving her an impromptu lesson on how to tell the real cattlemen from the city dudes. She noticed, to her satisfaction, that Jeffrey had begun to talk to the boy from his school.

Though all the events were rough-and-tumble, it was the bull-riding event that really made Blair wince. "Now, *this* looks dangerous," she murmured to the congenial cattleman next to her.

"Oh, no, ma'am. Them bulls are tough. They don't get hurt."

She gaped at him. "I wasn't talking about the bulls. I meant the riders. And those guys in the silly clothes and makeup who keep running in front of the bulls."

"They're called clowns, ma'am. Their main job is to try to keep the bulls off the riders once they're down."

She grimaced when a would-be rider went hurtling through the air to land hard in the dirt. The bull immediately turned, lowered his head and made a valiant effort to stomp the fallen cowboy, but the clowns' interference gave the cowboy time to scramble to his feet and over the fence. "You aren't telling me those guys never get hurt?"

"Well, no. Broken bones are as much a part of rodeo as boots and spurs," her new friend admitted with a crooked grin. "Back when I was young enough and dumb enough to do some riding, I broke both arms, an ankle, a whole bunch of ribs and my tailbone—now *that* hurt," he added reflectively.

Her attention split between the action in the arena and her talkative companion, Blair asked curiously, "Then why did you do it?"

His self-deprecating grin was charming. "Why, for the fun of it, darlin'."

She wrinkled her nose. "If that's your idea of fun..."

A familiar name spoken over the loudspeaker suddenly caught her attention. "Did he just say—"

"Aunt Blair, Scott's riding next!" Jeffrey said excitedly.

Before she could recover from her surprise, the gate opened and a massive black bull exploded into the arena with Scott McKay straddling its back. His gloved right hand was secured beneath the rope around the creature's neck, and he held his left arm suspended in the air for balance. A dusty black hat was pulled low over his face. Along with the leather vest, denim shirt, chaps and boots, the ensemble made him look the exact opposite of the man in the suit and silk tie that Blair had bought at the bachelor auction. She could hardly believe she'd been so mistaken about him.

The bull bucked and twisted, furiously trying to rid itself of its human burden. Dirt flew beneath its slashing hooves and Blair could only imagine the damage those hooves could do to a human body. Scott shifted dangerously to one side, seeming in imminent risk of sliding directly beneath the animal. Blair covered her face with her hands, watching through her fingers as he somehow recovered his balance.

It seemed like forever before a buzzer indicated that eight seconds had passed. The clowns ran toward the bull as the crowd cheered and Jeffrey crowed with pleasure.

"He made it, ma'am. The full eight. He can dismount now."

But just as the rancher spoke so confidently, the bull gave a huge lunge and twist that sent Scott flying. He landed some distance away with a bone-jarring thud and billowing clouds of dust. Blair's breathing stopped when Scott didn't immediately move.

The clowns ran the bull through a gate and out of the arena while a couple of guys ran toward Scott.

"Is he hurt, Aunt Blair?" Jeffrey asked in a small voice.

"I don't know, sweetie," she said, covering his hand with hers.

They both sighed in relief when Scott sat up, waving away the two men who would have helped him to his feet. He stood on his own power, although his movements were somewhat stiff. The crowd applauded as he limped away, pausing to scoop his hat off the ground and then wave it at the cheering audience, a showman to the end.

"He's okay, Aunt Blair," Jeffrey said, then looked to her for confirmation.

She managed a smile. "Yes, he seems to be."

At least he was until she got hold of him and ripped a piece off his hide for scaring her—for scaring Jeffrey so badly, she corrected herself.

"Friend of yours, ma'am?" the rancher inquired.

She nodded, unsure exactly how to describe her connection with Scott McKay.

"He done real good. He's made it to the finals."

She turned to him in disbelief, ignoring the ride that had just started in the arena. "You mean he's going to do that *again?*"

"Well, yes, ma'am. There were two other riders so far who hung on for eight seconds."

She groaned and wondered if she should leave right then rather than go through that traumatic experience again.

Her new friend smiled and patted her knee in a fatherly fashion. "Don't you worry, darlin'. Your friend looked like he knows what he's doing."

Was that before or after he'd eaten dirt? Blair wanted to ask as she shifted on the hard seat and braced herself for the finals.

SCOTT WINCED A LITTLE when he climbed out of his Yukon in Blair's driveway that evening. His body was reminding him graphically of the two hard falls he'd taken earlier that day. The first had mostly just knocked the wind out of him. The next—after only five seconds on that mean SOB he'd been assigned for the second ride—had hurt. No broken bones this time, fortunately, only a few ugly bruises, but he ached all over.

It occurred to him that he was getting a bit too old for some of the activities he had enjoyed in the past, but he dismissed that thought immediately. He had a lot of life in him yet, he decided firmly, and several things still to try. He wasn't quite ready for a rocking chair.

He eyed the doorbell, wondering how Blair would react to having seen him ride. He hadn't told her he would be participating in the rodeo—yet another charity contribution on his part. He'd thought it amusing to surprise her. Of course, he'd have preferred to land victoriously on his feet rather than ignobly on his face. He'd hoped to find Blair and Jeffrey after the rodeo, but by the time he'd gotten checked out and cleaned up, they had already gone.

Since Blair had last seen him filthy and bedraggled, he'd taken pains with his appearance this evening, choosing a gray, tweedy sport coat and navy slacks with an open-necked pale blue shirt. He'd debated for a time about whether he should add a tie—after all, it had been a tie that had prompted Blair to bid on him at the auction—but he'd decided to skip it. He'd been making an effort to introduce Blair to the real Scott McKay, rather than the illusion she'd purchased, and a tie wasn't a typical part of the picture.

He pushed her doorbell and donned his most charming smile.

The smile became genuine when Jeffrey opened the door, holding his cat in his arms. "Well, hi, partner. How's it going? I thought you'd be at your great-aunt's house."

"She's staying with me here. You were so cool at the rodeo today, Scott."

He smiled wryly. "I lost, Jeff."

"Yeah, but you should have won," the boy insisted loyally. "Those other guys got easier bulls than you for the second ride."

It wasn't entirely accurate, but Scott appreciated the support. "Well, that's the game. Sometimes you win the buckle, other times you're face down in dung."

"Eeww, gross," Jeffrey said with relish. "Are you okay, Scott? You sure fell hard."

"Yeah, just a few bruises. Guess you know how that feels, hmm?" he added, gently touching the bruise on Jeffrey's face.

Jeffrey wrinkled his nose, looking a lot like his aunt at that moment. "Yeah, it's kinda sore."

"Uh-huh. Me, too."

"Invite the gentleman in, Jeffrey. Don't just leave him standing on the doorstep."

In response to the woman's voice from behind him, Jeffrey flushed and moved quickly aside. "Sorry. Come in, Scott."

"Thank you." He crossed the threshold and glanced toward the broad-hipped, gray-haired, pleasant-faced woman in the living room doorway. "Will you introduce us, Jeff?"

Looking quite important, Jeffrey squared his shoulders. "Aunt Wanda, this is my friend, Scott McKay. Scott, this is my great-aunt Wanda. Er, Mrs. Townsend," he added quickly.

Wanda nodded approvingly to the boy before extending her right hand to Scott. "It's a pleasure to meet you, Mr. McKay. I've heard a great deal about you."

"The pleasure is mine, Mrs. Townsend."

"Jeffrey told me he saw you ride in a rodeo this morning."

"A charity event," he explained. "The coordinator is an old acquaintance who talked me into participating."

"That was very generous of you. You've donated a great deal of your time to charity lately."

Scott shrugged. "It was just a coincidence that two charity functions fell almost back-to-back."

"Please, won't you have a seat?" She motioned toward the sofa. "I'm afraid Blair's tied up with a telephone call from one of her clients. I'm sure she'll try to hurry. In the meantime, can I get you something to drink?"

"No, thank you." He waited until she was seated, then took a place on the couch. Jeffrey immediately sat beside him, just a bit closer than absolutely necessary.

"When did you learn to ride, Scott?" the boy demanded eagerly. "Was it scary the first time? Have you ever been stepped on?"

"I was a teenager, and yes, it was pretty scary. And no, I haven't been stepped on—at least, not full weight. I've been kicked by a hoof or two, and grazed by a couple of horns, but on the whole I've been pretty lucky. But then, I've never pursued rodeo full time—not like Shane Daniels or the other rodeo stars. For me, it's always been just a hobby."

"An insane hobby." Blair entered the room with that dry comment, looking fresh and pretty in a purple pantsuit in some soft, silky fabric that made his palms itch to feel it.

He rose to his feet, hiding the dull protests from his assorted bruises. "You look great," he greeted her. "All finished with business for the evening?"

"Yes. At least, I hope so," she added, crossing her

fingers. "I have a slightly hysterical client who thinks I should be on call twenty-four hours a day."

Wanda smiled faintly. "Your uncle had a few of those—probably the same ones you're dealing with. I can't tell you how many dinners and movies were interrupted by calls for him."

Scott shook his head. "The best way to deal with that sort of thing is to make your office hours very clear and refuse to discuss business during your personal hours."

"I'm afraid that's not always possible," Blair said lightly. "Some problems simply can't be handled Monday through Friday from nine to five."

He lifted a shoulder. "From my experience, there are few situations that can't be put off until later."

A frown that might have expressed disapproval crossed Blair's face, but she smoothed it quickly. "Are you ready to go?"

"Yes." He turned to her aunt. "It was very nice to meet you, Mrs. Townsend. I predict we will meet again."

"I'll look forward to it," she said with a smile.

Blair glanced at her nephew, who stood close to Scott's side. "Jeffrey, be good for Aunt Wanda. Don't give her any grief about bedtime."

"Okay." He was obviously reluctant for Scott to leave. "When will I see you again, Scott?"

"How about next weekend?" Scott suggested. "That is, if it's okay with your aunt."

Jeffrey was nearly beside himself with excitement. "Please, please, Aunt Blair. Can we go?"

Although Blair didn't look happy about being put on the spot, she hesitantly nodded. "I don't really see why not."

"Then it's settled," Scott said, ruffling the boy's

shaggy hair, feeling a wave of affection go through him. Jeffrey was a cute kid, despite his problems. He was young enough to turn himself around and bright enough to have a fine future ahead of him. Scott was glad to make any contribution to that future he could.

Looking extremely satisfied, Jeffrey allowed them to leave without further delay.

Outside, Scott opened the passenger door to his Yukon and helped Blair into the high seat. He closed her door for her, then loped a bit stiffly around the front of the vehicle to his own side. He was determined to conceal any discomfort he felt this evening. He suspected that Blair might not be overly sympathetic, unlike the buckle bunnies who spent so much time and energy kissing the bruises of major rodeo stars.

Apparently, he wasn't quite as good an actor as he had thought. "You were hurt this morning, weren't you?" she demanded as soon as he had settled behind the wheel and fastened his seat belt.

He started the engine. "No. Couple of bruises, that's all."

"It's a miracle you didn't break your neck."

Backing out of the driveway, he kept his voice casual. "One of the first things you learn in rodeo is to fall as safely as possible. Serious injuries happen, of course, but they're rare, considering how many participate in the sport."

"I saw that movie—the one about the handsome young rodeo star who died when he was gored by a bull." Her tone was so accusatory, Scott felt almost as if she blamed *him* for the tragedy.

"That was one of the rare incidents I mentioned. Accidents happen, Blair. In rodeo—and in everyday life."

"Especially in *your* type of everyday life. Riding

bulls, racing cars, jumping out of planes—I'm beginning to wonder if you value your life at all.''

"More than you could possibly understand," he responded gently. "I'm not trying to shorten my life, Blair. I'm trying to experience it to the fullest."

"And yet you have no serious bonds with anyone else because you don't want anyone to worry about you or grieve for you if you don't survive."

He grimaced in response to her all-too-accurate summation of things he had said to her. "Something like that," he agreed.

"Then there's an important part of life you *aren't* experiencing, isn't there?" she countered logically.

He gave a resigned, half-amused shake of his head. "You're still in lawyer mode. You're trying to trap me with my own words."

"I'm not trying to trap you in any way," she replied quietly.

After a somewhat tense pause, Scott cleared his throat. "So, other than thinking of all the entrants as reckless fools, how did you like your first rodeo?"

"It was…interesting. A very nice man sitting next to me explained some of the things that were going on— the origins of the events and how they have evolved, how they're scored and so on."

"A very nice man?" Scott repeated, not liking the sound of that. "Anyone I know?"

"I don't know, he didn't say. His name is Ben and he's a local rancher. About sixty, I would guess. Average height, but considerably overweight. Plainspoken, but pleasant."

Relaxing again, Scott shook his head. "No, I can't say I know him. Did Jeff have a good time?"

"He enjoyed it very much. He spent a lot of time

talking to a boy from his school. Maybe he'll start making more friends if he attends more local events.''

"Baseball season starts in the next couple of weeks. Have you considered signing him up?"

"I tried to talk him into it, but he refused. He said he didn't see the point since he doesn't expect to be in Lightning Creek for the entire season.''

"Because he thinks his father will be back for him?" She nodded.

"Have you ever suggested to the kid that his father might not be back for a long time? That he should be prepared to make a life for himself here with you?"

"I've hinted. He refuses to hear it. To push it any further would only make him angry and defensive again.''

"You could be right," Scott conceded. Despite his own experiences, he was no expert on child psychology. Blair had to trust her instincts on this.

"Where are we going?" She was looking out the side window in curiosity, as if she'd only just become aware that they had left Lightning Creek, and its limited selection of dining establishments, behind.

"Someplace where we can have a delicious meal and a relaxing, private atmosphere in which to enjoy it. My ranch.''

She half turned on her seat to face him. "We're going to *your* place? How far is it?"

"Another forty minutes or so. I hope you aren't starving.''

"Are you cooking dinner for us?"

He shook his head with a laugh. "I said we're going to have delicious food, remember? That pretty much disqualifies me, since grilled trout is my only company dish, and I've already made that for you. My house-

keeper is preparing a meal for us. She's a great cook. I
think you'll enjoy it."

"Your housekeeper?"

He nodded. "Margaret. She's a treasure. She's been
with me for fifteen years, ever since her husband died
of cancer. Her children were grown and have moved
away and she wanted a home to take care of—and
maybe someone new to mother," he added ironically.
"I suppose you could say she found both with me."

"She lives with you?"

"Yes, she has a small suite at the back of the house—
a bedroom, bath and sitting room. She says it's all she
needs."

"Does anyone else live on the ranch?"

"My ranch foreman and his wife have a bungalow
not far from the main house. The hands live in the bunkhouse, of course. And then there's Carolyn, my assistant.
She has a bedroom and sitting room upstairs in the main
house."

That seemed to startle Blair more than anything he'd
said so far. "Your assistant lives with you?"

"She lives in the same house," he corrected her. "Remember, I'm not there that often. Carolyn keeps things
running smoothly while I'm gone—not the ranch oper-
ations, my foreman takes care of that—the bookkeeping
and correspondence and payroll and everyday business
things like that. She also keeps track of my earnings
from the outside investments my parents left me."

"She doesn't have a family?"

"No. She's related to my housekeeper—the daughter
of a cousin. That's how I found her. Margaret brought
her to me."

Though she still looked a bit confused, Blair didn't

ask any more questions. Scott knew she would understand better when she met Carolyn.

"It sounds as if you're responsible for the livelihood of quite a few people."

He wasn't sure he would have worded it quite that way. "The ranch supports quite a few people," he amended.

"Don't you own the ranch?"

"Since my grandparents died and left it to me, yes."

"Then you're responsible."

Growing even more uncomfortable, he murmured, "The ranch gets along just fine without me, for the most part."

"Hmm."

He wasn't sure what that sound meant, but he didn't really want to ask just then. "How's Jeffrey's suspension going?" he asked instead.

"I haven't let it become a vacation. He's worked harder on his studies during the past few days than he has in the whole six months he's lived with me."

"I'm sure it's been an educational experience for him in many ways."

"I hope so."

So much for that conversation. "He's still happy with his cat?"

"They're practically joined at the hip."

"Jeffrey's following through taking care of her so far?"

"Yes, he's almost hovering over her. I still expect the novelty to wear off some, but so far it's working out very well."

They made casual conversation along those lines during the remainder of the drive, but were never quite as comfortable together as Scott would have liked. Blair seemed to have erected a barrier of some sort between them. He felt almost as if he might encounter an invisible force field if he should try to reach out to touch her.

What was going on? Did this have something to do with the rodeo this morning? When he and Blair had last parted, it had been with a kiss. She sure wasn't encouraging him to kiss her now.

He hoped to change that before the evening ended.

CHAPTER ELEVEN

BLAIR DIDN'T KNOW what she'd expected from Scott's ranch house, but it wasn't the large, sprawling, buff brick, two-story structure he parked in front of. It looked like a comfortable, upper-class family home, she thought as he opened her door for her. Yet she knew no family lived in it, nor did Scott seem in any hurry to change that.

"Hey, Scott. The crew got that new fence finished this afternoon," someone hollered from behind them.

Both Scott and Blair turned in response to the voice. A tall, gangly-limbed man with a weathered face and a beer belly ambled toward them, his features illuminated by numerous security lights. A big, somewhat dopey-looking yellow dog loped along at his heels. Scott slipped a hand beneath Blair's arm. "Here's someone you should meet," he said. "Blair Townsend, this is my foreman, Jake Gordon."

"Nice to meet you, Miz Townsend," the older man drawled. "Want I should take you aside and warn you about the scoundrel you're dining with this evening?"

She laughed and shook her head. "Thank you, but that won't be necessary, Mr. Gordon. I doubt there's much you can tell me that I haven't already figured out for myself."

"Got yourself a smart one here, boy," the foreman

said to Scott, his mouth crooking into a grin. "That's a right refreshing change."

"Okay, you can drop the Gary Cooper routine now," Scott answered dryly, looking up from the dog, who was eagerly trying to climb him to lick his face. "Blair's sharp enough to know an old fake when she meets one."

The foreman chuckled and winked at Blair.

"This is Cooper," Scott said, rising and holding the dog down with a hand on his massive head to keep him from jumping on him. "You heard me tell Jeffrey about him."

Blair nodded and tentatively patted the friendly dog. "Is he named after Gary Cooper?"

"Of course. I was hoping the name would give him some dignity. It didn't work."

Grinning, the foreman moved on, whistling for the dog to follow him, then calling over his shoulder that it had been a pleasure to meet Blair.

"I like him," Blair murmured as Scott escorted her up the front steps.

"Yeah. He's a great guy. A real clown. And I'm firing him tomorrow for not showing me enough respect."

"Don't you dare."

Chuckling to show he was only kidding, he led her into an airy foyer done in light woods and polished marble. A curving staircase led to an open gallery area, and a brass-and-crystal chandelier gleamed overhead. It wasn't opulent, but warmly welcoming, she decided. "Did your grandmother decorate?"

He shook his head. "I had everything redone after her death. She preferred darker colors and heavy antiques."

Blair wondered if Scott had contributed to the new look or if he'd simply left everything in a decorator's hands. "It's lovely."

"Thank you. Oh, Margaret, there you are. This is my friend Blair Townsend. Blair, Margaret O'Connell, the treasure of my life."

Margaret appeared to be in her late fifties. Her hair was a faded red mixed liberally with gray, her skin was lined and freckled, and she was almost as broad as she was tall. Her smile was wide and friendly, and her blue eyes were kind behind the thick lenses of her glasses. "How do you do, Ms. Townsend?"

"It's a pleasure to meet you, Mrs. O'Connell. Scott has spoken very highly of you."

"He's a sweet boy," she responded fondly, patting Scott's cheek with her chubby hand as though he were no older than Jeffrey. "And, please, call me Margaret. Everyone does."

Blair liked the woman immediately. It wasn't hard to tell why there had been so much affection in Scott's voice when he'd mentioned her.

"Dinner's ready whenever you'd like to eat, Scott," Margaret added, her tone easily familiar. "I'll keep it warm if you and Ms. Townsend would like to have a cocktail before dining."

Scott looked inquiringly at Blair. She smiled and shook her head. "Actually, I'm starving," she admitted. "Lunch was a hot dog at the rodeo arena, and that was hours ago."

"Then allow me to escort you to the dining room," he said, offering his arm.

She hesitated only a moment before slipping her hand beneath his arm. Before Scott had picked her up, she'd made a decision to keep him at a distance this evening. The kisses had to stop, she had told herself, before they led to something that couldn't possibly end well.

Seeing him at the rodeo had only underscored how

very different their lives were. And while she didn't want to interfere with the bond that had formed between Jeffrey and Scott, she had also vowed to be somewhat more careful about letting her nephew be influenced by Scott. Although Scott had made a success of himself since his time at Lost Springs, his was certainly not a life-style Blair wanted Jeffrey to emulate.

They had just stepped into a wide hallway when a woman in a wheelchair glided toward them from the other end. The woman was probably in her mid-forties, fair-haired and light complexioned. She seemed to have full use of her body from the waist up, but her legs were stick thin and obviously useless. She smiled when she caught Blair's eyes. "You must be Blair Townsend. I'm Carolyn Roberts. We spoke on the phone."

"Of course. It's nice to meet you."

Scott released Blair to rest a gentle hand on Carolyn's shoulder. "This place would literally fall apart without Carolyn. She keeps us all in line."

"Speaking of which," Carolyn replied, "will you *please* make time to meet with me tomorrow, Scott? We have to look over those papers and I absolutely must have some decisions and signatures from you."

"Yeah. Okay."

"Promise me, Scott," she insisted, unconvinced.

He sighed. "I promise. How about one o'clock? Right after lunch."

She nodded in satisfaction. "I warn you, if you don't show, I'll come looking for you. And it won't be pretty when I find you."

"I'll be there," he repeated. "Jeez, what a grouch."

Unoffended by his good-natured gibe, Carolyn glanced apologetically at Blair. "I'm sorry to interfere with your evening, but he's here so rarely, I have to corner him whenever I get the chance. If he would come home a bit more often, there wouldn't be so many crises to take care of at once," she added pointedly.

So Scott *was* neglecting his responsibilities when he took off on his reckless adventures, Blair thought without surprise. And he was mistaken about something else, as well—there would be people who grieved if something happened to him. It was obvious that Jake and Margaret and Carolyn cared about him. And they depended on him. She imagined they worried about his dangerous behavior more than he suspected.

All the more reason for her not to get too deeply involved with him, she reminded herself.

"Are you joining us for dinner?" Blair asked Carolyn, thinking her presence would diffuse some of the awareness between Scott and herself.

But Carolyn shook her head. "I've already eaten, thank you. I was just on my way to my rooms to relax a bit before bedtime."

Scott leaned over to plant a kiss on top of her head. "Good night, Caro. Sleep well."

"Carolyn seems very nice," Blair said as Scott held her chair for her once they were in the beautifully decorated dining room. "Has she been with you long?"

"Four years. Things were really a mess around here before she took over. Now I don't know what we would do without her."

"And she's content to live here—at the office, so to speak?"

"She gets away occasionally to visit family, but she prefers to stay here for the most part. Her rooms are upstairs where she has more space and privacy—I had an elevator installed for her behind the main staircase.

She has a few health problems. Margaret cares for her when she's ill.''

"Has she always been in a wheelchair?"

Scott's expression turned grave. "No. She was in a terrible car accident seven years ago. Her husband and daughter were killed. Carolyn was hospitalized for a very long time. I'm told that it was practically a miracle that she's recovered as well as she has."

Blair's heart ached with sympathy for the other woman's tragedies—and admiration that she could still smile and tease and almost single-handedly manage Scott's office responsibilities. "You said the accident was seven years ago and she's been with you four years. Where did she live before she came here?"

"With her mother—Margaret's cousin. But Carolyn doesn't want to be cared for. She likes knowing she has an important job to fill."

That didn't surprise Blair. The woman she had just met looked like a person who would prefer to pull her own weight. And she seemed to do so quite admirably here.

Even as much as he relied on Carolyn, Scott was being very generous to provide her with a job and a home and facilities here—probably for as long as she needed them—just as he'd given Margaret a home, and who knew how many others. He'd donated his time to the bachelor auction and the charity rodeo, both for very worthy causes, and he'd been so kind to Jeffrey. It wasn't easy resisting this footloose, but undeniably generous, cowboy. Somehow, she was going to have to find a way.

Margaret entered the dining room then to serve dinner. She kept up a running dialogue with Scott while she did so, making Blair laugh at their witticisms. The meal was as delicious as Scott promised—crisp salads followed by glazed ham with garlic-roasted potatoes and tender asparagus spears.

"Leave room for dessert," Margaret ordered when she left them to their meals. "I've got strawberry shortcake."

"If I keep eating with you, I'm going to have to buy new clothes," Blair told Scott ruefully when Margaret returned to the kitchen. "My old ones are going to be too small."

He smiled at her. "I wouldn't worry about that. You don't have an extra ounce anywhere."

She hastily concentrated on her meal.

Margaret served the shortcake and then stepped back from the table. "Is there anything else I can do for you two this evening?"

"No, Margaret, you've already gone out of your way for us. Thank you," Scott replied warmly.

"I'll finish cleaning up the kitchen and then watch a little TV before bedtime. It was sure nice to meet you, Ms. Townsend."

"Please call me Blair," she said with a smile, uncomfortable with the formality in such an informal household. "The dinner was excellent, Margaret."

The compliment seemed to please her. "I'm real glad you enjoyed it, Ms.—Blair."

"She likes you," Scott confided when they were alone again.

"I like her, too. You've assembled a very nice family here."

He seemed taken aback by her wording. "It's hardly a family. This is my staff, Blair."

"Hmm," she murmured, more taken with her own description. It wasn't hard to envision Jake as a father figure for Scott, Margaret a mother to him and Carolyn an older sister. And the men in the bunkhouse—brothers? For a man who claimed to need no family ties, Scott had surrounded himself with them.

When they had finished their desserts, Scott stood. "Why don't we move to the den? I'll refill our coffee cups first."

That sounded quite cozy—too cozy, perhaps. She glanced at her watch as she rose to her feet. "It's getting rather late...."

He chuckled. "What's the matter, Blair? Did your aunt give you a curfew?"

"No," she admitted. "She said she would spend the night if I was very late, but—"

"Then let's go get comfortable."

She swallowed and nodded, finding no reasonable excuse.

Scott's den had obviously been furnished for maximum comfort. It was filled with oversize leather furniture, state-of-the-art entertainment equipment and shelves of books, videos and CDs. It was a completely self-indulgent room—as typical of Scott as his generous gestures and impulsive kindnesses.

"Very nice," she approved, sinking into a thickly cushioned leather sofa.

After shrugging out of his jacket and tossing it over the back of a chair, Scott settled on the couch beside her. "Thanks. I enjoy it."

"When you're here."

"When I'm here," he agreed blandly.

"Your staff obviously misses you when you're away."

"They get along very well without me."

Blair sipped her coffee, deciding not to argue with

him. After all, it was none of her business whether he took his responsibilities to his ranch and his employees seriously.

Scott set his coffee cup on the table in front of them. "Blair, what's wrong?"

She gazed into her coffee cup as though she saw something fascinating there. "I don't know what you mean."

"You've been acting a bit strangely all evening. Is something bothering you? Something from your work? The phone call you took before I picked you up?"

She shook her head. "No, my work is going fine. I'm handling a couple of sticky cases, but nothing I can't manage."

"Is it Jeff? Has he done something else to worry you?"

"No. Not since the fight he got into. He's been on very good behavior since then—at least, most of the time."

"Then what is it?"

"Really, there's nothing wrong."

"Blair." He took the cup out of her hands and set it beside his. Then he took both her hands in his, gazing deeply into her eyes. "I've known you for a very long time," he said gravely. "Through thick and thin, we've come a long way together. I know your every expression. I know when you're happy or sad or troubled or..."

She couldn't help but laugh. "You're so full of it."

His eyebrows rose comically. "I beg your pardon?"

"We've known each other less than a month. You don't know anything about me."

"Oh, no?" His thumbs moved slowly over the backs of her hands. "You might be surprised."

Heat was starting to course through her from her hands outward. It was hard to keep her tone light and casual when he was turning her into mush by just holding her hands. His thumbs circled her knuckles, dipping between them.... She barely suppressed a shiver.

"Would you like me to tell you what I know about you?"

She was still looking at their hands. "Mmm? Oh, no, that's not—"

"You have a big heart," he began, ignoring her protest—as usual. "You take your responsibilities very seriously—maybe a bit too seriously at times. You're intelligent and competent and occasionally a bit intimidating. You're prim and proper outside but warm and passionate on the inside—though you do your best to hide it, because you're rather afraid of that side of yourself."

She was growing uncomfortable. "Scott—"

"I think you've been disappointed in romance a time or two—probably by men who didn't understand you or weren't strong enough for you. You expect a lot from others—but no more than you demand of yourself. You worry too much and play too little, and you make me crazy when you wrinkle your nose and fuss at me."

She was in serious danger of melting right into his leather couch. "You're making me nervous."

His mouth crooked into a lopsided—and devastating—smile. "I like the sound of that."

She shook her head. "I really don't think—"

He silenced her with a finger across her lips. "The problem is that you think entirely too much. Sometimes it's better just to feel," he said, leaning closer. "To experience. To surrender..."

The last words were murmured against her lips. And

all of Blair's best intentions evaporated in the heat the kiss generated. She wrapped her arms around his neck, ignoring the mocking little voice that chided her for being so easily charmed by this man.

His hands began to wander, sliding across the silky pantsuit, inching into territory he hadn't explored before. For the first time, Blair knew what it was like to have his hands on her breasts, on her thighs. And for the first time, she allowed herself to touch in return. She slid a hand lingeringly across his solid chest and down to his flat, firm stomach. And then she dropped her hand to his knee and slid it slowly upward. His thighs were rock-solid, she noted with a thrill.

He would feel so strong and powerful against her, she thought, her mind filling with images that made her have to swallow a groan. She had no doubt that he would make her feel things she had never felt before. Things she had a sudden deep, desperate craving to feel.

Scott shifted his weight and Blair found herself on her back beneath him, resenting the layers of clothing that still separated them.

She wasn't entirely oblivious to their surroundings, though such details occupied only a small part of her mind. Her voice emerged as a breathy whisper. "Scott?"

"Mmm?" He had his face buried in the hollow of her throat, his lips moving against the pulse that hammered so erratically there.

Almost involuntarily, she arched into his hand as he slowly kneaded her right breast, his talented thumb rotating against her nipple. She nearly forgot what she had intended to say. "What about…your housekeeper?" she asked, remembering. "Your assistant?"

He scooted a couple of inches downward, bringing his mouth closer to her breasts. "They're both in bed," he assured her. "They consider this end of the house my private quarters, and they won't come in without my permission."

Which meant she and Scott had complete privacy. She couldn't use his staff as an excuse to bring this to an end. She would have to come up with another one.

The problem was, she thought as Scott kissed the soft skin just above her low scoop neckline, she didn't want it to end.

"Blair?"

She had to clear her throat to speak. "Yes?"

"My room is just down the hall."

She went very still, knowing she could no longer be a passive participant. Scott was asking her to make a choice—stay and pursue this to its natural conclusion or bring it to an end and have him drive her home.

She knew all the reasons she should choose the latter. There were many of them, and she had recited them to herself enough times to have them permanently engraved on her mind.

It couldn't go anywhere. Scott wasn't interested in long-term relationships, and he wasn't the type of man she wanted to be involved with, anyway. He couldn't stay long in one place, and she wasn't the type to wait patiently at home. She had a child to consider, and he had no responsibilities at all—at least, none that he seemed to take seriously. He was reckless and adventurous, she was careful and organized. There were so many reasons they were wrong for each other that she could spend the rest of the night listing them.

She could think of only one reason to stay—because she wanted him so badly her toenails ached.

Never in her life had she indulged in a one-night fling, and she had no reason to believe this would be anything more. She didn't approve of them, didn't trust them, didn't think she could give so much of herself without an emotional involvement that could only hurt her when it ended. Lovemaking wasn't casual for her, and it wasn't recreational. It was momentous.

So did she really want to take that step now, with Scott?

He had lifted his head and was studying the emotions playing across her face. "Is it so difficult a decision for you?" he asked quietly.

"Yes," she answered simply.

"Why?"

Was he accustomed to women who expected nothing from him beyond a night of pleasure? Did he really think it should be that easy? "Because I'm afraid," she admitted.

"Of me?"

"Of what I could feel for you...if I stop being careful."

His face softened. His eyes were warm when he cupped her cheek in his hand. "You don't think I'm afraid of the same thing? Of feeling too much for *you*?"

She imagined her dubious silence was answer enough for that improbable question.

He stroked her lower lip with the pad of his thumb. "If it means anything to you, I care for you, Blair. I like you. I admire you. I respect you. I think about you all the time. You make me want to make promises...and that's enough to scare the socks off me," he added ruefully.

"I don't want you to make promises," she whispered. Not unless he was prepared to keep them.

"Then what *do* you want, Blair? Do you want me to take you home now?"

Her breath hitched in her throat. The decision was hers. And for the first time in her adult life, she was tempted to give in to her Townsend recklessness—to throw consequences to the wind and take what she wanted. She had fallen hard for Scott McKay—there was no getting around that. When he drifted away, would she regret more that she *had* dared to find out what making love with him would be like...or that she had not had the courage to try?

Scott smiled faintly and kissed the end of her nose. "Don't look so worried and anxious, Counselor. You're making me feel like the big, bad wolf. I'll take you home."

Definitely the smart thing to do, she thought. And Blair had always made smart choices—at least until she'd impulsively purchased a cowboy at that bachelor auction. Yet something inside her seemed to have changed when she'd made the first bid. She'd discovered that she was a bit braver and more daring than she'd ever suspected.

"I'm not ready to go home just yet," she answered with a certainty in her voice that surprised even her. "I'd like to stay a little while longer."

His eyes glittered, but he held back. "You're sure?"

She slid a hand behind his neck. "I'm sure."

"Blair, I don't want you to be sorry—"

She couldn't help laughing a little at the sudden reversal of roles. "Do you want me to stay or not?"

"Oh, yeah," he answered with a groan that could only be described as heartfelt.

Her other hand slid slowly up his chest. "So what's your problem, McKay?"

His grin flashed. His shoulders relaxed. "Why, not a thing, ma'am."

"Then saddle up, cowboy," she murmured, giving him a look intended to sizzle his synapses.

Once Blair Townsend accepted a challenge, she gave it all she had, she thought in satisfaction.

Scott looked both surprised and delighted. "Yeehaw," he said, and smothered her smile beneath his.

SCOTT'S ROOM featured warm wood furnishings and dark, cozy plaids. Blair felt welcomed immediately—not that the decorating was solely responsible for that, she thought as Scott took her into his arms.

They fell to the bed together, their clothing accumulating in tumbled piles on the plush carpet. Blair discovered that Scott was every bit as firm and solid as she had fantasized. Her fingertips traced the muscles beneath his skin, pausing at an occasional scar that gave evidence of his adventurous pursuits. The dusting of hair on his chest was soft and springy. She traced his spine from his nape to the hollow above his hips. Every inch of him delighted her.

Scott seemed every bit as eager to explore her body. From the soft skin behind her ears to the ticklish arches of her feet, he caressed every part of her with tender fingers and lips. She was trembling and restless by the time he returned to her mouth, every centimeter of her body tingling and sensitized. There was a deep, powerful ache inside her, an emptiness she begged him in whispered requests to assuage.

After swiftly donning protection—that was one area in which she had no intention of acting recklessly—Scott fulfilled every fantasy Blair had secretly harbored since the first moment she had seen him standing in the Lost Springs arena.

And it was even better than she had dared to dream.

CHAPTER TWELVE

IT TOOK A WHILE for reality to displace the euphoria that lingered after Blair's sighs of pleasure had faded away. She forced her heavy eyelids open and found herself only inches from Scott. He lay on his stomach beside her, his face turned toward her, eyes closed, lips curved in a faint, satisfied smile. It was the realization that she had just tumbled the rest of the way into love with this irresistible cowboy that made her heart start to race again—this time with panic rather than passion.

She shoved herself upright, reaching for her clothing in the same movement. If they left now, it would be around midnight when she got home, she thought. That seemed like an appropriate time for a fantasy to end.

Her sudden activity startled Scott into opening his eyes. He reached out to catch her wrist. "Where are you going?"

"It's getting late. I should go home."

"What's the rush?"

"My aunt will be worried if I'm too late."

"I seriously doubt that. Your aunt seemed like the understanding type."

"Yes, well, I have some things to do tomorrow. I need to get some sleep tonight."

"You can sleep here," he suggested, sounding as if the idea had just occurred to him. "Call your aunt and tell her you'll be there in the morning. I'll take you home after we share a nice breakfast.''

Spend the night? Wake in his arms? Have him smile at her over the breakfast table? Oh, no. That was definitely not the way to rid herself of silly daydreams. It sounded, instead, more like a way to create them.

"No, I don't think that's a very good idea," she said, slipping out of his grasp. "I have to think about Jeffrey."

"I'm not going to change your mind, am I?" he asked in resignation as he watched her scramble into her underthings.

She pushed her arms into the sleeves of her pantsuit. "No."

Sighing, he rolled to the opposite edge of the bed. "Give me a few minutes and I'll take you home."

Blair kept her eyes on the floor as she searched for her missing left shoe. She heard Scott pad into the bathroom and close the door, followed by the sound of running water. By the time he came out, she was fully dressed, her hair was brushed and she had straightened his tumbled bed.

"In a bit of a hurry?" he asked, buttoning his shirt.

Again, she found she was having trouble meeting his eyes. She wished she had her antacids—she could use one right now. "It's getting late," she repeated, finding nothing new to say.

He stepped in front of her, his hands gently gripping her forearms. "Blair—take a deep breath."

Though she wasn't sure why he'd said that, it seemed easier to comply than to argue. She inhaled deeply, then released the air slowly. Some of the tension eased from her shoulders.

"Feel better?" he asked with a slight smile.

"I'm fine."

"Sudden regrets?"

"Not regrets," she corrected quietly. "Misgivings, perhaps."

"About what?"

She shrugged and tried to speak lightly. "Oh, you know me. I thrive on worry."

He didn't look amused. "I don't want to cause you anxiety."

There was no way she could honestly promise him she had no anxiety where their relationship was concerned. But she could assure him that she was fully capable of handling her own problems—especially those she had brought onto herself. She smiled faintly. "I'm fine," she repeated. "I just need to get home to Jeffrey."

He didn't look entirely satisfied, but he nodded. "I'll take you home."

As if sensing that she needed time to process what had happened between them, Scott kept the conversation breezy and impersonal during the hour-long drive to her house. He told her story after story of adventures he'd experienced during the past few years, often turning his humor against himself to make her laugh. It startled her that she *did* laugh more than once during the ride.

Scott didn't mention their lovemaking again until they were standing outside her door. He cupped her face gently in his hands. "We're going to have to talk about tonight, you know. We can't keep pretending nothing happened."

"I'm not pretending. I just need some time to decide exactly what *did* happen," she admitted ruefully.

Scott's smile was wry. "You're going to dissect and analyze every moment we've spent together tonight, aren't you, Counselor? You'll probably list pros and cons and project every possible outcome—and go through an entire roll of antacids in the process.''

She couldn't help smiling, though she felt her cheeks warm. "You're probably right.''

"I'm getting to know you better than you thought, hmm?''

"Perhaps.'' Did he know that she was in love with him? Did he care?

"Promise me one thing, Blair.''

"What?'' she asked warily.

"Analyze it all you want—but don't regret it. It was too special for regrets.''

"I won't regret it,'' she promised—and she meant it. She had made the decision earlier that she wanted to know what it was like to make love with Scott. She'd found out—it was heavenly. Even if heartache followed when he drifted on to another adventure, as she knew he would eventually, she could never regret knowing those feelings if only that one time.

"Good.'' He kissed her lingeringly, tenderly. And then he drew back, his expression reluctant. "I suppose you'd better go in to your family.''

It warmed her to think she had a family waiting for her inside. After so many years on her own, it felt good to have people to care for, and who cared for her in return. Did Scott feel that way about the people who shared his home with him, or did he feel alone even when surrounded by those he referred to as his staff?

"You have a long drive ahead of you,'' she said. "Be careful.''

His smile flashed in the soft porch lighting. "Driving home is hardly a dangerous activity.''

Compared to most of his pastimes, that was certainly

true, Blair thought with a grimace. "Be careful, any-way."

"You bet," he replied carelessly. "Tell Jeff I'll see him next weekend, if not before. And I'll call you to-morrow, okay?"

She nodded. "Good night, Scott."

"Good night, Blair. Sleep well."

She wasn't at all sure she could do that. She would probably lie awake and imagine what it would have been like to awaken in Scott's arms.

AS HE HAD PROMISED, Scott called the next evening. He and Blair chatted for forty-five minutes without ever once referring to their lovemaking. He also talked with Jeffrey, asking about the boy's day, telling him a couple of jokes and promising to see him the following week-end at his ranch.

He called again Monday evening and Tuesday eve-ning. Both times he included Jeffrey in the calls, and Jeffrey thrived on the attention, telling Scott about school, making plans for the ranch visit. It wasn't a mi-raculous transformation, but Blair could see several pos-itive changes in her nephew's attitude.

Several times she was tempted to warn Jeffrey not to get too attached to Scott, to remind him that Scott wasn't a member of the family and that he owed them nothing, including his time. But she couldn't bring herself to di-minish the pleasure Jeffrey had found in this new friend-ship—and she had to admit to herself that she didn't want to accept that Scott's interest in them was only a fleeting whim. She sincerely hoped that she and Jeffrey weren't both headed toward bitter disappointment.

Jeffrey pounced on the telephone when it rang just after dinner Thursday evening. "Hi, Scott!" he said, barely giving the caller time to identify himself. "Guess what—I got an A on my English test today. I've been making my *Q*s the way my teacher wants me to, and I studied and got all the answers right, so she gave me full credit."

He grinned at whatever Scott said in reply. "Yeah, I worked the system. And I guess it felt pretty good."

Jeffrey and Scott talked a few more minutes and then Jeffrey handed the phone to his aunt. "I'm going to play with Belle," he said, heading for the doorway.

"Make time for a bath before bedtime," she called after him, then lifted the phone to her ear. "Hello, Scott."

"I have plenty of time for a bath before bedtime," he murmured in her ear. "Want to come scrub my back?"

She swallowed, deliberately dispelling the erotic picture of Scott in a bathtub that sprang to mind. "I was talking to Jeffrey."

"Oh, darn."

"Did you only call to make lewd suggestions?" she asked, settling comfortably into a chair.

"Of course. Actually, I had this idea that involved a new rope, a set of chaps and a pair of spurs...."

"Forget it," she said with a chuckle. "Chaps make my thighs look fat."

"Who said you would be wearing the chaps? Or anything else, for that matter."

"So how are Margaret and Carolyn?" she asked, changing the subject before it *really* got embarrassing.

"Chicken," Scott grumbled.

"Have you noticed that you call me that a lot?"

"Yeah. It's almost like an endearment, isn't it?"

She sighed and shook her head, thinking that only Scott would believe that.

They talked for another half hour, the remainder of the conversation as light and flirtatious as the beginning. That was one of Scott's charms, Blair mused when the call ended. He could make her blush and giggle like an infatuated teenager—something she had never really been. She had been so young when it became apparent that someone in her family had to be serious and responsible—and the task had seemed to fall on her. Now that she was a serious and responsible adult, it felt good to be silly and frivolous for a change.

Jeffrey was still smiling at bedtime. Freshly scrubbed and dressed in his PJs, he allowed her to kiss him goodnight—a new habit they had adopted. "I'm going to ask Scott if he'll teach me to ride a bull at his ranch," he said, climbing into bed.

"I'm sure a horse would be more appropriate," Blair remarked, smoothing the covers over her nephew and making a mental note to absolutely forbid Scott to even *think* about putting this child on a bull.

"Aw, Aunt Blair, how can I get in a rodeo if I don't know how to ride a bull?"

"You'll have plenty of time to learn that when you're older." And when *she* was dead, she added silently with grim humor, because over her dead body was the only way she would let Jeffrey ride one of those beasts.

He was so excited about the upcoming visit to Scott's ranch. Blair had to admit she was looking forward to it herself, though she knew there would be no opportunity this time for her and Scott to be alone together. She knew she was headed for trouble when she found herself thinking with reckless optimism that there would be plenty of other opportunities for them to be alone.

Her fingers were crossed when she left Jeffrey's

room—an old, superstitious act that served no purpose except to divert her from her worry about the future.

THERE WAS a final parent-teacher conference at Jeffrey's school Thursday evening before the summer break. Blair attended, of course, crossing her fingers that the conference would go well. Jeffrey's teacher, Miss Greene, was a no-nonsense young woman who'd butted heads with Jeffrey more than once. She smiled smugly when Blair took a seat in the classroom while Jeffrey waited in the hallway. "Ms. Townsend," the teacher said smoothly. "I'm so glad you could make it this evening."

"I make it a point to be available for Jeffrey," Blair reminded the teacher, a bit annoyed that the other woman had sounded surprised she was there. Blair hadn't missed a school function in the entire six months Jeffrey had been with her.

"Of course. Anyway, I wanted to let you know that your nephew has improved significantly in both his schoolwork and his attitude during the past few weeks. I'm quite pleased with his progress."

Blair smiled. "Thank you."

Miss Greene gave a rather weary sigh in response. "I must admit it has been a difficult undertaking, but I'm happy to say my persistence is paying off."

The teacher was obviously taking full credit for Jeffrey's progress, Blair thought in exasperation. She seemed to have no concept of how hard Blair had worked with her nephew—or how much input Scott had had.

"It's actually too bad school is almost over," Ms. Greene added. "If I'd had a bit more time with Jeffrey, I'm sure I could have completely turned him around."

"Thank you for all you've done, Miss Greene, but

I'm sure my nephew and I will get along just fine in the future."

"Yes, well, I'm certain you're doing the best you can—considering that you've had no training to work with difficult children," the woman replied with a touch of condescension that set Blair's teeth on edge. She went on to show Blair Jeffrey's most recent papers and then usher her out of the room with the excuse that she had parents waiting—as opposed to a mere aunt, her tone seemed to imply.

"Twit," Blair muttered beneath her breath as she exited the classroom. No wonder Jeffrey had never bonded with his teacher. At least next term he would have someone new, and most of the teachers at Lander Elementary were very professional *and* friendly.

A giggle from behind her made her wince as she realized that her unflattering comment had been overheard. She was relieved to see that it was only Jeffrey who had heard her, even though she regretted her lack of restraint in front of him. "Do not repeat that."

"No, ma'am," he agreed, though he was still grinning.

"You will treat your teacher with respect during the remaining few days of the term, is that understood?"

"Yes, ma'am. I know how to work the system, remember?"

She sighed and placed a hand on his shoulder. "You're beginning to worry me, Jeffrey. You're starting to sound too much like Scott."

The comparison obviously delighted him. "Can we go home now?" he asked. "I want to play with Belle."

Blair readily agreed.

Jeffrey was in an exceptionally good mood that evening, even though both of them were somewhat disappointed that Scott didn't call. The good-night hug he gave her was impulsive but sincere. "One more day until we go to the ranch," he announced happily when he pulled away.

The very intensity of his anticipation worried Blair. He was expecting too much from a mere visit to Scott's ranch, she fretted. If anything went wrong, he would be so disappointed.

But Blair was unprepared for how very wrong things would go.

She was at her office when a call came in for her Friday afternoon. She recognized Carolyn Roberts's voice immediately—and with a sense of foreboding. "What can I do for you?" she asked.

"I have a message for you, Blair. From Scott."

Blair closed her eyes and rubbed her temple, somehow knowing what the message would be. "What is it?"

"He has been called out of the state for the weekend and won't be back until the middle of next week. He said to tell you he regrets the timing, but he wanted me to assure you that you and your nephew are still welcome to visit the ranch tomorrow as you had planned. Margaret and I would love to welcome you, and Margaret will prepare a nice lunch for you and Jeffrey. Jake will be available to show you around and to give your nephew a riding lesson—you, too, if you would be interested, of course."

Blair dreaded telling Jeffrey that Scott wasn't going to be there. It was seeing Scott again that Jeffrey had so looked forward to, much more than simply touring the ranch. "Where *is* Scott?" she asked, hoping it was at least important business that had called him away.

"He, um, had a chance to go surfing with some friends in Hawaii. Apparently, the waves are unusually large or something—I'm afraid I don't know much about surfing—and there's an amateur competition that Scott and his friends want to enter. He left early this morning.''

Blair could tell from Carolyn's tone that she knew it wasn't a very strong excuse. After promising for more than a week to host Blair and Jeffrey at the ranch, Scott had taken off to go surfing with some friends. He hadn't even called himself to explain.

Apparently growing uncomfortable with Blair's silence, Carolyn cleared her throat. ''So, can we expect you and Jeffrey to visit us in the morning?''

Her first impulse was to coolly decline. Blair had absolutely no interest in visiting the ranch now. But she could not refuse on Jeffrey's account without talking to him first. He would be unhappy that Scott wouldn't be there, but for all she knew, he might still like to see the ranch. It should be his decision, since the outing had been for his benefit all along.

As she courteously thanked Carolyn for calling—after all, it hadn't been her fault that Scott had let them down—Blair disconnected the call. She didn't look forward to telling Jeffrey the news. Once again an important man in his life had abandoned him without a goodbye to pursue his own frivolous interests—and left Blair to deal with the boy's anger and disappointment.

She had foolishly allowed herself to believe that Scott was different from Kirk. From her father. She had begun to hope that his promises meant something. That he cared for Jeffrey…and maybe even for her. Finding out that she had been so very wrong about him was devastating.

She rubbed a hand across her face, discovering only then that her cheeks were damp. Was she crying for

Jeffrey, or for herself? All she knew for certain at that moment was that Scott had shattered something very precious—a boy's trust. Not to mention a woman's heart, she added with a heavy sigh.

THE SCENE with Jeffrey was as painful as she had expected. He was terribly disappointed that Scott would not be spending the weekend with him. "But he promised," he wailed.

"He didn't actually promise, sweetie," Blair replied, her heart aching for him. "He thought he would be there, but his plans changed unexpectedly. He still wants us to visit his ranch. His foreman, Jake, will give you a riding lesson. I've met him, he's very nice. A real cowboy. And Margaret, the housekeeper, is a wonderful cook who has offered to make a special lunch for us."

His lip protruding, Jeffrey shook his head. "I don't want to go now. I don't know any of those people. I wanted Scott to be there."

"Yes, so did I, but he had other things to do this weekend. I'm sure he thought you would have a good time, anyway."

"I won't go," Jeffrey insisted. "I would rather stay here with Belle. At least she doesn't lie to me."

He was furious, his small body trembling with it. Blair knew exactly how he felt—and she was tired of defending Scott when what he had done was so inconsiderate. "You know what, Jeffrey?" she said with sudden spirit. "You don't have to go if you don't want to. Scott invited us to be his guests, and it was rude of him to abandon us this way. I'm as angry with him as you are. But you and I don't need him to entertain us this weekend. We can find plenty of fun things to do without him."

Mopping his face with the back of one hand, Jeffrey sniffled and looked at her. "Like what?"

"Anything you like. Roller-skating. Swimming. A movie or an arcade. Or we can go to another ranch and take a riding lesson together—there are plenty of other ranches and other cowboys who would be happy to teach us, I'm sure."

Though his lip still trembled, Jeffrey seemed intrigued. "We can do anything I want?"

"Anything—except ride bulls," she amended hastily.

He didn't quite smile, but his expression lightened a bit. "That sounds like it might be sort of fun. Just me and you, I mean."

"What would you like to do?"

"Can I think about it?"

"Of course. Let me know whenever you decide, in the morning if you like. I'll call Carolyn and tell her we won't be available tomorrow—if you're sure that's what you want me to do."

He nodded. "I don't want to go to Scott's ranch now."

"Then we won't go. Now, wash your face and play with Belle while I make the call, and then I'll start dinner."

"Can we have macaroni and cheese?"

"If that's what you want."

He nodded. "It sounds pretty good." He wandered out of the room, his little shoulders slumping.

Blair turned and slammed her fist into a sofa pillow.

BLAIR TUCKED JEFFREY into bed that night and bent to kiss his forehead. He was still subdued, but seemed to have gotten over the first crushing blow of disappointment. "Are you thinking about what you want to do tomorrow?" she asked.

He nodded against the pillow. "I still haven't decided."

She smoothed his hair. "There's no rush." She straightened then. "Good night, Jeffrey."

"Aunt Blair?"

"What is it, sweetie?"

"I really wanted to see Scott tomorrow."

Her throat tightened. "I know you did, Jeffrey. I'm sorry it didn't work out."

"I thought he liked us."

"I'm sure he does like us." He simply liked his freedom better, she thought sadly. "There were things he had to do tomorrow."

There she was defending him again, even though he didn't deserve it. She told herself she was doing so only for Jeffrey's sake.

"Aunt Blair?"

"Yes?"

"Do *you* still like Scott?"

She had to swallow hard before answering. "Of course. We shouldn't forget that he's been very nice to us, even if he disappointed us this time."

And if she ever saw him again, she might very well throttle him.

"Aunt Blair?"

"Yes, Jeffrey?" she asked patiently.

"Is Scott sort of like my dad? You know, he doesn't let anything tie him down?"

She wanted to hit something again. Preferably Kirk. Followed, of course, by Scott.

"I don't think Scott is exactly like anyone," she said, settling on an answer that neatly begged the question.

Jeffrey pulled the covers to his chin. "I'm pretty mad at both of them."

"So am I, sweetie. So am I," she muttered as she left the room.

TOO WIRED to sleep, she forced herself to concentrate on paperwork until she had finally relaxed enough to consider going to bed. She had just closed her briefcase when the telephone rang. Since it was nearly ten o'clock, the sound startled her. She snatched up the receiver before it could ring again and disturb Jeffrey. "Hello?"

"Hi." Scott's voice sounded a bit muffled. Far away. "Did you get my message?"

She took a deep breath and counted to ten before answering. "I got it."

"Good. Tell Jeff I'll come by and see him as soon as I get back in town, okay? I'll bring him some souvenirs from Hawaii. Maybe a grass skirt for you, if you'll promise to model it for me," he added with a chuckle she didn't respond to. He continued before she could speak. "I want the two of you to make yourselves at home at the ranch tomorrow. Don't hesitate to ask for anything you need. Everyone there will be available to—"

She finally managed to cut in. "Jeffrey and I won't be going to your ranch tomorrow. We're making other plans for the weekend."

There was a pause, and then he said, "But I thought the kid was looking forward to the visit."

Could he really be this dense? "He was looking forward to seeing *you*, Scott. Not a collection of buildings and animals. I don't blame you, I suppose, for leaving this weekend. After all, you don't owe us anything. But couldn't you at least have called Jeffrey to explain the change of plans? You certainly talked to him plenty of times when you were making them with him."

"You're angry with me."

"Let's just say I'm getting tired of being the one who has to dry his tears every time a man he counts on disappoints him."

"You're comparing me to your brother? Blair, that's hardly fair."

What was unfair was the devastated look in Jeffrey's eyes when he had gazed at her from his pillow, Blair thought. "Look, there's really no need for us to argue. Jeffrey was disappointed, but he'll get over it." Just as she would, eventually. "Thank you very much for everything you've done for us. I'm sure neither of us will ever forget the time we spent with you."

It was a jumbled and breathless goodbye speech, but the best she could do at the moment.

Scott sounded startled. "You're giving me a brush-off? *Now?* Damn it, Blair—"

"Let's face it, this is better for everyone involved. Jeffrey and I lead a quiet life here—much too quiet and structured for you. Your life is filled with spur-of-the-moment adventures that don't—that can't—include us. It's better for us to simply say goodbye now."

"I can't accept that."

"I'm afraid you'll have to. Jeffrey has to be my priority now. He needs me. I'm all he has. I won't let him be hurt again."

"Surely you know I would never hurt that boy—or you."

"Don't you understand, Scott?" she whispered sadly. "You already have."

"By postponing one outing?"

"No. By making us care about you. You said you

never wanted to leave anyone behind to miss you or worry about you, but that wasn't something you could control. Your staff loves you and misses you very deeply when you're gone. I can't live that way—and I won't accept it for Jeffrey, either. He gets enough of that from his father.''

"Blair, this isn't the time to talk about this. When I get back—"

"Nothing will have changed. You know I'm right. You simply haven't given it enough thought. Goodbye— and good luck with your surfing competition. I'm sure you'll enjoy it immensely.''

She hung up before he could argue further. And then she buried her face in her hands, wondering if she'd just done something very logical—or incredibly stupid. She had asked Scott not to call again, and there was a good chance he would accept her request. It was possible that she would never see him again.

And that thought broke her heart—just as she had known it would when this happened.

She had to think of Jeffrey first. He was so young, so vulnerable. He didn't deserve to be hurt time after time by men who placed their own pleasures before his feelings. It was up to her to protect him as much as possible. Which didn't mean she wouldn't grieve for the only grand romance she had experienced in her entire thirty years.

Her eyes were watering again. As disappointed as Jeffrey had been, Blair was even more so. She'd been completely unprepared for this. She hadn't believed that Scott would string Jeffrey along until the very last minute and then figuratively pull the rug out from under him.

To give him credit, he had seemed surprised by her anger. Maybe he simply hadn't understood how much his presence would have meant to Jeffrey—and to her. But wasn't that very lack of understanding only further proof of how wrong he was for them?

Gripped in the throes of her sadness, she wasn't aware at first that someone had joined her on the couch. And then a tentative meow made her lift her head. Belle, the little gray cat, sat on the cushion beside her, looking at her as if asking if there was anything she could do to help. Blair took the cat onto her lap, obligingly scratching her ears when she butted gently against her.

The cat began to purr, snuggling against Blair as if offering comfort. Blair sniffed and rested her wet cheek against Belle's soft head, thinking that perhaps there was something to the theory that pets were therapeutic. Cuddling the affectionate kitty didn't make her heart ache any less, but it sure beat grieving alone.

CHAPTER THIRTEEN

JEFFREY SLEPT later than usual the next morning. Blair didn't disturb him, thinking that perhaps he'd had a restless night. She'd gotten little enough sleep herself. Unintentionally or not, Scott McKay had interfered with her sleep since she'd met him. Maybe now that their brief relationship—it could hardly be called an affair—was over, she could get some rest.

Small comfort, but she would take what she could get.

When she heard Jeffrey moving around, she started cooking his favorite breakfast. By the time he shuffled into the kitchen, still yawning and rubbing his eyes, she had a stack of buckwheat pancakes and a bowl of fruit waiting for him. "Good morning," she said, sidestepping his cat as she finished setting the table.

"Morning. That looks good."

She smiled and poured a glass of milk for him. "Have you decided what you would like to do today?"

"Can we go to a movie? Or an arcade?"

"We can do both," she agreed. "It's turning out to be a beautiful day. Why don't we drive in to Casper this morning and play miniature golf, then have lunch wherever you like, then maybe go to an arcade and a movie?"

"All of that?" Jeffrey nodded. "Sounds good."

He seemed genuinely pleased, though not quite as excited as he'd been about the visit to Scott's ranch, she noted with a pang.

She settled across the table from him with her breakfast. "You know, of course, that I'm going to stomp you at miniature golf," she teased, hoping to make him smile.

She succeeded. "In your dreams," he retorted.

"I'll go easy on you, if you like. Maybe let you get a stroke or two ahead at the beginning. But in the end, victory will be mine."

Jeffrey rolled his eyes. "Aunt Blair, I'm going to blow you off the score card. I could beat you with my eyes closed and my hands tied behind my back."

"You think so?"

"Know so. After all, I'm young and sharp and you're...well." He grinned.

"You're calling me *old?*" She promptly threw her napkin at him, making him giggle. "You are so going to lose, boy."

"Maybe I'll let you win a game of air hockey at the arcade."

"You're toast, kid."

He giggled. "We'll see."

He finished every bite of his breakfast, looking considerably more cheerful than he had the night before. Blair feigned a carefree mood. While she was pleased that Jeffrey wanted to spend time with her and that he seemed to be getting past his disappointment about the ranch trip, her heart was still very heavy.

It was going to take her quite a bit longer to recover from her own disappointment.

The next few hours were the most pleasant time Blair and Jeffrey had spent alone together. After breakfast they set out immediately for Casper. It was a beautiful day for a drive. They played two rounds of miniature golf, selecting a different course the second time. Blair won the first round, and was pleased that Jeffrey took the close defeat well. Perhaps she could give credit to Scott for that, she thought with a renewed pang. But Jeffrey beat her the second game, to his obvious delight.

He wanted tacos and cheese dip for lunch, after which they spent a long time in a noisy, crowded arcade. Jeffrey slaughtered her at arcade games, of course, but Blair couldn't care less since he seemed to be having so much fun. He proudly carried out the stuffed monkey he won, a toy Blair could have bought for half the cost of winning it, but she didn't care about that, either.

Jeffrey selected an animated action movie—which wouldn't have been Blair's first choice—and they bought popcorn, soft drinks and chocolate-covered raisins to munch on during the film. Blair enjoyed the snacks more than the story, but Jeffrey was enthralled. He chattered about the characters and the cool weapons all the way home. Blair tried to remember enough about it to respond with some semblance of intelligence.

Listening to his prattling made her smile. So what if her brief fling with Scott hadn't worked out. She would recover. She had Jeffrey in her life now, and she would take great pleasure in helping him grow into a fine, upstanding man. A man who understood the meaning of responsibility and commitment. A man who wouldn't make promises he didn't intend to keep.

A man who would never disappoint a child who looked up to him.

Scott McKay was an idiot. An insensitive jerk. An aging Peter Pan who needed to grow up and start paying attention to other people besides himself. And those were the words of someone who was very fond of him—his loyal but exasperated assistant, Carolyn.

The things he had said to himself were even harsher.

He sat on the couch in Blair's living room, his only company the small gray cat that curled on his knee. He wasn't sure he deserved even her careless affection.

For perhaps the hundredth time that day—if not more—he glanced at his watch. He had no idea when to expect Blair and Jeffrey. It was nearly 9:00 p.m., and he'd been waiting since before noon, after spending all night sitting in airports and airplanes. Wanda Townsend had let him into Blair's house once he'd explained to her that it was urgent he talk to her niece and great-nephew as soon as they returned. Apparently, she wasn't aware he wasn't on their good side at the moment; she had seemed to think it would be perfectly fine with Blair if he waited inside.

Scott hoped Blair wouldn't be too upset with her overly trusting aunt for letting him in.

After an hour had passed with no sign of them, he'd called the ranch, thinking maybe they'd changed their minds and gone there, after all. That was when Carolyn had let him have it about his insensitive behavior.

"It's bad enough," she had chided, "that you leave everyone here missing you and wondering when they'll see you again—if you don't get yourself killed first. But to disappoint a little boy—not to mention the nicest woman you've met in a long time—well, that's just too much, Scott." She had gone on to call him selfish and thoughtless, and to predict a sad, lonely old age for him if he didn't reform his ways. "I only tell you these things," she had added, "because I care about you and I want you to be happy. And I don't think you've been truly happy for a long time."

Her words still ringing in his ears, he was tempted to start pacing, but he'd done so much of that already today that he was probably wearing a path in Blair's carpet. He couldn't stop remembering the finality in her voice when she had told him goodbye. He had known when she hung up that he had to do whatever it took to win her back. As Carolyn had so bluntly pointed out, Blair was the best thing that had happened to him in a long time. And he wasn't going to let his old fears about commitment drive him away this time.

He only hoped it wasn't too late.

When he heard her garage door go up, he stiffened, his sudden tension causing the little cat to look up with an inquiring meow. Blair and Jeffrey were home—and he had some fast talking to do to win back their confidence.

Hearing them enter the kitchen, he set the cat on the floor and stood, turning toward the doorway. The cat ran into the other room to greet them, but Scott remained where he was. Waiting.

Jeffrey was talking, his voice carrying from the other room. Whatever he and Blair had done that day, the boy had enjoyed it, judging from his obvious excitement. Scott couldn't help smiling a little, thinking that Jeffrey sounded exactly the way a ten-year-old boy *should* sound—noisy, enthusiastic, secure.

And then Jeffrey and his aunt walked into the living room and spotted Scott. Their smiles froze, then faded away.

It broke Scott's heart that Jeffrey was immediately transformed into the boy he had first met—angry, sullen, suspicious. Scott had done that to him this time, he realized sadly. The only difference was that, instead of huddling alone and withdrawn, the boy moved closer to his aunt, as if seeking support from the one person who had not yet betrayed him.

Blair's expression was stunned. If she felt any pleasure at seeing him, it was masked by her surprise. "What are you doing here?" she asked. "How did you get in?"

"Your aunt let me in. After I promised not to pilfer the silver."

Neither Blair nor Jeffrey smiled at his feeble attempt at a joke. They just kept looking at him, making him feel a bit like something that had slithered out from under a rock. He cleared his throat and looked at the boy, thinking he might be the easiest to appease. "What have you got there, Jeff? A stuffed monkey?"

The boy glared at him. "Me and Aunt Blair had fun today. We didn't need you—*or* your old ranch."

"Jeffrey." Blair rested a hand on his shoulder. "There's no call to be rude. Scott was very nice to make his ranch and his staff available to us, even though we chose to decline the invitation."

She made the word "nice" sound like an insult, Scott thought with a wince. He shook his head at her. "Let the boy speak his mind. Okay, Jeff, let me have it. Tell me what you think of me."

Jeffrey didn't waste time. "You lied to us. You said you would be there today and then you left. You just expected someone else to take care of us. That's what my dad always does. He makes promises and he never keeps them. And that's not *right!*" he added fiercely.

It was the first time Scott had ever heard Jeffrey express any anger toward his father. Judging from Blair's expression, she was as surprised as he was. It hurt that the boy had compared him to a man who had caused him so much pain, and yet he knew he deserved the blow. "No," he said quietly. "It isn't right when someone you trust lets you down."

"And you made my aunt cry," Jeffrey added, visibly startling Blair again. "I saw her, last night when she thought I was asleep. You gave *me* a hard time when I got lost and made her cry. You said she didn't deserve it."

Scott looked apologetically at Blair's flushed face. "No. She didn't deserve it from either of us."

He took a deep breath and went down on one knee to look eye-to-eye with the angry boy. "I'm sorry, Jeffrey. What I did was thoughtless and stupid. I didn't realize it was so important to you for me to be there today—I thought you just wanted to see the ranch. But that's no excuse. I invited you to visit me, and it was wrong of me to desert you that way."

Jeffrey was making a valiant effort not to cry, but one tear escaped him. He dashed impatiently at it. "Then why *did* you?"

Scott wished he could understand that better himself. "My only excuse is that I've been on my own for so long that I've gotten selfish. When my buddy called to invite me to go surfing, it was just habit to grab a bag and take off. I thought you'd be happy with your aunt and my staff and my foreman, Jake. I even left instructions for my favorite horse to be available to you. I just didn't understand that you really wanted me to be there, too. I was a jerk, Jeff, and I'm very sorry. I hope you can forgive me."

Jeffrey shot a quick look at his aunt. He was obviously swayed by Scott's apology, but he wasn't a child who trusted easily. For good reason. But Blair didn't give him an answer. Her silence made it clear that it was up to

Jeffrey to decide whether to forgive Scott for hurting him.

Jeffrey drew a deep breath. "Okay," he said a bit grudgingly. "But don't ever do that again," he added with a shake of his finger.

"I won't," Scott said. "From now on, if I make you a promise, you can count on it. It would take a major emergency to cause me to let you down again. Something involving fire or blood or winds in excess of seventy-five miles per hour, at least."

To his satisfaction, a reluctant smile tugged at the boy's lips. "Okay, I get the point."

Scott straightened and extended his hand. "Thanks, Jeff. I appreciate you giving me a second chance."

Jeffrey slipped his small hand into Scott's, shaking it solemnly. Scott had to swallow a lump in his throat.

Blair cleared her throat as if she was affected in a similar manner. "Jeffrey, why don't you run over to Aunt Wanda's and tell her how much fun we had today? I'll call you in about an hour to come home."

"Are you going to yell at Scott?"

"I don't know. Maybe."

"Okay." He smiled at her, then gave her a quick hug. "I had a great time today. Thank you."

"I had a good time, too." She rested her cheek against the top of his head, and Scott couldn't help noticing how much more comfortable they looked together now than they had when he'd first met them. He wanted to believe he'd had some part in that, though he didn't like to think they had drawn closer partly as a reaction to his disappointing them.

Blair walked Jeffrey out to the front porch, then watched until he was safely across the yard and inside his great-aunt's house. Only then did she rejoin Scott, closing the front door behind her, her expression closed. "Why did you come here, Scott?" she asked wearily. "I thought you had a competition in Hawaii."

"I didn't enter it. After I talked to you, I dropped everything and headed back here."

"Is that grand gesture supposed to impress me?"

He winced. He'd known Blair would be harder to bring around than Jeffrey. He had hurt her—that was bad enough. But he had also hurt the nephew she had made a commitment to raise and protect—and that she would find much harder to forgive.

BLAIR REGRETTED her words as soon as she said them. She shook her head. "I'm sorry. As I said to Jeffrey earlier, there's no call for either of us to be rude to you."

"And I'll tell you the same thing I said to Jeff. Say whatever you want to me."

"Fine." She crossed her arms over her chest. "I'm sure you meant well by coming all this way to apologize, but it would have been better if you'd stayed where you were. I haven't changed my mind about us."

"You still think it best if we say goodbye."

"Yes," she said, finding it every bit as hard to say this time—maybe even harder after he'd made up so sweetly with Jeffrey.

"Because you think I'll continue to disappoint you? That I can't be trusted to follow through on my promises to you and Jeff? You think I'm another self-centered wanderer like your brother and your father?"

"I...didn't say that."

"You didn't have to."

"The thing is," she said, determined to stay focused on logic and reason, "you and I are all wrong for each other. What happened this weekend is a perfect example of that. You weren't obligated to be at the ranch to host us this weekend. You had every right to go to Hawaii with your friends. You very generously made arrangements for us to have a lovely day at your ranch, but it wasn't enough for us. Jeffrey and I can't seem to help wanting more from you, and you're a man who doesn't want any ties or commitments. We need order and security, and you crave freedom and adventure. It simply can't work."

"It can if I'm willing to change," he said quietly.

Her chest tightened. "I haven't asked you to change. There's no reason for you to—"

"I've already changed." He reached out to pull her hands into his. "Blair, why do you think I panicked enough to run all the way to Hawaii?"

"You went to Hawaii to surf."

"I went to prove that I was free to do so," he corrected. "When Bobby called, my first instinct was to turn him down. To tell him that I had a prior commitment for the weekend. Because that reaction was so new to me—and so momentous—it scared me into telling him I would be there."

When she only looked at him in confusion, he laughed ruefully and tightened his grip on her hands. "Don't you see? There's never been anything so important to me that I couldn't just ditch it if a better offer came along."

That made her frown and pull at her hands. "I understand. You wanted to go surfing in Hawaii more than you wanted to play tour guide for us at your ranch."

"No, you don't understand. There was *nothing* I wanted to do more than play tour guide for you and Jeff—including surfing in Hawaii. I knew the minute I got on the plane that I'd made the wrong choice for myself. What I didn't understand was that I had let you and Jeff down so badly.''

"Surely you knew how much we wanted you to be there."

His smile turned crooked. "I guess I'm not accustomed to thinking of my presence as being particularly important to anyone."

As far as she was concerned, he had just made her point. "That's exactly what I meant by differing expectations."

"I'm trying to tell you our expectations aren't as different as you think. I don't want to spend the rest of my life chasing one meaningless adventure after another, having no one who really cares if I ever return. I've had my reasons for living the way I have, but now it's time for me to change my priorities. I'm not like your brother, Blair. I know it's going to take time to prove that to you, especially after my stupid mistake this weekend, but I'm asking you to give me that time."

She didn't exactly understand what he was asking. "Why would you want to change your whole life? Why would you want to give up the freedom you've had to go wherever you want, whenever you want, to do whatever you feel like doing?"

"Before your nephew moved in with you, you were free to do whatever you wanted, right? Except for your commitment to your work, you could come and go as you liked, responsible for no one but yourself. Given a chance, would you go back to that now? Would you send Jeffrey away so you could have your freedom back?"

"No, of course not."

"Why?" he asked simply.

Although she suspected he already knew the reason, she answered anyway. "Because I love my nephew. I like having him with me. And because it makes me feel good to know I can make a difference in his life.''

He smiled at her as if she were a pupil who'd just given him a very clever answer. "Exactly. And now you know why I'm willing to make changes in my life.''

"No...why?"

"Because I love you," he replied gently. "I like having you in my life. And because I hope I have something to offer you in return.''

His words hit her like a blow. She took an instinctive step backward, jerking her hands from his and holding them up as if to ward off another attack. "Scott, don't—"

"Don't what, Blair? Don't love you? It's too late for that. Don't tell you? I've already done that, too.''

She was shaking her head, resisting a childish impulse to cover her ears. Hearing Scott tell her he loved her was simply too painful when she was so afraid to trust him with her heart. "You don't know what you're saying. It's too soon. You can't possibly—"

"You think I don't know what I feel?" He shook his head. "Blair, I've spent most of my life running from love. Now that it's finally caught up with me, I know exactly what it is.''

"It's too soon," she repeated helplessly. "You've known me such a short time. You can't—"

"Are you telling me it's too soon for you to have any feelings for *me?*" he interrupted gently.

She bit her lip and remained silent, unable to confess the truth.

"Blair? Are you saying our lovemaking meant nothing to you? That there's nothing I can do to make you fall in love with me?''

How was she supposed to answer that without making

herself completely vulnerable to him? "I...have feelings for you, Scott. I told you that before we made love. And I told you, as well, that those feelings frightened me because they seemed so ill-fated. I haven't changed my mind. I still worry that someone is going to be hurt. One or both of us—or, even worse, Jeffrey."

"I love you, Blair."

Her eyes closed and she moaned quietly. "Please, don't..."

He cupped her face in his hands, bringing his mouth close to hers. "I love you."

"Scott..."

His lips brushed against hers when he said it again. "I love you."

Her breath left her in a sigh. "Oh, Scott..."

His mouth closed over hers, and her resistance melted away. He sounded so sincere. So certain. So convincing. And even though she was still terrified by the potential for disaster, she was only human. And she loved him.

"I'll make this weekend up to you, Blair," he muttered against her mouth, pulling her almost roughly into his arms. "I'll prove to you that you can trust me, that I'm free to love you now."

She curled her fingers into his travel-wrinkled shirt. "This is crazy."

"No. This is the first sane thing I've done in years. I've been a fool in a lot of ways for a long time, Blair, but I'm not dumb enough to throw away the best thing that ever happened to me."

She couldn't resist returning his kisses, sliding her arms around his neck. But she hadn't surrendered entirely to the madness. "Scott?"

He slid his mouth across her cheek, pausing at her ear. "Mmm?"

"I want to take this slowly. I don't want either of us to make promises we can't keep."

"I never make promises I can't keep. That's why I've never been willing to make promises before. I'm willing to do so now."

She shook her head. "I'm not ready to hear them. Not yet."

"I understand. You want me to prove myself to you."

"No, that's not what I meant. I just want to be sure...."

He kissed her again, slowly and thoroughly, and then lifted his head to smile at her. "I'll prove myself, anyway. You're going to find me impossible to resist for long, Counselor."

She sighed. "I've found you hard to resist since the day I bought you, cowboy. And that's what makes me so nervous."

He seemed satisfied for the moment. "Let's go get Jeff. I've got a way to go to win him back yet."

Blair hoped he didn't consider her completely won over. He had a way to go with her yet, too.

CHAPTER FOURTEEN

WHATEVER SCOTT was trying to prove during the next few weeks, he went all out to do it. He was on Blair's doorstep almost every evening when she got home from her office. He had dinner with them, took Jeffrey on "guy" outings when Blair had other plans, played board games with them and generally made himself a part of their lives. He sent flowers and balloons to her office, called just to tell her he was thinking about her and made sure he was never far from her thoughts. As if she could ever forget him...

Jeffrey blossomed under all the attention. His tantrums declined in both frequency and intensity—especially when school dismissed for the term—and his moods were less volatile. He laughed more and mentioned his father less. He didn't become a perfect child, nor would Blair have expected that, but the improvement was so marked that both Blair and Wanda were delighted.

Scott, of course, took his full share of credit for the improvement. If there was one thing Scott was not, she thought wryly, it was self-effacing.

She tried very hard to protect herself from his charms. But she was no more able to hold Scott at arm's length than her nephew was. She laughed at his jokes, she sighed over his romantic gestures and she melted every time he kissed her. Because she was so determined to go slowly this time—and because Jeffrey was usually with them—there was no more lovemaking. Which didn't mean she didn't think about it. Often.

They spent an entire weekend at his ranch, three weeks after the first attempt failed. Jeffrey was thoroughly spoiled by Scott's staff—mothered by Margaret and Carolyn, treated like a favorite grandson by Jake and a cute mascot by the other hands. Jeffrey spent the entire time tagging along at Scott's heels as faithfully as Cooper, the yellow lab, and was acting like an old cowhand before the first day ended.

"Your nephew is delightful," Carolyn said to Blair when they found themselves alone together late Saturday afternoon. "He's so bright. And so polite."

Though her heart swelled with pride, Blair couldn't help laughing a little. "There are those who would be stunned to hear you say that."

Carolyn looked surprised. "I'm sure he's a normal ten-year-old boy who misbehaves occasionally, but on the whole he's a dear."

"Only a few months ago, he was a holy terror," Blair admitted. "He came to me very angry and sullen and rebellious. He has come a long way in the past weeks, and I have to give Scott quite a bit of credit for that."

Carolyn smiled at her. "I think a great deal of the credit has to go to *you*. Jeffrey's not the only one who has changed because of you. I've never seen Scott pay so much attention to his responsibilities here at the ranch and his other business holdings. It certainly makes my job easier. To be more honest than I probably should, I was beginning to wonder about his financial future the way he was running through money and caring so little about…well, never mind that. By the way, I've never seen him pay so much attention to a woman, either," she added teasingly, "and I'm delighted."

Blair blushed like a schoolgirl.

Excusing herself from Carolyn, she found Scott and Jeffrey at the main corral, where Jeffrey was riding a well-mannered paint while Scott looked on. "Look at me, Aunt Blair!" Jeffrey called, grinning at her from beneath the brim of a youth-size Stetson Scott had given him. "Scott says I'm almost ready for a real trail ride."

"We'll be very careful," Scott said quickly when Blair looked at him.

She chuckled. "I know. Jeffrey hasn't had a new bruise in days."

He slipped an arm around her shoulders and nestled her comfortably against his side. "He seems to like it here."

"Are you kidding? He loves it here. You would think he'd been born on a ranch instead of in a Midwestern city."

Scott smiled, but his eyes were serious. "He should probably spend more time here, then."

"I'm sure he would be delighted to come anytime he's invited."

"I'm talking about a regular basis, Blair. I'd like both you and Jeffrey to start thinking of the ranch as a second home."

She moistened her lips. "That's very gracious of you," she said, a bit lamely.

He scowled and dropped his arm, turning to face her with his chin tucked and his eyes narrowed. "Don't do that, Blair. I think we're beyond that now."

"Don't do what?" she asked, startled by the sudden, rare flash of anger in his voice and in his expression.

"Don't treat me like a generous stranger. I'm not extending a gracious invitation, I'm asking you to consider living part time with me. And if that shocks you—and

I can see by your expression that it does—wait until you hear about the more permanent arrangement I have in mind.''

She clutched the fence rail in front of her, her knuckles white. "You're not...you aren't..."

"Proposing?" He smiled again, though it was a crooked smile. "No. Not until you trust me enough to hear it without losing all the color in your face. I guess you could say I'm just preparing you for the eventuality."

She swallowed, asking herself what she would have said if he *had* proposed then. Wondering what she would say when—*if*—he ever did.

"I love you, Blair," Scott murmured, reaching out to touch her cheek, his momentary anger replaced by a rather sympathetic amusement. "And I *will* teach you to trust me that much—no matter how long it takes."

Or until he grew tired of trying and was off on another of his adventures? Blair realized how far she still had to go in her trust when that unwelcome question crossed her mind.

"Scott. Aunt Blair. Watch me canter," Jeffrey called, bringing the disturbing conversation to an end.

The questions continued to echo in Blair's mind as she turned to admire her nephew's new equestrian skills. Unfortunately, she had no answers.

SCOTT CAME to her room that evening after everyone else had gone to bed. She was sitting in a wonderful old rocking chair, a hand-crocheted afghan across her lap, looking out the window at the glittering Wyoming sky, when he suddenly appeared in front of her like a spirit out of the shadows.

"You really are very good at slipping in and out of

bedrooms, aren't you, cowboy?'' she murmured, remembering something he had said during that weekend at his cabin—the first weekend they had spent together.

"There's only one bedroom I want to slip into these days,'' he murmured, smiling at her in the moonlight. "Yours.''

"Don't you think you should wait for an invitation?''

"If you want me to leave, just say the word and I'm gone.''

She studied him standing there, so lean and beautiful in the soft light filtering in from outside. He wore nothing but a pair of jeans, and it was all she could do not to run her hands over every delicious inch of exposed skin. She was thinking of doing just that when she said, "No, don't go yet.''

He knelt beside her chair. "Do you know how beautiful you look sitting here in the moonlight?''

She smiled and reached out to smooth his hair. "I was just thinking the same thing about you.''

Catching her hand, he pulled it to his lips. "Do you know how difficult it's been for me to spend the past three weeks with you and not make love to you?''

Her hand trembled. "I know exactly how difficult it has been.''

"I love you, Blair.''

She let out a soft sigh of surrender. "I love you, too. But you know that, don't you?''

He kissed her knuckles. "I knew. I just wasn't sure *you* did.''

"Arrogant cowboy.''

"Not arrogant. Desperate. I've waited a long time to find you. I can't imagine living without you now.''

"It's still so risky.''

His smile was the dimpled, endearing one that had

made her fall in love with him at the auction. "What's life without a little adventure?"

That was what worried her, of course. "What makes you think you'll find enough adventure with me?" she whispered.

His smile warmed, deepened, sending a quiver through her. "I have no doubt that I will. I want to help you raise your nephew, Blair. To build a family with you. I can't imagine a greater—or more terrifying—challenge than that."

Her eyes filled suddenly with tears. Scott had just revealed a dream she had secretly harbored for a long time but had almost given up. A family of her own. Making that commitment with Scott would be the ultimate gesture of trust in him. Did she dare risk that much?

"Maybe it's a little too soon to talk about that," she said, her voice tremulous.

His low laugh was shaky. "You think this isn't scaring me spitless? But it's right, Blair. I know it."

He was kneeling so close to her chair, looking at her through his lashes, bare shoulders gleaming so invitingly. Blair had resisted as long as she could. She was only human, after all.

"Convince me," she murmured, and wrapped her arms around his neck.

He pulled her right out of the chair and into his arms, rolling her beneath him on the carpeted floor. And then he swiftly transformed her startled laughter into blissful sighs of pleasure.

They eventually made it to the bed, leaving tangled piles of clothing scattered on the floor. Sated and exhausted, they lay draped across each other, their breathing slowly returning to normal. "All the adventure I could possibly want," Scott murmured.

Blair's euphoria faded a bit. "For now, perhaps," she whispered.

"For always, Blair," he said firmly.

She lifted her head. "How could you possibly know that? You've spent so many years chasing excitement, taking off at a moment's notice, avoiding any ties or commitments. What makes you think you won't regret giving that up to take on the day-to-day responsibility of raising a family?"

Scott stared at the ceiling, his expression suddenly pensive. "Did you ever wonder *why* I spent so many years living that way? Trying everything that came along, regardless of how crazy or how risky it seemed to everyone else?"

"I just assumed it was your way of rebelling against your unhappy childhood."

He shook his head, still looking somewhere into the past rather than at her. "I was trying to cram as many experiences as possible into however many years I was given to live. It was my way of living for my little brother, who didn't have a chance to have any adventures of his own, and for my parents, who died so young and so unfairly. I didn't want to die with anything untried, anything untasted, and I didn't want to leave anyone to grieve for me as I grieved for them. And I didn't want to risk loving someone that much again and being in danger of losing so much again."

He looked at her then, his expression wry, his tone self-deprecating. "I came to this self-awareness during the night I spent trying to get back to you from Hawaii. I kept asking myself why I'd done such a stupid thing, why I'd felt the need to run just when I'd found something so precious...and that was the conclusion I came to. Brilliant, huh? And so damned original."

"I didn't know you lost a brother," she said, her heart breaking at the expression on his face.

"He was six. His name was Phillip. Cutest kid you ever saw, all dimples and freckles and giggles. He was riding in the back seat of my parents' car when a drunk driver hit them head-on after crossing the median. My family never had a chance. They had dropped me off at a friend's house for a birthday party ten minutes before they died."

"You must have been devastated."

"I was enraged. At the drunk, at fate—at my grand-parents, who kept telling me I had to hold my chin up and get on with my life. I didn't know why they couldn't understand that my life ended the night my family died."

"Survivor guilt," she murmured.

"That's what a string of child shrinks called it at the time. Of course, I told them what they could do with their pithy analyses."

She rested a hand against his cheek. "I'm so sorry."

"It was a long time ago," he said, suddenly sounding a bit weary. "And I've been letting it control me for too long. I'm tired of running from the past, Blair. Tired of feeling sorry for myself—and guilty for being alive. I want to live my own life for a change, and make it mean something."

"You think your life hasn't had meaning?" She smiled tenderly at him. "You're wrong, Scott. You are one of the kindest, most generous men I've ever met. You've given a home and a purpose to Carolyn and Margaret, who love living and working here. They've told me a great deal about you this weekend, while you've been spending so much time making my nephew happy. I know about the financial contributions you make to a great many charities. I know about the teenagers you hire during the summers, and the time you spend with them when you're here. I know that you're helping at least two of those boys with their college education, and that you're looking into setting up a scholarship foundation for residents of Lost Springs. Yes, you've avoided personal ties, but there are so many people who depend on you. Who love you. And despite your wanderlust, you've never seriously let any of them down."

Scott was frowning now. "Margaret and Carolyn told you that?"

"And Jake and his wife. And that sweet little man who cooks for your ranch hands, and the veterinarian who visited this morning while you took Jeffrey for a ride over the ranch in that cute two-seater airplane you keep here."

"Damn," he muttered, apparently uncomfortable that he'd been the topic of so many conversations.

Her smile deepened. "You needn't worry. No one said anything against you. Everyone agreed that they worry about you, they sometimes want to hit you in the head and they wish you would be a bit more helpful making plans and schedules, but every one of them admires and respects you. Some of them even love you. And they don't seem like people who give their respect foolishly."

She had finally figured out that Scott was the one who thought of himself as unworthy and undependable, not those who cared about him. What had his embittered grandparents said to him that had made him feel that way? What had he said to himself?

As daring and reckless and charming and successful as he had become in the past twenty-odd years, there was still a very small part of him that was an angry, lost boy who needed to be loved. Who needed a home and a family to make him feel worthwhile. And she knew just the woman to give him those things. A woman who needed them every bit as badly for herself.

"I love you, Scott," she murmured, leaning over to kiss him. "And, just as important, I trust you."

His eyes gleamed bright in the shadows. "I've been waiting a long time to hear you say that."

She couldn't help laughing a little. "A long time? Hardly. We've only known each other a couple of months."

He shook his head. "I've been waiting all my life for you," he said simply.

That made her smile waver. "I know the feeling," she murmured, and lowered her mouth to his again.

He put a hand behind her head to hold her to him, kissing her with renewed urgency. "Blair," he said with a gasp when he finally drew back for air. "We can have the longest engagement in history if you want, but you've got to say you'll marry me. Give me that much, at least."

Funny how easy the decision was, after all. Especially considering how much she'd worried about this moment. "I'll marry you. And, although I want to take our time and do this right, I don't think it will be the longest engagement in history."

Scott looked stunned for a moment, and then elated. "That was a yes."

"That was a yes," she confirmed.

And then giggled when he rolled her beneath him and proceeded to show her exactly how much her answer had pleased him.

JEFFREY DID NOT want to leave the ranch Sunday afternoon, even though Blair reminded him that she had to work the next day, and he had been invited to a birthday party that he'd seemed interested in attending. He was on the verge of one of his infamous tantrums when Scott skillfully interceded, promising him that he could come back the very next weekend.

"And when your aunt and I get married, you'll spend as much time here as you like, okay?"

That got his attention. He went still, his jaw dropping. Blair sighed. She and Scott had agreed not to announce their engagement immediately, until she'd had time to get used to the idea herself. She had known when he'd solemnly assured her he understood that he wouldn't keep quiet about it for long.

Scott was still the fast-talking crazy man she'd tagged him the first day she met him. And she wouldn't have him any other way.

"You guys are getting married?" Jeffrey demanded, looking from Blair to Scott and back again.

"We're discussing it," she replied, searching his expression for his reaction.

"You said I could ask her out," Scott reminded Jeffrey with a grin.

"I just said you could date her," the boy retorted.

"I tend to get carried away with things occasionally."

Jeffrey snorted. "No kidding."

"So...how do you feel about it?"

The boy tilted his head, considering the question. Blair held her breath.

"Am I still going to live with you?" he asked her.

"You have a home with me for as long as you want," she answered firmly. "Nothing will ever change that."

"I feel the same way, Jeff," Scott seconded. "I think we make a great team, don't you?"

Jeffrey scratched his chin and looked speculatively around the ranch. "Are we going to live here?"

"We'll have to work out the details later," Scott admitted. "Your aunt has a business in Lightning Creek to consider. We may have to spend part of our time there and part of our time here, something along those lines."

"What about Belle?"

"Belle is part of the deal," Scott assured him with a grin.

"It's okay, then," Jeffrey pronounced with a nod. "But do we have to go home now, Aunt Blair? Can't you take tomorrow off?"

She rolled her eyes. So much for the grand reaction to her engagement. Jeffrey was taking up the argument exactly where he'd left off. "We have to go home now," she replied. "And that's the end of it. Belle's going to be wondering where you are. I'm sure she likes staying with Aunt Wanda, but I'll bet she really misses you."

He sighed heavily. "All right. But this stinks. I wanted to ride Mercury again."

"You'll have plenty of time to ride Mercury later," Scott replied, opening the back door of his Yukon and ushering Jeffrey inside. "After all, he's your horse."

"Mine?" the boy squeaked as Scott closed the door and headed for the driver's seat. "Mercury's *mine?*"

Scott climbed behind the wheel, winking at Blair, who'd just belted herself into the passenger seat. "That's what I said. Mercury's been needing a boy for a while. I went out and found him one. I thought it was very clever of me."

"Oh, man." Jeffrey sank back into the seat, looking dazed.

"You know, of course, that there's a long list of conditions involved here."

"There always are," the boy replied dryly. "But it's worth it. Thanks, Scott. I'll take really good care of him."

"You bet you will, or you'll have me to answer to."

Blair noticed that Jeffrey didn't look notably worried.

Scott reached out and took her hand during the drive to her house, giving her a loving, wicked-edged smile. She wondered if it was possible to be any happier than she was at that moment.

And then she worried that maybe she was too happy. Wasn't she just inviting disappointment by letting herself want so much?

Telling herself she was being both paranoid and pessimistic, she made herself stop thinking along those lines and simply enjoy the moment, her fingers curling around Scott's as he and Jeffrey kept up a teasing give-and-take during the remainder of the drive.

She was afraid her fears had been justified when she, Scott and Jeffrey entered her aunt's house a while later to find her brother, Kirk, waiting for them there. He stood and grinned at them, his handsome face creased with his usual careless smile. "Hi, Jeffrey," he said, looking immediately toward his son. "Daddy's home."

SCOTT WAS WATCHING Blair when Jeffrey ran across the room and threw himself into his father's arms. She looked devastated, he thought, beginning to scowl. And the expression on her face made him hook his thumbs in his belt, spread his boots and narrow his eyes. His first instinct was to protect. He turned to look at her brother, who was giving his son a casual hug.

Blair cleared her throat. "Scott, this is my brother, Kirk Townsend. Kirk, I'd like you to meet my fiancé, Scott McKay."

"Fiancé?" Keeping his left arm loosely draped around Jeffrey's shoulders, Kirk extended his right hand. "This is a surprise. Nice to meet you, Scott. I'm Blair's shiftless older brother, as I'm sure she's told you."

"Not in so many words," Scott answered smoothly. "But I have heard quite a bit about you."

"Fiancé?" Wanda clapped her hands together, looking pleased. "When did this happen?"

"Yesterday," Scott answered, smiling fondly at Blair's aunt.

"That's wonderful," she said sincerely, kissing his cheek and then hugging and kissing her niece. "I'm so happy for both of you. I knew you made a good couple."

Jeffrey pulled away from his father to scoop up his cat, who'd come running to greet him. "Dad, this is Belle. She's mine."

"Yeah? Cool." Kirk turned to Blair then. "Looks like you've been taking real good care of him, sis. I appreciate it."

Blair cleared her throat. "I've enjoyed having him. Um, how long are you in town for this time, Kirk?"

"I've got an opportunity lined up in Argentina. Chance of a lifetime, Blair. I think this one's really going to pay off."

She nodded, looking as though she'd heard that many times before. "I hope it works out for you."

"I was going to stop by and give the kid some presents, make sure he's okay before I take off again. But with you getting married and all...well, I guess you'll be too busy for baby-sitting. So—how would you like to go to Argentina with me, boy?"

"Argentina?" Jeffrey bit his lip.

Scott drew a deep breath, thinking that this was it. The kid had been waiting a long time for a chance to take off with his dad. There was a good possibility that he would grab it while he could—even though it would break Blair's heart.

But Jeffrey didn't look as delighted as Scott might have expected. "Where would we live, Dad? Where would I go to school? Who would I stay with when you're busy with other stuff?"

Kirk looked baffled. "I'm sure we can work something out," he said vaguely. "I can always hire someone to help us out. And you're a pretty big boy now, right? You don't need a baby-sitter all the time."

Blair made a muffled sound and started forward. Scott caught her wrist, thinking they should wait and let Jeffrey make this decision. He only hoped the boy would make the right one.

Jeffrey looked at the cat cradled in his arms. "What about Belle?"

"The cat? You probably better leave it here with Aunt Blair, son. That's a long trip for a cat. But you can visit it, if you want, whenever we get back into the area to see Blair and Aunt Wanda."

"I have a horse, Dad. His name is Mercury. He lives on Scott's ranch."

Kirk chuckled. "Definitely the horse stays here. Maybe we'll get you a pet in Argentina, okay? I know they've got dogs and cats and horses there."

Jeffrey looked at Blair and Scott, who were watching him so quietly, Blair with a rather pleading expression on her face. "Dad?" he said in a small voice. "Would you mind too much if I stay here? I'm sort of settled here, and I think I might be in your way."

What could only be described as regretful relief crossed Kirk's face, but he didn't speak immediately. He looked at Blair instead. "Uh, sis?"

"I would love to have Jeffrey stay here," she answered quickly. Sincerely. "And so would Scott."

Scott nodded, his eyes on the boy's somber face. "Yeah. I'd like him to stay...if he wants to."

"He has a good life here, Kirk," Wanda chimed in. "He and Blair have gotten along wonderfully."

Kirk turned to Jeffrey. "Sounds like you got a good thing here, Jeffrey. I'd love to take you with me, but I've got to think of your best interests...and it sounds like it might be better for you here."

Jeffrey nodded. "Maybe I'll go with you another time, okay, Dad?"

"You bet." Kirk reached out to ruffle the boy's hair with easy affection. "Some other time."

Scott could almost see Blair relax. "Before you leave this time, I'd like you to sign some papers," she murmured, choosing her words carefully.

Kirk studied her face. "Legal guardianship?"

At least he wasn't as stupid as he was irresponsible, Scott couldn't help thinking.

Blair nodded. "It would make things easier for me...and for Jeffrey."

Kirk hesitated a moment, looking at his son, then shrugged. "You're the lawyer, Blair. You do whatever you think is best for the boy."

Blair reached out to take Scott's hand, and he could feel the faintest tremor in her fingers. He thought of the expensive gesture she had made at the bachelor auction—the one that had brought him and Blair together. He thought of her constant worrying about her nephew, the way she had put Jeffrey's needs before her own desires. And he thought of how much love she had given to the boy—and to him.

"She's always done that, Kirk," he said. "And she

always will. We'll both take care of Jeffrey—that's a promise.''

Blair smiled mistily at him. When he glanced at Jeffrey, the boy was smiling, too.

The absolute trust in their eyes filled a painful emptiness that had gnawed inside Scott for a very long time.

EPILOGUE

BLAIR WATCHED with a wince as her nephew and her husband scrambled over rocks and limbs, skidding perilously on slick spots, stumbling in occasional holes, shouting challenges at each other. It was an all-out race to the vacation cabin, similar to the one they'd engaged in a year earlier and to many races since. She followed more sedately, picking her way carefully over the familiar path, slowed somewhat by the awkwardness of early pregnancy.

Scott had given her everything he had promised, she thought with a happy smile, resting a hand on her stomach.

Jeffrey won the race. He did so by slipping through a narrow crevice much too small for Scott to get through. By the time Scott went around the massive rocks Jeffrey had scrambled over, the boy was almost to the porch. He got there a full two seconds before Scott.

"I win!" he shouted, planting his boots and pumping the air with his fist. "I finally figured out how to win—even though your legs are still longer than mine."

Scott grinned, looped an arm around the boy's neck and gave him an affectionately rough hug. "Yeah, kid, you won."

"I used my natural advantage. Just like you taught me," Jeffrey said, grinning impudently at him. "But I will congratulate you on running a good race."

Scott laughed and rubbed his knuckles against the boy's head, initiating a giggling wrestling match.

Finally reaching the porch, Blair leaned against a post and sighed, shaking her head.

Scott looked at her, flashing his wicked, dimpled grin. "What are you looking at?"

"A couple of crazy cowboys."

Her guys stood side by side, hands on their hips, smiling at her, and her breath lodged in her throat.

"Any complaints?" Scott asked, his voice a warm drawl.

"Not a one," she answered with all her heart.

She'd come to realize that this cowboy had been just what she had needed all along.

continues with

HITCHED BY CHRISTMAS

by

Jule McBride

Luke Lydell was supposed to be Claire Buchanan's last fling before her Christmas wedding—a gift from her sisters. But Claire told herself she didn't want him...not *that* way. She didn't need his hard body, she didn't need the passion that sizzled between them. She needed him to find her missing fiancé!

Available in December

Here's a preview!

"THOSE WILD LITTLE sisters of yours obviously think you need a fling with a dangerous man," Luke said.

Claire's heart hammered. Just what had her fool sisters said? "They said I needed a *what?*"

"You heard. That's why they *procured* me." Luke glanced away and when his eyes seared into hers again, their liquid blue heat ran right through her veins. "Procured," he continued. "I think that's the word Emma Jane used."

"They…" Her cheeks suddenly felt boiling hot, and she stared at Luke, taking in his irritating, mildly-bemused expression, and how the breeze lifted his fine blue-black hair. "Procured you…"

"Like a stud bull, Claire."

His lips suddenly twitched, and as much as she fought it, Claire almost smiled, herself. "They wanted us to go on a…like a…date?"

Date was definitely better than whatever "stud bull" implied. Still, one look at Luke made Claire's mind start running to hot musty haylofts and steamy summer nights in the grasslands.

He was shaking his head. "Not a date, Claire. They said they were paying for a fling," he continued, his lips still curled in faint bemusement. "There's a difference."

"As if I didn't know." Ignoring the crazy jitters of her insides, Claire managed a shrug. She wasn't about to allow Luke to rile her passions again, just so he could watch her flounder like a fool. "Well, just consider yourself off the hook."

"Mighty kind of you."

"I'm not *kind,*" she tossed back mildly. "I'm engaged."

"So I hear."

He looked as if the news hadn't affected him a bit, and she hated the fact that she wanted it to. Raising her hand, she waved away a buzzing fly more energetically than was necessary. "You could at least say congratulations."

"Congratulations."

Something unexpectedly terse in his tone made her say, "You have a problem with my getting married?"

"None whatsoever. Girls get married."

Girls, she noticed, not women. Now she definitely knew he was trying to goad her. He was thirty, not that much older than she. "I'm twenty-six."

"All grown-up."

"Grown-up enough not to let you take potshots, Luke."

"Sorry," He said, squinting those incredible eyes at her, "But you came barreling over here like you had an ax to grind, Claire."

"Maybe I do."

"Now, don't go having a conniption fit. It's not my fault your sisters bid for me."

She felt more unwanted color pour into her cheeks. "Well, the way you were parading around, Luke, I guess you were asking for it."

He surveyed her another long moment. "Was I?"

Her heart fluttered as she remembered how good he'd looked flexing his muscles. "Yes," she returned, thinking it was the wrong time to remember they'd been near this spot the last time they'd been together. It was years ago, after another fund-raiser, but even now, Claire could feel both the heat of his kisses and the sting of his rejection. Watching him sober, Claire felt her throat ache with something she couldn't quite name—maybe regret for what she'd once thought they might share, maybe longing.

He said, "Been a while since we've talked, hasn't it?"

Her lips lifted at the corners. "Hmm. And I thought we were just baiting each other."

He chuckled softly.

Suddenly it seemed easier to study her boots than his broad-shouldered, half-naked body, and she toed the dust a second before lifting her gaze again. "Really, Luke...Tex wanted to make a contribution to Lost Springs, and he would have, whether my sisters bought a—a bachelor—or not." Somehow, calling him a bachelor hurt. Wasn't Luke ever lonely, living by himself when he could so easily find a woman to look after him? To love him? Glancing away again, Claire suppressed the emotions, taking in the soothing wash of pale summer colors she loved—the cerulean sky, the burnt umber and sienna in the bone-dry arid land.

"The way I figure it, Claire," Luke said when she looked at him again. "Tex paid good money for a service so, no matter how we feel about it, we've got no choice but for me to oblige."

The comment was so unexpected that Claire almost burst out laughing. She didn't know what possessed her, but she said, "Whoa. Let me get this straight, Lydell. You're offering stud services?"

He grinned.

Her heart did a three-sixty in her chest and she stared at him, wondering if he was serious, and chastising the part of herself that so desperately wished he was.

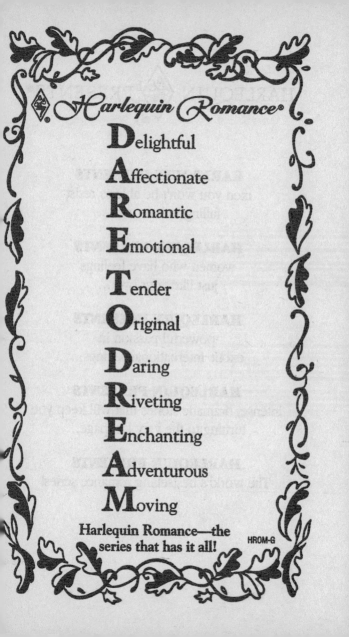

Harlequin Romance®

Delightful

Affectionate

Romantic

Emotional

Tender

Original

Daring

Riveting

Enchanting

Adventurous

Moving

Harlequin Romance—the
series that has it all!

HROM-G

HARLEQUIN PRESENTS®

HARLEQUIN PRESENTS
men you won't be able to resist
falling in love with...

HARLEQUIN PRESENTS
women who have feelings
just like your own...

HARLEQUIN PRESENTS
powerful passion in
exotic international settings...

HARLEQUIN PRESENTS
intense, dramatic stories that will keep you
turning to the very last page...

HARLEQUIN PRESENTS
The world's bestselling romance series!

Harlequin® Historical

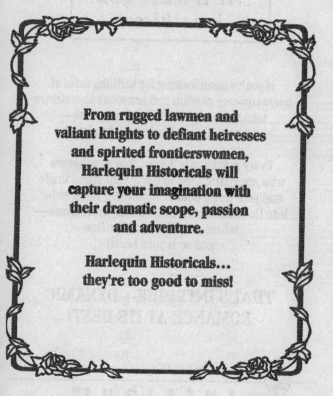

From rugged lawmen and
valiant knights to defiant heiresses
and spirited frontierswomen,
Harlequin Historicals will
capture your imagination with
their dramatic scope, passion
and adventure.

Harlequin Historicals...
they're too good to miss!

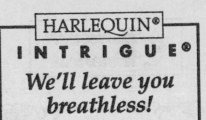

LOOK FOR OUR FOUR FABULOUS MEN!

Each month some of today's bestselling authors bring four new fabulous men to Harlequin American Romance. Whether they're rebel ranchers, millionaire power brokers or sexy single dads, they're all gallant princes—and they're all ready to sweep you into lighthearted fantasies and contemporary fairy tales where anything is possible and where all your dreams come true!

You don't even have to make a wish...
Harlequin American Romance will grant your every desire!

Look for Harlequin American Romance
wherever Harlequin books are sold!

$\mathcal{S}$ HARLEQUIN SUPERROMANCE®

...there's more to the story!

Superromance. A *big* satisfying read about unforget-
table characters. Each month we offer
four very different stories that range from family
drama to adventure and mystery, from highly emotional stories to romantic comedies—and
much more! Stories about people you'll
believe in and care about. Stories too
compelling to put down....

Our authors are among today's *best* romance writ-
ers. You'll find familiar names and
talented newcomers. Many of them are
award winners—and you'll see why!

If you want the biggest and best
in romance fiction, you'll get it
from Superromance!

Available wherever Harlequin books are sold.